HORRIFICA

by Sheldon Woodbury

Nightmare Press
Shepherdsville, KY

To LuAnn and Will

I love you so much it's scary

HORRIFICA

by Sheldon Woodbury

INTRODUCTION

Imagine a place called Horrifica that's as infinite as the mystery of dreams, but it's just out of sight, hidden in our nightmares and lurking in the shadows like ghosts. It's the place where all that's creepy prowls, a midnight scream away, where darkness is sacred, and the glory of horror is everywhere. This is where you'll find the trinity of fear, the misbegotten secrets that haunt our world.

The GROTESQUERIES are the freaks that rage against nature and order. The MONSTROSITIES are the savage offspring of a blasphemous god. The DEPRAVITIES are rarely glimpsed, their deeds so perverse they hide from even the dimmest glimmer of light. Each has its own gloomy allure in a wasteland that worships the wicked above all else.

There's no map or marker for where it is because fear and dread are never bounded by the illusionary constraints of time and place. You can call it another dimension, the nightmare realm, or the secret soul of who you really are. Whatever distinction you want to use, Horrifica haunts our world with its macabre marvels of horror and fear.

THE GROTESQUERIES

Family Reunion
Dark as Hell
A Tattered Black Shroud
Bones in a City Graveyard
The God of Flesh
A Gift from the Stars
Down Where Her Nightmares Dwell
The Last Horror Show
Hard to Get

THE MONSTROCITIES

Behold My Son
The Monster Maker
The Holy Ghost
Magic Macabre
A White Farewell with a Splash of Red
Underworld
The Last Halloween
A Beautiful Horror
We Have Our Ways
Extinction
Eternal

THE DEPRAVITIES

Midnight Town
Uncommon Pleasures
The VIP Club
In the Darkest of Places
Between Heaven and Hell
Last Call
A Dream Come True
Johnny Hell
Love Never Dies
Dirty Minds
Missing

THE GROTESQUERIES

A gathering of the brutal and bizarre

FAMILY REUNION

As Reverend Isaiah stood backstage waiting to make his entrance, he knew he was a dying breed, a wrinkled relic clinging to the remnants of his glorious past.

There was a time, many decades ago, when he'd toyed with the idea of leaving his calling and becoming an actor, because he'd been blessed with the physical tools and skills that made any stage a place where he could perform his holy roller magic. Back then, he had a mane of thick black hair, and a booming voice, along with a natural instinct for the right gesture or turn of phrase to excite a crowd and bring the audience exploding to their feet.

He'd started out as a lowly country preacher, then ascended the religious ladder step by step: next as a truck driving evangelist, then a tent filling revivalist, until he finally became a miracle worker billed as a chosen messenger of God.

For the last forty years he'd traveled endless highways and backwoods roads, bringing his fire and brimstone show to downtrodden audiences desperate for the tiniest promise of hope and salvation. But the best return was always going big and bold with his mostly poor audiences.

His specialty was using the power of faith to cure untreatable diseases - a high-wire act requiring a special kind of performance skill and unshakable confidence.

He'd grown up poor, on a dusty dirt farm in Alabama, in the lingering shadow of the Great Depression. His parents were god-fearing country folk who clung to religion like a life raft, hoping it would keep them afloat in a constant storm of unbearable hardships. The greatest was the passing of his younger twin sisters, who died when they were six from a severe case of chicken pox. This almost broke his parents' already withered spirits, but their faith kept them trudging onward.

It also gave them a new focus for their religious fervor. They saw that their only son had been spared, so they jointly decided this must be a divine message they couldn't ignore. From this point on, his destiny was preordained, and he followed it without disagreement or discussion, dedicating his life to spreading the holy word.

And now it was sixty years later, and he was a tired relic ready to retire.

Like any business, his had evolved into something brand new, and he could barely recognize it anymore. While he was still playing to crowds in rented halls and movie theaters, his younger counterparts were preaching to millions on TV and the internet. They'd discovered a better way to sell their product, but he was too old to learn these new age tricks.

For him, it had always been about being up close with the true believers hungering for a miracle, pressing his flesh against theirs to make it happen.

Billy hobbled over with his pre-show shot of bourbon. Billy had been with him from the very beginning as his right-hand man, a childhood friend from the same small town. He'd had polio as a child, so his skinny frame staggered like he was always drunk. The fact that he was always drunk only added to his unsteadiness.

"Knock 'em dead," Billy rasped, handing him the plastic cup with a wobbly hand.

"I feel a little tired tonight," he confessed.

"I've heard prayer always helps," Billy slurred.

This brought a smile to his weary face.

With Billy he'd long ago dropped the pretense that he was toiling away, selflessly doing

God's work. Now it was just a job, much like the acting profession he'd toyed with decades ago. He was playing the part of a heavenly anointed miracle worker because it paid the bills, and it came with other fringe benefits he'd always enjoyed.

He'd started out in a cheap black suit when he was a lowly country preacher, but now he was draped in a thousand-dollar midnight black robe that glowed mystically in the shimmering lights. His long black hair was shorter now, a silvery white. His booming voice had aged too, losing a good bit of its power.

But when the bourbon rolled down his throat with a fiery burn, he felt that glorious confidence surge back. He waited for the canned religious music to end, then he strode on stage with his hands raised high. There was an explosion of shouting and clapping. Looking down, he always knew where the loudest ovation was coming from.

And, yes, there it was.

Stretched out in front of the stage was a ragged line of trembling sick people hungering for a miracle. With the fiery bourbon still burning in his throat, he dropped his wrinkled old hands down from the heavens, because it was time to go big and bold.

She'd driven for most of the day on sun baked roads from her home outside Kansas City on a personal pilgrimage. Her destination was a small city in northern Texas called Wichita Falls. It had just turned a dusky twilight when she turned into the parking lot of the rundown motel. As she carried her overnight bag from the car, she saw a giant night sky was already slipping in overhead.

She was thirty years old, but the trip had still been exhausting, a long-distance trek with just a brown bag lunch to get her there. But now her energy and spirits were climbing, eager to embrace the night ahead.

When she opened the door and walked inside the musty motel room, she began to feel a surge of hope that bordered on ecstasy. She quickly unpacked and took a hot shower, imagining the scalding waters were a baptism of sorts and tonight would be a new beginning.

She knew that others had taken the pilgrimage too, leaving their squalid small towns in search of a miracle. They'd all been victims that had been handed a cruel fate, forced to live a ghost-like life of frailty and sickness.

As she got dressed in front of a dirty cracked mirror, she also knew she was luckier than most. There was no doubt that her face was a wonderful creation, so she always showcased it in the best way possible. Her hair was long and dark, falling in lush curls across her shoulders and down the long slope of her back. There was a luminous glitter to her green eyes that made her face even more alluring. She covered the rest of her body in clothes that revealed nothing. This choice of dress wasn't because of modesty or shyness, but because of her affliction. While a part of her body

4

was undeniably beautiful, the rest of her was undeniably not.

When she saw the dusty marquee of the movie theater, her heart stuttered with anticipation.

One Night Only
REVEREND ISAIAH
Faith Heals

She parked in the lot behind the theater, joined the jostling crowd strolling on the sidewalk to the front entrance. The giant night sky was pitch black now, sweeping and silent overhead.

She shuffled inside and heard "Amazing Grace" thundering out from the speakers in the theater. Excitement surged inside her again. She'd been carrying around an abysmal pain in her body and soul that had poisoned her life, but she had faith that her encounter tonight would remedy that.

Then she wondered if the same song had been playing thirty years ago, when her beloved mother had come. She'd heard the story on a stormy summer night just a week before her mother died, and she'd carried it locked in her grieving heart ever since. Back then, the doctors didn't even have a name for the disease her mother had because it was so rare. Every avenue of treatment they had at the time hit a dead end, and that's what finally brought her mother in a white cotton dress to the man that promised miracles.

Even now, as she joined the ragged line of trembling people in front of the stage, she could still remember her mother's whispery voice as she described that night. She talked about a man with long black hair like a lion's mane, and a booming voice that could soar out from the stage and caress your soul. The man on the stage in front of her now was a much older version of that, but it was still the same man.

The line in front of her staggered forward, as one by one, they ascended up the wooden steps to the stage. It was a sad parade of the sick and afflicted. When each one reached the stage and stood in front of the silver haired man in the glowing black robe, their eyes were brimming with hope.

It was finally her turn.

She walked slowly up the stairs and was led across the stage to the Reverend Isaiah. He took both her hands, stared deeply into her glittering green eyes, and she felt a sudden shudder course through her body. He must have liked what he saw because he stared even longer.

Then, with a sudden and dramatic movement, he swept his hands on top of her head, pressing flesh against flesh, and shouted out, "Glory be to God!" As the crowd cheered and clapped, he reached into his robe and slipped a card in her hand with a final squeeze. "I'm also available for private appointments," he whispered in her ear. "God tells me this is something your ailment requires."

Yes, she thought as she was led away offstage. He was much older than the man her mother's dying voice had described, but he hadn't changed a bit.

She'd returned to the rundown motel and placed the call right away. She wanted tonight to be the night. After all these years her pain-racked heart couldn't wait any longer. He answered his phone with the familiar voice that sounded like it came straight from

6

the heavens, commanding and soft at the same time, caressing and caring. She explained she needed to see him right away. She said he was right; her affliction was so ferocious and strong it required more of his anointed attention.

"Of course, my child, I understand. I'll come to you directly."

She immediately slipped out of her long white dress and hurried into the shower, letting the scorching water wash over her naked body again. She wanted to be freshly scrubbed and clean, as pure as she could be. The Bible says the body is a temple, so she prepared hers for the encounter ahead, like a sacramental offering.

When the knock thumped against her door, she was sitting on the bed, her warm hands folded neatly in her lap. She'd worked extra hard on her make-up, applying it in expert brushstrokes across her beautiful face. The part of her that wasn't beautiful was again covered up in a long white dress.

She opened the door and was instantly greeted with the wafting smell of bourbon, as he stumbled into the room. The magnificent black robe was gone, replaced by wrinkled brown pants and a stained yellow shirt. Away from the radiant lights, he didn't look divine at all.

"Let me look at you, child. You're a blessed young woman." She didn't answer, except for the faster beating of her heart. "Forgive me, but I'm overcome by the glory of your God-given beauty..."

He stumbled closer, pressed his saggy flesh against hers, bringing his whiskey-soaked mouth down to her lips. She reached over and flicked off the lights, plunging the small motel room into darkness. She could feel his fingers crawling over her body, unbuttoning buttons, rubbing against her, hungry and desperate for an encounter he'd had hundreds of times before.

"I'm sick," she whispered.

"I know my child... that's why I'm here..."

He'd pulled off her white cotton dress, dropping it to the floor like an unwanted rag, leaving her naked in the darkness.

And now they came at the stroke of midnight, stumbling and crawling down the motel hallway just as they'd planned. It had taken her years to find them, pouring over the history of Reverend Isaiah's holy-roller tours. Most were living in secluded hovels, hiding away from the rest of the world, because there was no part of their body that was beautiful.

Together, they were a secret congregation, not of faith, but of indescribable misery and pain. All of them had been born to mothers with a morbid illness, so their physical forms came out of the diseased wombs ravaged and hideous. She'd been luckier than most, with at least one part of her body not desecrated. But the part of her body that was not beautiful was shockingly gruesome.

They poured in through the door in a writhing, twisted mass, grabbing the Reverend

Isaiah with a flurry of clawing hands. They dragged his screaming flesh from the musty room, then down the long hallway to a door, then outside to an open field that was barren and rocky.

"*Father*..." came the croaking chorus from the twisted mass.

They dragged him to the middle of the empty field, so the savage ceremony could be witnessed from the heavens. The sky was still pitch black, sweeping and silent. The Bible preached an eye for an eye, so that was their guide for the holy ritual they'd planned.

"Oh God... please stop..."

He kept screaming it over and over again in a drunken wail, as the mob of monstrosities took an eye, then an arm, then a whole lot more. He tried to fight back, but deep in his hypocritical heart, he knew his punishment was righteous and just. His heart kept pounding in his blood-soaked chest with unrelenting pain and fear, then his howling children ripped that out too.

DARK AS HELL

He was slouched next to her in the transport, his pale, dazed eyes staring straight ahead.

Her first thought had been surprise at how small he was: just barely over three feet, and so skinny his skin hung limply on his bones. He was also much quieter than she'd expected. She thought all children were loud and boisterous, but not him. When he spoke, his mumbled words were barely above a whisper.

They'd met in the tiny tomb-like reception area just a short time before. A young woman in a somber black uniform had marched her down the hall and stopped in front of a doorway, soft voices murmuring on the other side.

"His name is Klyle," the young woman said. "But you can change it if you like."

No, she wouldn't change it, she'd decided right away, because she was smart enough to know that's what they wanted.

Klyle...

It was an easy name to remember. That was good, It'd be an easy name to forget, and that was better.

It was another government program; that's what she hated most of all. In a world that was already drowning in complications, she hated intrusions of any kind, and this program was exactly that. "Population Control," it was called. In the last fifty years, a strange and unexpected new social movement had suddenly sprouted. More and more women were making a choice, and that choice was not to have children. The population was flat and would soon be shrinking at an increasingly faster rate.

That was the problem.

But why?

In place of hard facts, there was the usual surplus of wild guesses and lunatic theories. Some believed it was simply the destiny of the species, there was a secret suicide note hidden somewhere deep in our DNA. Others believed the cause was environmental, the culprit some new strain of microbe that had somehow affected the maternal instinct. Whatever the reason, women were choosing not to do what they had always done, and the size of that group was growing like an out-of-control virus.

Her name was Consuelo Bonne.

She'd made her decision like so many others. Exactly why, she wasn't even sure herself. After all, she'd grown up with a brother and a sister, and parents she'd loved. It didn't matter. The decision seemed natural, so she didn't feel a need to investigate. It came from somewhere deep inside, that's all she knew.

"Petra, I don't want to have children," she'd revealed a few weeks before they were bonded.

An awkward discussion had followed, but not a very long one. Petra tried to change her mind, but quickly saw he couldn't. His decision was to respect her choice, even if he couldn't completely understand it.

The government had made a decision too, one that was much less tolerant of this troublesome new movement. It couldn't force women to have children, but there were other options that might prove beneficial.

11

Consuela had been expecting the notification for some time. Their childless status was sure to be identified. The government's stance was firm. Given the current conditions, if a woman chose not to have children, that woman should at least be given the opportunity to clearly see what that decision deleted from her life.

So, the few orphaned children were given a very special government duty. They were assigned to childless couples for a designated period of cohabitation. The benefits were deemed positive for all involved. The children were given a succession of temporary guardians, and the childless couples were given a child that would hopefully prompt them towards a biological duty they had chosen to ignore.

Looking out the soot-covered window of the transport, Consuela could see the jagged haze of the landscape blurring past. It was a dark world she lived in.

Dark as hell, she often thought.

The landscape was an endless stain of crumbling, misshapen constructs that were a brutal assault on the soul. Looming overhead were more of the same, churning clouds of sooty black after-burn darkening every corner of the chemically scorched sky. But there was always light too. It was off in the distance, the mysterious, shimmering static that snapped and crackled on the horizon.

Consuela could also see the reflection of the frail boy floating ghost-like in the window. He was slumped next to her, his withered legs hanging weakly towards the floor. Like her, he was staring outside at the endless darkness and shimmering gloom.

Consuela sat still, but a nudging anger had been growing inside her from the very first moment she received notification. The boy would be living in their home like a tiny intruder, sent by the government on a mission. As she stared at his strange little face floating in front of her, she was suddenly startled by the fierceness she felt.

Deep in her heart, she despised him already.

It was solemn and quiet as the unwelcome intruder was introduced to his new home.

Their quarters were beneath the southern rim of the city in a sagging mega-structure that appeared close to final collapse. They lived on one of the lower levels where the scorching stench was almost unbearable, and a noxious chemical fog had been hovering for as long as she could remember. Their home was small, but clean. Like a jail-cell, Petra liked to joke. The boy was given a corner on the floor to sleep. Consuela had decided that would be enough.

From the outset, communication was kept to a minimum. They'd agreed on a unified front. No special kindnesses would be offered, or curiosities revealed. The unwanted child was just another temporary government intrusion, nothing more.

The first morning Consuela was allowed to sleep but was still up and dressed before the boy stirred. Petra had already left much earlier, but she'd been given temporary leave for the purposes of the program.

On the first day, she decided to let the boy do as he pleased, not encouraging him toward any activity, or restricting his movement within the cramped walls of their home. She kept her distance, using the time as her own. It also became apparent that the boy's persona would be equally distant. After wandering through the quarters a few times, he stumbled back to his makeshift bed in the corner and slumped against the wall. From that position, he spent the rest of the day staring at the strange looking woman he was now living with.

His listless behavior was so overwhelming Consuela began to wonder about its cause.

Maybe he's retarded, she thought. The faraway look that was fixed in his eyes might indicate this, but she couldn't be sure, and she wasn't about to probe him for information.

As she moved about, she knew the boy's silent gaze followed her progress. His presence didn't make her nervous, but it didn't provide the pleasure of companionship either. For that, she was grateful. She didn't want the boy's companionship and wouldn't have trusted it even if offered. She reminded herself that the frail body slumped on the floor was a temporary intrusion, nothing more.

At the end of the first day, it was a peculiar looking group that circled around the meal table. The boy's pale eyes barely cleared the top edge of the small table, and his ashen skin seemed completely drained of color. It was the most delicate looking skin Consuela had ever seen, like something ancient that would crumble to dust if touched. She had already come to a private determination. His sullen sluggishness was more like someone approaching the end of a life, not the beginning.

But the boy's appearance did present a modest offering in which she could take comfort. She and Petra had hunched backs because of their torturous work. Their skin was discolored and scabrous from long-term exposure to the poisonous air. What she found comforting was how different the child looked from them. There was no aspect or detail of his appearance she felt any kind of connection to. She could snatch glimpses of him with complete indifference.

As the meal continued, the only sound at the table was the soft clatter of utensils scraping against plates. The unwelcome intruder never said a word.

Quiet and somber it remained, until the third day when Consuela got her first glimpse of how fragile the boy really was. Like the previous two days, he'd spent most of the third sitting mutely on the floor, lost inside some private inner world. *What's he thinking about?* Consuela wondered. *Does he know how much I don't want him here, and that's why he's so solemn and still?*

It was late in the day when the listless silence was suddenly shattered. Consuela was passing through the quarters when she heard a whimpering scream.

"Oooooowwwwww..."

Turning around, she saw the boy was falling. She was only a short distance away, but it was still too far to help him. His back hit the hard floor. He let out another whimpering scream.

"Oooooowwwwww..."

Consuela rushed to the boy's body sprawled on the floor. "I have to see what happened," she said quickly, pulling his tiny hands away from his head. Blood was already flowing from a ruby red cut. Looking up, she could see the sharp corner where his forehead hit.

"It hurts..." he whispered in anguish.

The flesh around the cut had turned crimson. Consuela shoved her hands under the boy's body, lifted him up, and carried him to the meal table. His skin was damp, his eyes half-closed. She pushed away the soggy clumps of hair matted around the wound. More blood streamed out.

She hurried away, came back with medication and a wet cloth. She wiped away the blood, smeared the medication on the boy's damp head. His skin was trembling and feverish to the touch. She stayed with him until he fell asleep, then slowly carried him to his place on the floor.

That evening, she decided to let the child continue to sleep, as she and Petra ate alone. His troubled moans were just loud enough to hear, as they silently ate.

Earlier, Consuela had come to another conclusion about the real cause of the accident.

The problem was clearly his weak physical condition, and for that she blamed the Center that was supposed to care for him. The child needed nourishment. If he couldn't even walk across the floor without falling, he needed strength.

When they finished eating, Consuela carried scraps of food to the boy still sleeping on the floor. She nudged him awake with her foot, so his eyes saw the food. She hated the sight of him, but no purpose would be served in letting him die.

Later that night, after waking from a deep sleep, she found herself back in the room with the sleeping boy. She'd slipped out of bed without much thought, then shuffled groggily to the corner where he slept.

Why was she here? She wasn't sure.

Maybe it was to finally study the child when he wasn't staring back with those dazed, pale eyes. Maybe she just wanted to make sure he was sleeping. Moving closer, she could see he was. But even asleep, he seemed on the verge of death.

Then she suddenly became angry.

The boy's body was curled up at her feet, so near she could touch it – and that's why she was angry. She was angry that she wasn't in bed with her husband, but was standing alone in the dark, wondering about the welfare of a child she had vowed to hate. The unwelcome intruder.

She shuffled quickly back to bed.

The next morning, Consuela slept later than the previous three days, but she still felt a vague uneasiness when she awoke. The remainder of the night had not been restful, her sleep troubled by a succession of murky dreams that lingered until morning.

She dressed slowly, giving herself time to think. She was worried that the boy had somehow crept into her thoughts, and she couldn't push him back out, no matter how hard she tried. She was concerned about his welfare. She couldn't deny it. But she was also angry she felt that way and decided to focus on that instead.

The anger.

Before leaving her room, she renewed her vow. The boy was an intruder, nothing more. Her behavior would not be outwardly hostile, but it would leave no room for misinterpretation. No special kindnesses would be offered, or curiosities revealed.

So went the day.

Through the morning, and into the last moments of the afternoon, Consuela kept to her vow. If the boy was slumped on the floor, she busied herself in another part of the quarters. If the boy moved, then so did she, quickly moving off in the opposite direction. When contact or proximity was unavoidable, she was careful not to linger too long on the boy's pale gaze.

In her heart, of course, she didn't really hate the child, but she did detest the reason for his presence. Why were all power structures so obsessed with self-preservation? That's what this program was really all about. She wasn't sure what faction of the Triad was currently in majority because that knowledge was negligible. They were all the same, only their constant mistakes were different.

She hadn't ventured outside since the boy arrived, so she wondered what fresh horrors would be lurking when she did. With so much grimy science around, the new horrors were always ghastly and sordid.

Like the previous nights, little was said as they sat around the meal table. The boy kept his gaze low, quietly taking nibble-size bites and small sips from the offerings in front of him.

The injury looked better. The swelling was down, and the medicine had healed the cut, leaving only a reddish line as a scar.

But he's so pitiful looking, Consuela found herself thinking. His droopy hair needed cutting. His gaunt body needed some of the wild, frantic energy that all little boys had.

And that was the real mystery, wasn't it?

If this was the child who was supposed to change her maternal mind, he seemed blatantly counterfeit.

His chronological years were the same as a normal child, but so much else was missing.

"Aaaaaahhhhhh..." the boy suddenly cried out in another whimpering scream.

Petra was out of his chair first, then Consuela. The boy had a knife in his hand, which had now clattered to the table. It must have slipped while he was eating, slicing into the sagging flesh below the thumb. The boy looked up in shock, his pain-stricken face now as shockingly white as a tiny full moon.

"It hurts..." came the whisper.

Petra was already gone, stumbling off for medication, as Consuela began to move, shuffling quickly around the table, reaching out, being pulled towards the whispery, moon-faced child by some unseen force she was just barely beginning to understand.

So it went.

Perhaps, Consuela should have realized sooner what was happening, but she didn't. They'd bandaged the hand, then she sat vigil again, as the boy curled up into a fitful sleep.

The next day there was more blood, and the next, and the next. When he woke the fourth day, it was smeared on his face and arms. The bandage on his hand rubbed off during the night, and blood had dripped until morning. The boy started coughing, and there was blood there too, splashed on the hand he held at his mouth. The next day, his legs gave out as he was walking to the bathroom, and he plunged to the floor, banging his knees.

"It hurts..."

19

Those were the only words the child whispered as the mishaps continued. A few days before, the boy had seemed feeble and frail, now he was much worse.

Consuela tried continuously to contact the Center but could never reach anyone to answer her questions. She found herself sitting with the boy, doing what she could to comfort him. Then, finally, she was able to reach a gruff voice at the Center who could answer her questions. That's when she was reminded of something she'd been too distracted to think about.

The boy was leaving.

Tomorrow he was scheduled to be returned.

It was later that night, when Consuela woke up, and slipped out of bed without making a sound. It may have been a muffled noise that stirred her awake, or a nagging fear that had been building for days. But something had nudged her eyes open, then pulled her into the room with the boy.

When she got there, he was waiting for her.

Standing in the middle of the room, there was just enough light for Consuela to see his slender, frail form, and see what he had done with the gleaming metal knife he'd found just minutes before she arrived. How long she stood there, she didn't know, but it was long enough to finally see the truth about the boy. Everything about him was a brutal reflection of the government that sent him. He was silent and naked, his trembling body covered with blood. He had taken the knife and wandered over his ghostly-white skin, randomly cutting and slicing at the limp flesh.

Consuela was too shocked to move, until an achingly small voice drifted through the shadows and hit her in the heart.

"It hurts..."

Just those two words and Consuela suddenly realized her whole world had changed.

He's won.

The intruder had won, and she was powerless to stop him. Tears came against her will, as she also realized much more about the dark puzzle of the child. She guessed his body had scars from all his other visits too, probably hundreds scattered across his tortured skin, and they'd all been removed, just like these would be too.

As Consuela stood there, her heart ached at the sight, and she wanted more than anything to grab the frail boy in her arms and comfort him. But she also knew that's exactly what the Center wanted.

In the darkness of the room, with the bloody child a few steps away, an image flashed in her mind. She imagined the despicable cadre of social scientists who'd schemed together and come up with the plan. After all, what woman could resist the helpless plea of a child in pain? And what child could resist the grimy science that would easily turn them into a willing participant?

Yes, she had been tricked into caring about the boy, so now she would have to find someone else to care for when he left. In a few weeks, she would have to confide to Petra she wanted to have a baby. It was all such a perfect plan; the surprise is that it didn't work.

That's because Consuela had a secret of her own. In her heart, she was already a mother, but she refused to bring a child she would love more than life itself

21

into a world it would despise. This was the origin of her decision not to give birth. It had seemed so natural and right, but she'd never understood the real reason why.

Now she did.

Like all the others, she had been protecting her unborn from the horrors of the world, like any good mother would.

Tears were still streaming down her cheeks, as she moved through the darkness. She reached the boy, and gently tugged the knife from his shivering hand. Holding it tight, she turned and shuffled away, disappearing around a corner where the boy couldn't see her. She stood still for a few moments, gathering her strength, and maternal rage. Then she held the knife over her pounding heart. She didn't want the boy to see her, because she had to do something he wouldn't understand. He was young, so he wasn't yet aware of the true nature of his world.

But she knew all too well.

It was dark as hell.

And only another woman would understand the sacrifices you have to make for your children.

A TATTERED BLACK SHROUD

If darkness is the absence of light, then this was a darkness of endless depths. Down here there was no sense of time, just a raging struggle to cling to life. It was raw and primal, scary, and scurrying, more rabid than any beast.

But in the not-too-distant past, something new had seeped into the black caverns where that concept had lost all meaning. At the bottom of the craggy tunnels burrowed down from the surface eons ago, an odor had oozed in - the odor of death.

That stench was everywhere, more a part of this life than life itself. Gnawed chunks of flesh were strewn like rubble in the crushing murk, quickly decaying into grime and dirt. But this new odor was even more rancid and rank, as if the excruciating savagery of ending life had spewed an onslaught of sputtering fumes. The smell had crept out into the steaming caverns, then exploded up like a billowing fog, because this was dying on a gargantuan scale, the death-rattle-groan of a once grand giant.

If memory is keeping the past alive, then the glowing eyed creatures had slowly killed it long ago. They knew nothing of their past, except for the bottomless hunger that had always eaten at them.

It was hunger that had pushed them deeper and deeper into the earth, searching for sustenance. Life always clings to life with a consuming ferocity, and that's what had driven them underground on their dark scavenger hunt.

Along the way they'd been forced to evolve, but that memory was also gone. They weren't aware of what they were now because the suffocating darkness cloaked their decrepit forms. Their bulging eyes glimmered, but that's all that was visible as they scurried around with raspy desperation. They were nothing more than a will to live in a simmering underworld of noxious death.

Now they'd reached their final dead end, having burrowed all the way down, consuming and destroying until there was nothing left except madness and extinction. But instinct is always more powerful than reason, so the exodus began as the gargantuan death rattle shuddered around them. They scampered away in the only direction remaining, back up from where they came forgotten eons ago. The gaseous spew that gushed out from somewhere even deeper smelled like the end of the world – and it was.

The creature had no reason left, but instinct said it was being pushed along by a creature that belonged to it. There was no concept of family, that was part of the unknown past. There was only the trembling hunger to survive, which was always hidden in the abusive and unforgiving darkness.

But instinct said the creature nudging it had come from within, so it stumbled along, rising up in one of the vein-like tunnels in the forgotten maze. The other creature was younger and stronger with larger eyes. It was pushed higher, struggling up through the rocky wasteland of death.

The ferocious hunger that had always been the whole of its existence had finally become too much to bear. All it could do was crawl and shiver, lapping weakly at the rock and grime. It tried to hide the weakness, because the scent of any weakness would mean its end would come with a flurry of chomping teeth. They were one of many, a vast swarm rising out of the depths below. They'd long ago been scorched to a blistery crust by the smoldering heat, so they looked like a scuttling flood of burning red eyes.

They swelled into the ragged tunnels and crumbling caverns with the billowing smell churning behind them. They had no sense of where they were going, driven only by the need to flee the deathly stank erupting below. Their ascent was grim and arduous, clawing back up through the massive netherworld of choking smoke. It still wanted to live, but its trembling body was now a traitor, desperately clinging to the earthen walls. But the younger creature continued to guide it up with the rising mass, pushed by an instinct it didn't understand.

All lives have meaning, and everything is alive, including this colossal creation spinning through space. It had always been grand, with a complexity impossible to fathom, like life itself. It had been there from the very beginning, speaking a language all its own, of air and wind, water and oceans, mountains, and earth. It also had an instinct to survive, and this is what it had whispered to those who would listen.

But the whisper had grown fainter as the gorging assaults on its majestic form had increased in scope. The humans had always roamed its surface with a wanton cruelty, completely unaware of what survival was really about.

Its destruction was gradual, but steadfast and determined. It had been desecrated and devoured from

25

the very beginning, until it had finally become little more than a skeletal husk. The whisper was gone with all its past glory. Now there was just the death rattle from its core.

The black mass oozed from the simmering depths below, rising higher and higher to where the heat was not as stark and stinging. The fumes still chugged around them, seeking higher ground too.

The ravenous hunger worsened. The swarm traveled back up the way they'd descended, a barren graveyard as forgotten as all else in their existence.

The craggy terrain began to change. The rising mass climbed over ancient crumbling structures from a mysterious sanctuary deep underground. They had no sense of what it was, only that it was different from the molten rock and sputtering crud deeper below.

Still lapping weakly at the strange new ground, it knew it was dying, still surrounded by the flood of luminescent eyes, but now rising up with a slower crawl. They'd become acclimated to the sulfurous air in the depths. It had always fought to survive, but now the end was near, a trembling kind of darkness creeping over its skeletal form.

The younger creature was still pushing it up, but it stumbled and fell, splaying flat. A charred chunk from the mass quickly broke off, eager to feed. The younger creature was an instant shield, thrashing them away with a fury it could only watch with a flickering gaze.

It was too weak to take notice of the crumbling structures from long ago. Something had lived here, but now they were abandoned like everything else. There were strange marks telling a story from when memory remained. They were gargantuan and gory, a mysterious plea from another life.

But the scorched creatures didn't see it, and they wouldn't have understood it even if they had. They wouldn't have recognized the pictures of creatures who fled underground to find food and a new place to live. They wouldn't have remembered that's what they'd looked like before their descent into madness.

If darkness is the absence of light, then a life lived in darkness is startled by light. They had journeyed for what seemed an eternity, but only because it was measured in pain. They were climbing through the crumbling structures when it appeared with a stinging strangeness.

It was only a tiny splash hitting the ground, but the force sent a shivering ripple through the black swarm.

They felt a gush of air that was different too, not as steamy and stifling, but still rancid and raw. They clawed up through the tunnels, the misty light leading the way. The younger creature still urged it along, but now it was more dead than alive.

The exodus was finally done as the black swarm crawled out of colossal black holes and blasted craters. The underground darkness was gone, replaced by a glimmering glow that was eerie and ghostlike. The landscape didn't look that different from the depths below, just a more visible wasteland.

In the shivering light, the black swarm blinked wildly in every direction. It was still alive, but just barely, and it gazed at the younger creature hovering close by. It had never known love or hate, only the burning hunger to survive in darkness and decay. But this younger creature seemed different, as if it knew what surviving was about.

But it was too late for that.

It lay down to die, but it wasn't alone, because the vast black swarm collapsed to the ground with a splattering thud. Their instinct told them nothing could survive in a world like this, a world that had been eaten alive one gnawing bite at a time. There was a final shudder beneath them, then nothing else. And then there was just the darkness of death everywhere, as the black swarm covered the ground like a tattered black shroud.

BONES IN A CITY GRAVEYARD

She was downtown, below 14th Street, standing on the corner of Bowery and Broome. She'd been standing there for some time, a harsh cold rain whipping around her. The walk to the drugstore had only been four blocks, but she stopped because she needed to rest. Her legs ached, and the stinging rain mixed with the sweat soaking her body. She glanced at her watch. Almost six o'clock. She was running late. She tugged her frayed raincoat tighter and thought about how best to allocate the time when she returned home.

First, she would take an extra hot bath to melt away the icy chill, then the long soothing ritual of oils and creams. Maybe tonight she would sprinkle rose petals in the water for good luck and apply her make-up by the warm soothing glow of candlelight.

Yes, she decided. *That would set the mood perfectly*.

She started walking again, turning off Broome onto Bowery. She had purposely avoided this street earlier but was now too tired to take the longer way back home. She kept her head down, dreading what might be ahead.

If the surly bodega owner was slouched in his doorway, he'd watch her like a hawk, then shake his head and spit in disgust. She looked up. The doorway was empty. Beyond that, she saw the upside-down crates where the domino players sat. The rain kept them inside too. Good. They loved to shout at her in

29

Spanish and throw empty beer cans whenever she passed. She didn't see any teenagers either, and that was even better. There was usually a small group slouched in front of the pizza shop with scowling faces. They were always the cruelest of all. They'd howl and point whenever she passed, then follow her for a block or two, making "oink, oink" sounds and yelping like a pack of hyenas.

Like always, she wondered how hard they'd all laugh if they knew the real joke.

She used to be beautiful.

But she was also another person back then. In fact, she was no longer sure about the details, because so much about her life had changed.

But she did remember this.

She came from Ohio, because she wanted to be famous. She always thought she was special, because that's what everybody told her when she was growing up. Her beauty sprouted early and propelled her towards a destiny she thought was hers. She was the head cheerleader, the Prom Queen, and voted most beautiful in the yearbook. You should be in movies, and on the cover of magazines, everybody said. It was a small-town chorus she heard so often it had to be true.

So, the summer she graduated from high school, she climbed up the steps of a bus and came to New York City.

She remembered this too.

She had tried.

She had tried as hard as she possibly could, but the dream never got far. Audition after audition, meeting after meeting, day after day, year after year, in a city so big and overwhelming it forced the brightly colored memory of her hometown to get smaller and hazier.

There had been a few small successes, just enough to keep the dream alive, as the years tumbled by. For most of those years she had tried to be patient, always believing her "big break" was right around the corner. But the occasional modeling jobs never led anywhere, and the small parts in off-Broadway plays never lasted long enough to get attention from "the right kind of people."

Then, late one night, she finally understood what had happened, the reason for all her bad luck. It came to her in a nightmare. Her life had obviously been cursed, and this curse was responsible for everything. That's what the nightmare told her.

The curse had probably lured her to this cruel city in the first place, shrewdly disguising itself as an innocent dream. Pain and punishment, that's what the curse was really all about. What else could explain her brutal misfortune? She had only been in the city a few years when the curse had suddenly killed both her parents back in Ohio. Evidently, the curse loved blood and the horrible smell of burning flesh, because the accident was a head-on collision in broad daylight.

But that was just the beginning.

Pain and punishment. Punishment and pain.

Month after month. Year after year.

None of it made any sense, but the curse was relentless. It brought bad boyfriends and wrinkles, two rapes, and three muggings. Most of all, it brought endless bad luck and missed opportunities, until the only comfort she had left was the little bit of money her parents had left her. It was barely enough to live on, but that was part of the curse's diabolical plan. It wanted her to be desperate. It wanted her to live in filth and darkness.

So, this is what it did.

It pushed her.

The island of Manhattan was long and slender, jagged on the edges. When she first moved to the city, she found a five floor walk-up on West End Avenue in the nineties. The neighbors were friendly, but the rent kept going up and her succession of crappy jobs couldn't keep pace. Her next apartment was in the fifties, another walk-up, but she was only there a few years, unable to afford that either. Her next apartment was farther south, and the one after that, farther still. But the curse kept pushing and pushing, until she finally ended up all the way downtown, with the rats and the rumble, in the grimy black shadows of the Bowery.

And lately, the curse had been sending her a brand-new message, whispering it in the darkest hours of the night.

Playtime is over, now I want you dead.

She was scared, of course, but she also came up with a plan. She needed a partner. The curse was on the verge of winning, so she desperately needed someone to help her fight back. After all, she kept telling herself, she just needed what most women already had.

She needed a man.

For the past year she'd been placing a personal ad in small magazines and newspapers. The response had been encouraging. Actually, she'd been surprised by the number. *But it's a big city*, she told herself, *so there's probably a large number of just about anything, including men who responded to personal ads.*

So far, the encounters had been disappointing, but she wasn't about to give up hope.

Her trip down the block had been without incident. She turned the corner. The doorway to her building was a short distance away, so she tried to accelerate her lumbering pace. On this block there were no bright lights or passing cars. There was only darkness and dirt, despair and desperation, sordid secrets the rest of the city knew nothing about.

She climbed the two crumbling steps, then pushed open the door of her dilapidated building. The entryway was as dark as a cave. The only escape was the shadowy stairway rising in front of her. She stared at it for almost a minute. This was always the part of the trip she hated the most.

Her rain-soaked foot landed on the first step with a soggy thud. She took a deep breath, then raised her other foot. The zigzagging climb up the six flights of stairs would take another twenty minutes. She took another step, then another, then another. The old wooden boards groaned from the strain, and her legs were already on fire.

Yes, the curse was evil alright.

It had ruined her life by turning her into the kind of freak drunken old men threw beer cans at. She stopped at the landing, utterly exhausted, but she still had five more flights to go. She sucked in another wheezing breath, then she climbed and climbed, stopping again and again, the shadowy stairway moaning and groaning with each heavy step. When the torturous ascent was finally completed, her trunk-like legs were shivering with pain and her body was a blubbery swamp of stink and sweat.

Why?

Because evil always takes away what you love the most and this is what the curse had accomplished. It had taken away her beauty by smothering it beneath hundreds of pounds of suffocating flesh. She came to the city with youth and beauty, and she came because she wanted to be famous. But it was now more than twenty years later, and she weighed almost four hundred pounds.

Drenched with rain and sweat, she stopped in front of the grimy door to her apartment. Her exhaustion was so ferocious, the dusty air was swirling around her. She fell against the wall for support. When the wave finally passed, she took out her keys and unlocked the door.

Lumbering inside, a single hope was all that gave her the strength to keep going.

Maybe tonight would be the night she fell in love.

He was late.

When the buzzer finally shrilled, she had been anxiously waiting for almost an hour, but the sudden sound was magic. A warm tingle washed over her body in a rush, and her growing doubts about the night instantly disappeared. She pushed herself up from the sofa and shuffled to the buzzer that would open the downstairs door.

At least she'd put the time waiting to good use.

The apartment was cramped and musty, with a permanent smell that lingered like a fog. Outside, decay was all around, so she treated her meager living

34

space like a private sanctuary she could control. She'd spent most of the last hour sweeping and dusting, obsessively searching for dirt and grime.

Sitting on a small table was a bottle of red wine and a plate with cheese. She always explained she preferred a quiet evening at home on a first date, and most of the men readily agreed.

She put her ear against the door, better to hear the footsteps slowly climbing the stairs. Her skin was still tingling like it always did. It was tingling with excitement and hope. But there were darker thoughts nagging for attention too.

She felt ugly.

It was a constant feeling she couldn't shake, always clawing inside her, tearing away at her heart and soul. At first, the weight came slowly, a few pounds at a time. But then it began to appear with a monotonous consistency, day after day, week after week. It was somewhere around three hundred pounds when the other changes came too, the more drastic mutations in her appearance. This is where the curse had demonstrated its spectacular eye for detail and brilliant talent for punishment.

Men worshipped beauty in women, so the curse had gleefully pushed her into a body that was the exact opposite of what men considered beautiful. Her face was now as plump and round as a perfect full moon, and her bright blue eyes had turned murky and dark. The weight of her flesh had bent her spine forward. Even her hair seemed heavy, hanging like a fright wig around her mushy face.

On the phone he'd said he was an electrician and he lived in Queens.

The knock on the door was sharp and loud. She opened it slowly, and the sight that greeted her was not unpleasant. He was dressed in a black leather jacket and a black cowboy shirt. She normally didn't like mustaches, but his was trimmed and neat. What she did like was he was still standing in front of the open door smiling, after he had clearly witnessed her appearance.

"Hi."

"Hello."

"You must be Phil."

"That's me alright.

"It's nice to meet you Phil."

"Same here, doll. It's a real pleasure."

Now she was smiling too, because this brief exchange had lasted longer than most of her past dates. He followed her inside.

This is when her fantasy took flight.

They sat together in the cramped living room, he in the chair, she on the tattered brown sofa. He quickly opened the wine and filled their glasses.

Yes, she thought, *he could very well be the one, my own Prince Charming*. He had climbed the winding staircase to rescue her like a hero in a fairytale. He was going to fight the curse and win.

Her heart began to soar.

But only for another few seconds.

He finished his wine in a single gulp, then rose from the chair and stumbled towards her. He fell down next to her on the sofa, mumbling something she couldn't understand. She smelled the harsh stink of whiskey on his breath. He rolled on top of her, shoving his hand under her dress. His calloused thick fingers crawled between her thighs like a spider.

"Stop..."

"C'mon, honey, let's have some fun."

"Please..."

"Hey... don't be a bitch... relax..."

But she couldn't relax, because now she was scared.

After all these years, she had finally gained a small advantage in her battle against the curse. She could sense when it was near. She felt it now. It was close. It was very, very close. He was still riding on top of her like a drunken cowboy, one hand jammed between her thighs, the other roughly groping her massive breast.

She closed her eyes.

It's time, the curse whispered. *It's time.*

The curse snapped her knees shut with a stunning force. The cheese knife was now in her

hand. His shocked expression was followed by bloodcurdling screams and death wails as she stabbed him repeatedly with a strength only the curse could give her. The sounds were deafening, but all she heard was the evil sound of the curse happily giggling with wicked glee.

The two cops had gotten the call from the precinct house a few minutes earlier. The Hispanic super met them at the door. Climbing the stairs, he continued his story in angry streams of broken English.

Not much made sense to the officers, but it had something to do with a fat lady and a locked door. For the past few days, neighbors had been complaining about a "terrible smell," and the super had finally gotten around to calling the police. At the fifth-floor landing, the older cop stopped to catch his breath. His name was Ramirez, and he knew this much already. He hated climbing stairs, and he hated that smell, because he knew what it was.

On the sixth floor, the super stopped in front of a grungy brown door. He swung a key ring from the back of his pants and flipped through the keys. The first few tries didn't work. Finally, one did. The super mumbled angrily to himself as he pushed open the door, then switched on the light.

Ramirez turned around and looked at his partner. He was hard to read. *Welcome to the graveyard*, Ramirez thought. But that talk would come later. Every job has its own unique rite-of-passage, and Ramirez guessed his rookie partner was about to have his. The younger cop was an Irish kid named Rafferty. He'd just graduated from the academy six weeks earlier, so he was a virgin with all his naïve assumptions still intact.

Inside the apartment, the smell was overwhelming, as oppressive as smog.

The super was already standing in front of another closed door, pointing out the obvious.

The smell was coming from behind this door, but he didn't have a key to open it. The older cop nodded to the rookie. That's why they brought the crowbar. The rookie was a strong kid, a few inches over six feet. He shoved the crowbar in deep at the door's edge. Leaning low, he shoved hard once, then again, and the door popped open.

The rookie quickly straightened, giving him the first look at the contents of the room. When he turned back around, his face was drained of color.

Ramirez walked past the kid, into the room. What hit him first was a stronger smell, stomach turning and much worse than the outer room. Then he saw what was lying on the bed. The body was naked and decomposed, rotting into grayness. It was a huge, blubbery mass of human flesh. Right now, only one rat was visible, quietly nibbling at one of the toes, but there must have been others. The nose and ears were gone, most of the fingers too.

Turning around, Ramirez saw the super had already stumbled back a few steps, cursing in Spanish. The kid was still standing in the same place, clutching the crowbar. His face was drained of everything but shock. Every job has its own unique rite-of-passage, and the rookie cop had just had his.

Ramirez smiled grimly, turned back to the room.

Time to go to work.

Looking around, he saw a lamp on a small table next to the bed. Putting a handkerchief over his nose and mouth, he walked across the room. The light from the lamp didn't make the sight on the bed any prettier, but it sent the rat scurrying out of sight.

Ramirez walked around the perimeter of the bed, randomly poking the giant corpse with a pencil. The smell was almost unbearable, even with the handkerchief. The skin was tough and leathery, but spongy too. He was looking for evidence. A bullet hole, a knife wound, needle marks, whatever. A couple more pokes, then he stopped.

So far, cause of death unknown.

He turned his attention to the room. Not much there either: a bureau, old movie magazines, make-up, plastic bottles, perfume, shoes, newspapers.

He walked to the closet and opened the door.

What he found were pieces of a ghastly jigsaw puzzle. Hundreds of bones spilled out and clattered to the floor. Skulls, leg bones, ribcages, thigh bones, every kind imaginable, and all of them, every single one, was completely white and impossibly smooth.

What Ramirez had to explain to his rookie partner was the legend of "The Graveyard." He did it four nights later at Morans, the neighborhood bar down the block from the precinct house.

Ramirez led him through the chattering crowd to the quieter room in the back. Its nickname was the blue room, because that's where the cops always sat. For the first couple of beers the conversation wandered over the usual topics of sports, women, and precinct politics.

Then Ramirez brought up Monday's events.

They had already talked over the facts that had accumulated in the last few days.

The medical examiner had determined no foul play was involved in the death. The cause was a sudden heart attack brought on by the women's extreme obesity. But the medical examiner had also discovered something else in his autopsy - traces of human flesh in the woman's digestive tract. The connection to the smooth white bones hidden in the closet was horrifically clear.

The final piece of evidence was found during another search of the apartment. Stashed under the bed, in tightly bound bundles, were letters from dozens of different men, and copies of the personal ad she'd used to attract them. In the ad she'd described herself as Rubenesque.

The rookie shook his head and grabbed his beer. "What I don't understand is why the newspapers aren't jumping all over this story."

"Actually, that's what I wanted to talk to you about."

Ramirez glanced around at the nearby tables. It was time to educate his virgin partner, but it wasn't the kind of story he wanted strangers to overhear.

The "Graveyard" was the macabre term the powers-that-be in city government coined for the decaying blocks hidden in the crumbling gloom behind the Bowery. It was called the Graveyard because that's where all the dregs of the city eventually landed. Accepting this, the powers-that-be also recognized what happened in the Graveyard was so far beyond the limits of normalcy, it was in the best interests of the city to withhold selected information about the day-to-day crime rate.

But the cops obviously knew because their job was to contain the problem.

In the graveyard, sick things happened every single day, because some of its inhabitants were known to adopt lifestyles that had mutated far beyond the scope of public tolerance. It was a place where delusion and insanity were the medication of choice. Simply put, the Graveyard was the neighborhood where the monsters lived.

That was the story he had to tell.

Before he started, Ramirez leaned back in his chair and took a leisurely look at the face in front of him. His new partner was twenty-one years old. He probably grew up watching cop shows on TV, just like Ramirez. He'd already told him becoming a cop was his childhood dream. But Ramirez had learned a terrifying fact in the last twenty years. This is real life, not TV, and this was New York City, not anywhere else.

"Welcome to the Graveyard," he began.

THE GOD OF FLESH

He stood before rows of eager young faces and raised his hands overhead like an old-time preacher, waiting until every eye was staring at him with rapt attention, then he made his usual pronouncement.

"Are you ready to become a God?"

There were a few giggles and smiles, but that was okay, because he had a slashing smile too. His course in surgical techniques was renowned because he was so unlike the other professors, who didn't have a smidgen of his dramatic flair. He kept his hair long and always wore black, a very different look from the rumpled blandness of the other instructors. He had tattoos too, the dark etchings of some unknown design creeping out above his collar and at the ends of his sleeves.

Due to his reputation, the room was always charged with buzzing excitement when he strode in and took his place at the lectern, looming for a moment with a piercing gaze. He was only a decade older than the students, but conducted himself with an air of unshakable superiority as he lectured about the blood-soaked mysteries of the human body. Every year they came to him like naïve lumps of clay, and he performed his transformative magic, slicing away what was weak and tentative and replacing it with a much higher power. What he'd said hadn't been a joke at all, but a belief he embraced with every part of his being.

He'd come to a rapturous realization years ago. The human body was a holy temple and true healers deserved to be worshipped like a god. This was the secret craving most medical students kept hidden inside, deep in that place where they locked away their most primal desires. They wanted to have the power of life over death; they wanted to perform miracles far beyond the reaches of mortal men; they wanted to ascend to a higher place where their ability to heal was nothing less than astonishing.

In the other classes, medicine was taught as little more than a job to be learned, not much different from building a house or fixing a car. But he knew with a feverish fierceness that the human body wasn't a house or a car, but a mystical vessel of flesh and blood, infinitely more mysterious. Of course, there were the usual skeptical looks scattered among the young faces, but it never deterred him from what he saw as his singular mission.

"If you don't want to be a God, then ask yourself this. If it was your dying body hovering above the horrible black chasm of death, would you want a doctor who believed he could do the impossible, or a doctor who had no faith in himself?"

This always brought more nods and smiles.

He was not thought of fondly by the rest of the faculty, but he'd made his peace with that. When you can see and do what others can't, the result is always dislike and distrust. The rest of the faculty thought he was arrogant and strange, not worthy of being at such an esteemed institution, but he accepted this as a badge of his unrivaled uniqueness. He went to their stupid

44

meetings and prattling cocktail parties, but only to take enjoyment in how desperately they wanted to ask him about his mysterious tattoos. It was a private matter, so he wouldn't have answered the question even if they'd asked. In another moment of rapture, he'd decided to cover his flesh with black gothic scrawls that were a quote from the Bible.

Heal the sick, raise the dead

Unlike the faculty, most of his students revered him. So, this is where he chose to spend his free time, meeting with a chosen few at the local watering hole, regaling them with his surgical tales of life and death, huddled next to a crackling fire that made them all glow with a ghostly brightness. Even the faculty couldn't deny his amazing accomplishments, which is why he was hired. And this is where his dramatic gifts were even more evident, as he took the ghostly group deep inside a dying body and described how his swiftly moving hands raced like lightning through the gushing blood and throbbing organs to drag dying flesh back to life.

When each tale of his medical miracle was finished, he always liked to wave to the waitress for another round of drinks, because the booze and crackling fire added a radiant touch to his words. And this is also where his growing legion of disciples was enlisted, their young faces brimming with wide-eyed wonder and worship. But the calendar showed six months had passed, so on this night he wouldn't be joining them. Tonight, he would once again engage in his most sacred battle against his archenemy death.

He began as he always did, with a scalding hot shower almost blistering enough to burn his flesh, leaving it red and raw, except for the parts covered with tattoos. The result was always exactly what he wanted: a burning baptism infusing his body with a searing pain that made his senses even more intense and alert. He'd learned long ago you need to experience the anguish of pain to fully appreciate the ecstasy of pleasure, and you need to witness the horror of death to fully appreciate the wonder of life.

He quickly dressed in clothes he kept hanging in his closet specifically for this night. They were expensive, but bland and muted, very different from the dark attire he usually wore, more like that of the other instructors. Then he always drove a good distance, rumbling quickly through the night, making a random choice with no discernable pattern to where he'd gone six months before, and six months before that, going back many years.

On this night, the trip was over an hour, and he chose a roadside bar near a local airport. His ruse was always the same, strolling in like he was a weary traveler just passing through. He never made his move until he'd secretly studied the single women milling about, quietly searching for one with a specific physical feature. It might be a pair of soft blue eyes, a freckled nose, or a falling swirl of lush red hair. But it had to evoke the heavenly face always glowing in the darkness of his mind. When he spotted the right woman in the mingling crowd, his heart began to pound with a feeling very close to love, but a lot more complicated.

This time it wasn't a physical feature, but a quiet laugh that attracted his attention, because it echoed a sound he could still hear from that time years ago.

"I'm Arthur," he said.

"I'm Cheryl," she smiled back.

46

It never took longer than an hour or so before they were strolling out the door together. Whenever they learned he was a doctor, which he always revealed in the most casual way, it was a certainty he was the kind of man they were seeking. They thought they were going back to his motel room, but they were never conscious long enough to question why he raced back to the highway instead, an unseen dose of chloral hydrate in their drink always doing the trick.

His rules of waiting at least six months between each selection and choosing random locations were necessary precautions for those who would question his medical methods. Every god has to deal with non-believers, and the procedure could only be appreciated by those with his glorious vision and unique knowledge of life and death.

He drove through the night trying not to speed, his heart racing with a thumping excitement. He felt this way before a challenging operation, but never to this extreme. The pain from the scorching shower had long faded, but now his senses were even more on fire, because in one way, she had never left him, still living a haunting life in all his dark places. But he desperately needed more than that, which is the reason he became a doctor.

It was a rain-splattered night when he'd lost her physical body in a car accident. They'd met freshman year in college and for him it had been love at first sight, and not just love, but a feeling even more profound. Her beauty was ethereal, like a girl from another time and place - pale blue eyes, freckled white skin, and red hair that fell like a waterfall. He was going to marry her, of course, he had no doubt about that.

But the skidding truck slamming into their car put a screaming end to all that as her beautiful body lay bloody and mangled beside him. In the flickering light inside the car, he saw her organs spilling out and he knew that would be certain death, so he pushed them back inside, desperately trying to stop the gushing blood with nothing but his flailing bare hands. But he was just a kid back then, so there were no miracles to come, just a howling and gruesome death to the girl he cherished more than life itself.

His decision to become a doctor came soon after that, when he was still in the throes of a bottomless despair. A faint glimmer of hope kept him alive, and that's why he became a surgeon, knowing her dead flesh could only be healed by someone with a special power beyond an ordinary man.

Being a grave robber was another one of his methods the non-believers wouldn't support, so he'd kept that a secret too, performing the midnight rescue on a moonless night. If there was a God, and he had to believe there was, then surely there must be some way to get back what should never have been taken in the first place. His training as a surgeon had given him the idea, and his growing awareness of his own godly powers provided the rest. Faith was a crucial element too, a piece of the puzzle that surged even stronger into a raging force.

As he dragged the unconscious body from his car to his house, the memories of his past efforts crept into his brain. He always chose a woman with a feature that reminded him of his beloved, because it heightened what was to come, like the scalding hot baptism earlier.

And now everything was on fire inside him, as he dragged her body across the polished floor to the closed basement door. He lived in an isolated house at the end of a one-way street, surrounded by a thick sprawl of woods, so he didn't have to worry about being interrupted by any non-believers. He dragged her down the wooden stairs like he had all the others, her unconscious flesh thumping down to his operating room.

The house was grand and ornate, befitting his stature, so the basement was spacious too. But he'd made peculiar changes to suit his needs. He'd ripped away the white walls to expose the craggy black brick behind it, wanting a look closer to a medieval dungeon. His life in the years following the accident had been a brutal torture only he knew, so he wanted the sanctum for his release from this agony to be a symbol of the horror he'd had to endure.

He stripped off his clothes and lit the giant iron torches. His nakedness was necessary because it revealed the sacred tattoos that proclaimed his faith like a divine commandment covering his flesh.

Heal the sick, raise the dead

And now, after another excruciating wait, there was holy work to be done, to give life back to the decomposed body he couldn't live without. He wanted her back, and not just in those dark places where she smoldered like a mangled memory. She was lying on a surgical table he treated like a slab between heaven and hell, her body stuffed with transplanted organs from all his past futile efforts. There was little left of her original body, but that was the sacrifice that had to be made.

He hoisted the unconscious body on top of the table next to her and tugged on his rubber gloves. If tonight was the night his horrific nightmare finally became a dream-come-true, a part of him wanted one of his students to witness his greatest achievement. But all he had was the gory row of dead women slumped against the blood-speckled walls, their bodies sliced open with expert precision.

His back was turned to gather his surgical instruments when he suddenly heard a sound behind him and spun back around. The body on the table was stirring.

"Arrggggg..." she suddenly spat out in a guttural gasp.

Her eyes shot open, instantly filled with confusion and fear, gaping around at the dungeon-like space that clearly wasn't a motel room. She roared out a booming shriek when she saw the dead women, all staring back with black eyes and gutted bodies, a gory line-up of one-night stands gone bad.

He stared back in surprise, because this had never happened before. But he also knew the human body was a maze of blood-soaked caverns filled with infinite mysteries, so he accepted this twist without further thought. The woman named Cheryl had a will to live he hadn't previously witnessed. This also meant she might have the elusive body part he'd needed all this time.

But she didn't want any part of that.

"You motherfucker," she screamed in the same shrieking voice, scrambling off the steel slab and facing him on the black stone floor. Her green eyes were wild, her short brown hair a sloppy mess, all of which filled him with an aching sadness. There was nothing about her that reminded him of his beloved anymore. He remembered it was her quiet laugh, but he knew he wouldn't be hearing that down here.

He laughed to himself as he stared back at her, the burning torches on the walls casting eerie black shadows and crackling light inside the room. She was a screaming woman who wanted to live, but he was holding a scalpel that could slice through clothes and flesh with just a flick of his wrist. It obviously wasn't going to be a fair fight, but that was okay, because his beloved was waiting.

It was a chaotic and bloody affair that should have ended a lot quicker than it did, but she wouldn't give up. She fought back with more screams and shrieks, flailing arms and kicking legs, as he methodically did what he always did best, slice into the holy vessel of her flesh. But on she fought when she should have fallen to the red-stained floor in a lifeless heap. Rage and anguish burned in her eyes as she continued to flail with her bloody arms at the slicing figure she could barely see.

"*But who will take care of my son...*" she yelled in a blaring cry fiercer than any sound he had ever heard. It was a sound that could only have come from her heart, a war cry that held a power and fury that startled him.

And that's when he saw it, the scalpel she'd grabbed from the table holding his holy instruments. She lunged at him with fire in her eyes and rammed the scalpel into his flesh. She had none of his expertise or skill, but the fire was the love she had for her son, and that was enough.

The torches sputtered and burned as he collapsed to the floor, seized by an icy darkness spreading inside him. For all these years, he'd been convinced he was a god on a holy mission to bring his beloved back from the dead, but he'd only created more death.

He stared at the mutilated bodies slumped on the floor and realized he wasn't a god at all, but something evil, an unthinkable monster. And if he'd brought her back, she'd be a monster too, an unwanted creation cobbled together from other chunks of death.

It was the trembling mother who refused to die who truly believed in the sanctity of life, because that's what real love is. For a terrible second, he gazed around at his dungeon walls, the crackling torches, and the sickening sight of senseless death.

"Forgive me..." he muttered in a whispery gasp.

His last thought, as the icy darkness dragged him away, was the Bible quote he should have tattooed on his flesh instead... *Physician, heal thyself.*

A GIFT FROM THE STARS

Dear Clark Ashton Smith,
  I am writing this letter because I believe you're the only person with an imagination immense enough to accept what I'm about to reveal. My fear is if I disclose this to others, their dull minds will dismiss it as the delusional drivel of a madman, but I've learned that madness is a term misused by those with no knowledge of the hidden terrors lurking in our world. I say this as someone who has witnessed these terrors and embraced madness as the only appropriate response. Madness is simply the acknowledgement of our insane world's true nature.

My mother's descent was slow and torturous, especially to the eyes of an impressionable young boy. After my father's mental collapse, hers was more gradual and painful to behold. Her gaze became strange and murky, as if some inner light was dying and something dark was taking its place. She continued to be my mother, but there was a gradual metamorphosis that severed a part of who she was and replaced it with something inhuman. I know how this sounds, but I have no other way to describe what I saw.

What I've never revealed are the private times we spent in her shadowy room when her shocking madness was fully unleashed. I shudder even now when I recall it, because the memory of her otherworldly voice still sends shivers to my soul.

At first, there were only random murmurs and garbled whispers that were like gibberish from some unknown language. It was as if this frail old woman was becoming a transmitter for a distant message from some strange beyond. My young mind had no way to fathom what it meant. I concluded that her mental decline had opened a psychic portal that allowed her to see the unseen.

In her candlelit room, she rambled on in a croaky hush about a cosmos that was infinitely more terrifying than anyone had ever suspected. It was teeming with monsters and unnamed horrors that dwarfed our planet with their gargantuan girth and hideous majesty. I sat there with trembling hands as she described how insignificant and hopeless our puny lives were. She made it clear in no uncertain terms that the universe belonged to these colossal monsters and not to us. Equally startling was the creeping transformation that began to alter her frail form. Her murky eyes grew bigger and more luminous. Her wispy breathing turned watery and wet, like some prowling monster from the depths of the sea.

Yes, my dear friend, I'm sure you've made the connection that's been my secret for all these years. My stories don't come from my own inner fears, but from my mother's mad ramblings and whispery rants. But I hope you don't think any less of me as a writer, because I've strived to commit to paper in the most vivid way possible the terrifying scope of the cosmic horror that was revealed to me.

And now I must ask you to indulge me for a few moments longer, because of a recent occurrence I will now relate. It happened a fortnight ago, but I am only now sufficiently able to describe the blasphemy that will forever haunt my life. When my mother's decline plunged to its lowest depths, I was left with no choice but to commit her to an asylum in my hometown of Providence to be with others like her. It's a tomb-like place in a tragic state of disrepair, but the only facility in New England willing to care for her extreme condition.

A pummeling rain was thrashing outside when I was suddenly summoned to come to the asylum without delay. No details were given, except that it was of the utmost urgency, so I rushed through the rain with a pounding heart. My mother's troubles had never diminished my love for her but had only complicated it with a heart-wrenching sadness. We'd always had a connection that couldn't be put into words, even though words are the only true skill I've ever had.

I arrived at the hospital with gasping breaths, for a reason I could only conclude was the fear pounding louder in my heart. My father was dead, and my mother was all I had left. The possibility of her demise filled me with an aching dread, and this is the fear I carried with me into the crumbling asylum.

My dearest friend, I've already confessed the connection between my stories and my mother's madness, and now I must take you with me into this horrid sanctuary where the blasphemous event occurred. I'd been there during the day, but never at night, and the ominous feeling that washed over me was a startling jolt. There were more black shadows than glimmers of light, more dust and grime than breathable air. I was drenched from the pounding rain, and this only added to my misery.

I was promptly led by a mute attendant down a long dark hallway, then up a clattering elevator to the uppermost floor. I knew this is where the most depraved patients were kept, which was the reason for the massive locks on every door. And that's when I heard a familiar sound, a mumbling chorus of moans and wails, all of them watery and wet. It sent a cold chill up my spine, as the drenching rain on my shaking body splattered to the floor.

The mute attendant unlocked my mother's door and pushed it open with a groaning creak. I walked in with squishy steps and peered down at the strange new form she'd become. She was still vaguely human, but now other creatures seemed to be part of her body too. Her luminous eyes were bulging, much too big for the wrinkled flesh drooping around them. Her skin was scaly and limp, hanging on her bones with no strength left. Small webs stretched between her fluttering fingers, and sharp teeth were mostly hidden in the black gash of her mouth. The horrible love and anguish in my pounding heart was ready to explode.

Yes, my dear friend, this was true horror, but now is when I need your celebrated imagination to accept what I'm about to say next.

"My dearest, Howard," she croaked in a watery whisper. "I'm dying, but there's a final gift I want to leave you..."

I uttered no words because I'd suddenly lost the ability to speak. I watched my mother's bizarre new form rise up from the bed with a shivering shakiness. The human part scarcely remained, replaced by some kind of mutated gruesomeness.

And now I heard dozens of rusted iron doors opening, and the watery howls gurgle into the hallway. My mother's bulging eyes stared at me as I was dragged from the room by a horde of creatures who

56

shared her misshapen condition. They were once human, but now they weren't. A tangle of mutated appendages and slimy tentacles carried me down the hallway by this mass of gurgling wretchedness.

My dear friend, please know that this was truly a horror beyond all others, because I was carried up a twisting flight of stairs by this abysmal assemblage to the asylum's roof. The pummeling rain was gone, and the rumbling black clouds had parted, revealing a full moon glowering down with a bright gaze. The eerie light from the moon revealed a construct that shouldn't have been there. A primitive temple was still dripping with rain, and it seemed to be fashioned out of cosmic materials not of this world.

"You'll be one of us now," a whispery voice croaked.

My mother came through the mass of creatures with a shivering gait. When the moonlight splashed on her face, it shattered my heart. There are no words to describe what she'd become. And now I saw another creature was with her, both of them coming to where I'd been thrown on the temple floor.

The other creature was much younger and appeared less extreme in her transmutation. She was still walking on two wobbly legs, with two arms hanging at her sides, but her blinking eyes were also huge and bulging. She stood for a moment in front of me and let her tattered hospital gown flutter down to the ground. Tentacles unwrapped from around her body and slithered towards me in the gloomy night air.

My dear friend, this is when I learned that horror has no boundaries but can always be stretched in macabre ways that are truly unimaginable.

She dropped down to the ground and ripped off my clothes with her swarming tentacles. Her human hands began to caress my body with an embrace close to tenderness, but her squirming tentacles invaded every part of my flesh with a lusty hunger that left me wailing. I realized this was a ritual of some kind, as our coupling was watched in sacred silence by the surrounding horde. The physical aspects were equal parts pain and pleasure, but on a scale that would be incomprehensible to a sane mind.

And this is when I understood the truly mundane nature of sanity. The ritual was blasphemous but liberating too. Like my mother, I suddenly felt a psychic portal burst open inside me, and I could now see the cosmos as it really was. Gaunt black creatures slithered through the swirling night air, and gargantuan monsters prowled the yawning black chasm of space. I had already learned from my mother that these beings had once roamed our planet in history before ours. But it was all so overwhelming I suddenly blacked out, slipping into an unconscious state where the ghastly visions continued to haunt my mind.

There is only one place as infinite and scary as space, and that's where I was with the monsters howling in my head. When I returned to consciousness, the horde of creatures was no longer there. It was only me and my nakedness violently shaking on the temple floor. When I gathered my clothes, the pummeling rain returned, and the full moon was covered again by the black clouds.

And now, my dear friend, I must leave you with this.

I have spent the last fortnight locked in my study contemplating what I've just described. My own physical changes have already begun and will surely follow the same torturous path as my mother's. My eyes have become dark and strange, my breathing raspy and wet. It won't be long before I reach the point when no cloaking disguise will be enough so I can venture outside.

I'll continue to write you when I can, but I've found that madness is a chaotic affair that shuns plans of any kind. But at least my madness will give me comfort as I face the greatest horror of all.

We've had this planet to ourselves since the dawn of our time, but a new age is coming when The Old Ones return. That, my dear friend, is what I've learned from my shattering journey to insanity. They won't be traveling across the yawning black chasm of space, they'll be spawned here on Earth. There's nothing we can do, so we might as well accept it. I'm sorry, my friend, but our time on this planet has run its course. If you don't hear from me, it's not because our friendship is any less important, but because other concerns are now more urgent.

And now I must ask one final favor.

In nine months' time, my child will be born on the uppermost floor of the crumbling asylum on the outskirts of Providence. By then I will surely be housebound in a heavily locked room, without the freedom to travel outside. So, I am going to leave my child to your loving care. Please be forewarned it's not going to be a normal offspring, but a gift from the stars, so it needs to be cared for in a very special way.

Yours forevermore,
Howard Phillips Lovecraft

DOWN WHERE HER NIGHTMARES DWELL

They say the greatest heartache a parent can have is to witness their child in pain and feel helpless to stop it. That misery is even worse when it echoes the same pain they felt as a child, because they know the agony being inflicted upon the flesh they created.

But what if that flesh is what causes the pain?

The childhood of Molly Stark was brutal in a way no child should ever have to endure. She'd been born with a face that was fat and sullen, with gloomy grey eyes, and a lumpy body. In her younger years, this condition created other abnormalities: a halting stutter, a nervous twitch, and a lumbering walk.

To make matters worse, she grew up in Los Angeles where physical beauty was worshipped above everything else. The siren call of Hollywood lured striking faces from far and wide. Prom queens and hunks strolled the streets in all their stunning glory, as gorgeous faces gazed down from billboards like fallen gods.

Her teenaged years were nothing less than a daily crucible of punishment and fear. She found out, in the most painful way possible, the cruelty of kids had no limits. Every day of her miserable life, she was tormented with sadistic taunts and horrible pranks. And that's when something began to fester inside her, a dark and secret creation that whispered at night. She didn't know what it was, only that it came from the hidden place where her nightmares dwelled.

The voice told her she had to change, no matter the drastic measures that needed to be taken.

Her course of action was obvious at first. She began to exercise with a frantic obsession, huffing and puffing in her tiny bedroom. It was a grueling ordeal, but necessary. She purchased stacks of beauty magazines and studied them by flashlight deep into the night. The glossy pictures and self-help articles became her sacred text, pointing the way to the promised land of physical beauty. Some modest gains were made, but that was all, some fat sweated off, a different hairdo, more pleasing make-up.

But even with that, the daily abuse didn't end, because once the mean girls and snarling bullies chose their prey, they wouldn't be fooled by modest changes.

So, in that secret place, the festering voice told her more radical steps were needed, because the problem was too severe for minor accomplishments. Her next needed step presented itself when a football player pushed her down a flight of stairs at school, and her plump face was horribly crushed by the tumbling fall. She was used to savage taunts and mocking sneers, but now it was obvious they wanted her dead. She was rushed to the hospital and that's when her life was changed forever. Under the bright lights in the operating room, she was introduced to the gleaming metal god that possessed the divine power to change human flesh.

Her face had been smashed to a bloody pulp, so bones were rearranged, sinew attached, and the battered skin was sewn back together. The operation was deemed a success, but now her face was even more revolting, a swollen atrocity mashed together with blood-crusted stitches.

The recovery process took months, another wrenching crucible of pain. When the healing was completed, the result was a surprise she didn't expect. Whether it had been the surgeon's miraculous skill, or just a lucky accident, her features weren't as dreadful as they were before the surgery. The transformation wasn't total, but it was far better than anything exercise and make-up had achieved.

All because of the gleaming god of surgical steel.

"This is your life..." she heard from that dark, secret place.

The insults and bullying persisted through her teenaged years, then finally eased up in college, only because the new torment was to make her invisible. The beautiful people decided this cruelty was more befitting, to pretend they didn't see her. By this time, she was so focused on becoming a doctor, the new torture could be ignored.

Her goal wasn't to be just any doctor, she wanted to worship the metal god that could transform flesh. She learned the blood-soaked mysteries of the human body in medical school, then studied the alchemy of plastic surgery. Late at night, in that secret place where her nightmares dwelled, the pain of her younger years still roared. But now she knew the blubbery slab of flesh that covered her body was not a prison, but merely a mushy facade that could easily be changed.

The years of study and building her practice were grueling, but when money finally came, she quickly utilized the benefits of her chosen profession, sculpting her face and figure into a form that was unrecognizable from the pitiful creature of her youth. She transformed her flesh into a captivating shape like those in the beauty magazines she used to study.

With her new allure, suitors flocked in, and she picked the one who seemed the most pleasant. She'd never been overly attracted to men because of the psychic pain that still burned inside, but she wanted a child, so she accepted marriage as a necessary choice.

When her daughter was born, the flesh of her flesh, she felt a joy she'd never experienced. Cradling the tiny bundle in her arms unleashed a part of her heart she never knew existed, the part where unbounded love was the most powerful feeling.

But one night, another emotion suddenly appeared when she realized her child was indeed, the flesh of her flesh, only like she was before her sculpted transformation. The child's eyes were becoming dark and gloomy, and her wiggling body was becoming lumpen too.

They say the greatest heartache a parent can feel is to witness their child in pain when it echoes the same pain they too felt as a child.

So down where her nightmares dwelled, a plan formed which she saw as the only course of action. No loving mother would ever allow cruelty to the flesh of her flesh, so if ugliness was going to be her daughter's inheritance, then changes had to be made.

She divorced her husband in case he didn't understand what needed to be done, then set up a make-shift operating room in the basement. She'd acquired skills that few people had, as a long-time worshipper of surgical steel.

The process was slow, but extreme and radical. She gradually transformed her daughter into a teenaged beauty, but it didn't stop there. She made her a bombshell beyond the limits of good taste, with a sexy figure, lusty lips, and cascading hair. She'd been attacked for being ugly, so she made the flesh of her flesh something totally new, seductive perfection in every way. And that's when it happened, the horror of horrors that no child should ever experience.

Her daughter came home in tears after a date with the captain of the football team, and the evidence was easy to see. Her clothes were ripped, and her body was bruised, but the assault had gone much deeper than that.

Down where her nightmares dwelled, her rage erupted to monstrous proportions and she prayed to the metal god for an appropriate response. It instantly came with a savage clarity, that she accepted for its unflinching justice. She needed her daughter's help, which she offered with the same need for payback and punishment.

With a soft and seductive voice, her daughter told the sickening football player how much she wanted another date. This feed his brutish ego like a game-winning touchdown.

"My Mom is away this weekend," she whispered in his ear at school. "Why don't you come over Friday and we can have more fun..."

He arrived lugging a bottle of cheap booze and flashing a horny grin. It was easy to knock him out with a powerful tranquilizer slipped into his drink. It took both the mother and daughter to drag his bulky body down the thumping stairs to the make-shift operating room in the basement, then lift him up to the surgical table. He was missing for a couple of days, because the operation was not an easy fix. He was one of the beautiful people, with sunny blonde hair, a square jaw, and sky-blue eyes.

Around midnight, his parents heard a scraping at the front door and stumbled downstairs. When they opened the door, it took a few seconds to see the whimpering thing on the stoop was their son, but now the flesh of their flesh was something brand new. He looked more like a pig than a human, with four stubby legs, a limp tail, pointed ears, and a snout that came from between his legs. The horror in his eyes was a pain no parent should ever have to see, but down where her nightmares dwelled, she knew the operation was a success.

THE LAST HORROR SHOW

Finally, his life had come to this, the end of the line. He was driving his car down a dusty dirt road. The desert landscape was silent and dark, like only a hot Texas night could be. He had left his trailer and was making his way to the TV station on the outskirts of town. The squat brick building appeared ahead.

The last few years had crept by as he felt his life fading away. There were still days when the past burned brighter than anything else. That's when he could remember it all, especially back to the time when he first fell in love with monsters.

It began with his father, who'd come home from work every day in a bad mood. He still looked like a regular guy as he quietly ate dinner and started drinking his whiskey. The change didn't happen every night. Sometimes he'd just fall asleep on the couch or stumble to bed with a bleary gaze. There were other nights though, when the bottle of whiskey didn't put him to sleep but woke up something frightening inside him. His face would twist into a furious scowl that belonged on the face of a terrifying beast. The sight filled him with a fear that changed him too. On those nights, this mutated monstrosity would stalk his mother around the house in a lumbering lurch, then stagger into his room with a slobbering growl. He'd cower in bed, shaking and crying under the covers, filled with a terror for his father that was impossible to describe.

When he was twelve his father died, just like that. He dropped dead at work and never came home again. Looking back, his fascination with monsters began with his father, who showed him how strange and shocking they could be.

During his teenaged years, his obsession began, watching the *Twilight Zone*, *The Outer Limits*, and any movie with scary creatures. He collected *Famous Monsters Magazine*, reading them over and over. He covered the walls of his room with Godzilla, King Kong, the Mummy, the Werewolf, and Dracula. While other boys were outside playing baseball, he was creating an army of miniature monsters from model kits. He could still remember the smell of the glue and the tingling thrill when he held the plastic model in his hand. His tiny room was a cluttered shrine to the glory of monsters.

After high school, there was never any doubt about where he was going. He went to a junior college in Los Angeles to be near Hollywood. His goal was to work in the kind of movies he loved. He dropped out when he got an entry level job at New World Pictures for Roger Corman. He ran errands, built sets, and anything else they asked him to do. There was barely enough money to live on, but it didn't matter. They were making his kind of movies, *Night of the Blood Beast, The Terror, The Dunwich Horror*, and *Creature from the Haunted Sea*.

It was a crazy time, without any rules, except for one. Get the movie made any way possible, so you could make the next one, churning them out, one after the other. He learned about special effects, wardrobe, and make-up, all the cobbled together parts that made a monster movie. The days and nights were long, each a grinding slog of drugs, booze and feverish dreams. It was as if they lived in a different world than everyone else, where making movies with monsters was all that mattered. The only goal was to bring shock and terror to a theater near you.

The years tumbled by, and then it happened, the night that would change the rest of his life. He was past forty now and married to a secretary he met at the company, working as the crew chief on *Galaxy of Terror*. They were north of the city for a night shoot and the rookie director rushed over with a panicked look. They were about to shoot a scene where the outer space creature attacked the astronauts, but the actor never showed up. It was a skeleton crew, and he was the right size for the creature suit. He'd done just about everything else, so he nodded and followed the director to make-up.

The rubber suit was a wobbly mess, with floppy tentacles, scaled skin, and plastic goggles for eyes. He could barely breathe or see, but the director told him what he needed to do and he was taken to the set. And then, as if in a kind of trance, he was struck with a feeling he'd never had before. He'd fallen in love with monsters back when he was a kid, but this was the first time he saw what it felt like to be one. When he lunged out and attacked the astronauts, he knew they were acting, but the flash of bulging fear in their eyes made him feel stronger than he'd ever felt. And that's when he realized this is what he'd always wanted, not to be scared of anything, and for everybody else to be scared of him.

After that, he pushed to do it again, taking acting lessons and getting his SAG card. He still worked with the crew, but he got what he wanted, playing other monsters and creatures. He lunged and staggered, chased and crawled, each time seeing how fear was stronger than any emotion. Nothing felt better than when he sat in the make-up chair and watched his aging body turned into a nightmare. It was all about the alchemy of transformation, leaving the mundane and ordinary behind for a frightening new form.

There were other pleasures too, like going to weekend horror conventions where fans treated him like a movie star. They'd line up for a picture and autograph, hanging on his every word, as if he knew secrets they desperately needed to know. He also loved doing interviews with horror magazines revealing behind-the-scenes stories and talking about monsters. It was a grand time knowing he'd become, in some small way, that very thing he'd idolized as a kid.

Maybe it changed him, or at least that's what his wife said when he came home one night. "I want a divorce. It's not the same anymore. You care more about those stupid creatures than you do about me." She'd already packed her clothes and left that night. But he didn't care. After work, he'd sit in the dark and drink whiskey just like his father did. He'd watch videos of his movies over and over, or roam through his collection of old magazines and models. As the night lurched on, he'd begin to hear voices, his father among them. Dad was his first monster and was still lurking somewhere inside him.

And then it was over when he became too old to do it anymore. All he could do was stagger around in front of the camera and that wasn't enough. He'd lost the strength and fierceness audiences wanted. He woke up one morning and his aching body told him that a feeble monster wasn't a monster anymore.

He still went to conventions to make some money, but the lines got shorter and he felt like a creaky old relic. The lines now formed in front of the younger monsters who had taken his place. Then another idea came late one night when he needed it most. He was watching *Shock Theater* on a local station, The host was a goofy creep in cheap vampire make-up. He wasn't scary at all and didn't seem to know anything about the movie he was showing. He remembered his room from his childhood, his cluttered shrine to horror and fear. If he couldn't be a movie monster anymore, he figured there was still a role he could play.

It took months of reading the trades and asking around, then he finally found a job as a late-night horror host at a small station in Nevada. Three weeks later, he was back in front of the camera, this time as Dr. Ghoul showing the movies he loved on *The Midnight Monster Show*. He'd spent days creating the make-up because it had to be just right. There was a bit of Lon Chaney, some Bela Lugosi, and Boris Karloff, a tribute to the old masters. It didn't matter the people at the station rolled their eyes and snickered whenever he came into the station. After all these years, he'd learned a valuable lesson, that monsters shouldn't be ignored.

But now, more than ever, he felt like he lived in a blurry realm different from everybody else, brought on, no doubt, by the flask he gulped when no one was looking. It belonged to his father and was in a box his mother had given him. There was other stuff too, like a stack of drawings about mystical places and imaginary beings his father drew when he was a kid. He never knew his father wanted to be an artist.

The jobs never lasted longer than a year or two before he was called in and fired. It was always the same story, just told by a different station manager that got younger and younger. "I'm sorry Dr. Ghoul, but I think it's time we part ways," the one in Nevada said without looking up from his cell phone. "The ratings just aren't what we need to get the right kind of advertisers."

After that he moved to a station in Arizona, then another in New Mexico, then Kansas after that, drifting farther away from the city of dreams. He never made any friends, living alone in crappy apartments with only the late-night voices to keep him company. He'd ended up at a small station in Texas, a scruffy desert town just north of the border. He'd been there for a month when he heard a soft knock on the door of his broken-down trailer, the only home he could afford.

The night voices hadn't crept in yet, so it was quiet and dark, just him and his unwashed cup of whisky. He stumbled to the door and stood for a moment, wary of opening it. He didn't trust his neighbors, or anyone else. He thought he heard whispers and shuffling feet outside. He shook his head because his foggy mind wasn't the same anymore. Along with the voices, he'd been seeing things that shouldn't be there.

"Who is it?" he finally asked in a slurry mumble.

"*It's us...*" the whispery voices came back.

He waited some more, turned back and took another gulp, then slowly cracked open the door. And there they were, a dozen or so kids huddled outside. They had dirty frayed shirts and ripped shorts, their gaunt young faces etched with an eerie paleness. They were mostly boys, but a few girls too, hunched

72

together in a shadowy pack. He could see their rusted bikes lying in the dirt behind them.

"What do you want?" he croaked.

The splattered moonlight cast them in a strange haze, like a desert mirage. The tallest was a boy, thin and bony, with chopped black hair hanging like dead weeds over his ears. "We're sorry to disturb you, but we've been watching your show. You're Dr. Ghoul, aren't you?"

He stood for a moment staring back, and this is when he saw a look in their eyes he'd almost forgotten. It was from that time long ago when there were lines of eager fans waiting to get his picture and autograph. Even in the heavy gloom of the night, he could see they were excited to see him.

"Yes..." he murmured.

And then it happened, just like it did back then. They moved closer and started asking him questions about horror movies and monsters, all of them packed together in front of his trailer door. His wrinkled old face was still smeared with the spooky make-up that never came all the way off anymore. He went back for his cup of whiskey and kept talking on and on, until the shadowy kids became so blurry he could barely see them.

"Good night," he finally mumbled. When he got back inside, he watched from the window as they climbed back on their rickety bikes and pedaled away like ghosts in the night.

But they came back a few nights later, and kept coming back. He'd hear a soft knock on the door and knew they were waiting outside. He came to know their names, and something about their lives, which were hard and luckless. Miguel was the tall bony one

73

and the rag doll next to him was his younger sister Sara. Tom-tom lived with his blind grandmother, Sofia walked with a limp, and Runt was missing some of his teeth. Their faces were dirty and grim, but they loved what he loved, and that's all that mattered. After a few weeks, they didn't have to knock on the door anymore, he'd dragged a chair outside and was waiting with his whiskey when they biked in. After they left, the voices would come telling him there wasn't much more of his life left. That's when he decided at least he could leave behind what he loved the most.

When they came the next night, there were paper bags plopped on the ground next to him. They arrived like they always did, a dusty whirlwind of spinning wheels and moonlit faces. He reached into one of the bags before they could get out the first question, and they all froze with eyes as wide as they could possibly be. He showed them some of the musty *Famous Monsters Magazine* he'd kept with him all this time. He handed them out with a shaky hand and they slowly flipped through the faded pages. A few crumbled from age as the kids stared at monsters from the past.

There were no questions that night, or the next, when he brought out the rest of his collection, along with his plastic army of misbegotten creatures. After that, their number seemed to grow as more bikes were left in the dirt, and more eerie young faces stretched out in front of him into the night.

Soon after that, they began to change, showing up with crude make-up they'd created themselves. Miguel smeared dirt around his eyes to look like the walking dead, and Sara wrapped herself in a tattered blanket like a creepy cocoon. Ketchup was used for blood and torn rags for mummy wrapping. This wasn't something he'd expected, but it didn't completely surprise him. They'd discovered the thrill of being a monster, leaving their hard lives behind.

But now it was over. He was driving his battered old car to his last show. The day before had been one of the worst of his life. He was summoned to the manager's office and given the usual spiel about moving in a different direction. When he left the office, the other workers were waiting in the hallway outside. They were wearing cheap Halloween masks and started singing "The Monster Mash." He could still hear them laughing and clapping as he staggered away. They obviously thought he was crazy old man who didn't belong here anymore.

When he parked the car, a light rain began to fall, adding a watery gloom. He took a gulp from the flask and thought about he'd never truly known his father. He wondered what he would think of his life, that he'd done what he wanted to do.

And then he went inside to show his last movie. He picked *The Galaxy of Terror*, the one when he first saw what it felt like to be a monster. He didn't leave right away, because the voices wanted him to watch it one last time. He got barely a glimpse from the other workers when he stumbled down the hall and pushed open the door.

And there they were, waiting outside. It was the kids who'd come to his trailer, and now their transformation was complete, but not just with dirt, ketchup, and rags. Miguel was clawing up from below ground, dead flesh hanging from his bones. Sara's cocoon-like blanket was gone, leathery wings lifted her up into the night. Teenaged werewolves howled at the moon and pale-faced vampires bared their fangs. His army of monsters was there too, twenty feet tall now, with a fire-breathing Godzilla and a chest-beating King Kong. The rain had suddenly turned into a downpour, but it couldn't hide the startling beauty of his monsters. It took him a few seconds to realize they weren't waiting for him, but for the others to leave from inside, because monsters should never be ignored.

HARD TO GET

Trevor Malone stepped out of his limo in front of a glass tower that soared to the sky like a monolithic temple. He was just past thirty with jet black hair slicked back, attired in a thousand-dollar custom made suit. He had the kind of life others could only dream about, a superstar hedge fund manager worth hundreds of millions of dollars.

As he strode to the building, a part of him wasn't sure he was doing the right thing, but he had reached a point in his life where he had all the millionaire toys and still wasn't happy. He'd confessed it to his best friend Rod after a couple of martinis. Rod was another Wall Street hotshot who was almost as rich as him.

"I know this sounds crazy, but I can have any woman I want and that's the problem. When they find out how rich I am nothing else matters. I'm their winning lottery ticket with a bank full of cash..."

They were sitting in the corner of a private club so exclusive you had to be worth more than some third-world countries. It was dimly lit with dark leather and polished wood, droopy-faced waiters in starched white jackets shuffling quietly through the room. The members had clawed their way to the top of the money mountain and looked down on everybody else.

Rod was tall with curly blonde hair and cold blue eyes that would suddenly twinkle when he crushed a big deal. They'd met at a conference in Vegas and bumped into each other later that night at a strip club that was super exclusive too, known only to those who knew the right people because they were the right people. They shared the same love for beautiful women and being filthy rich, a connection that brought them together from that night on.

"I hear you my friend, it's tough being us."

Trevor leaned back in his chair, knowing how he sounded. He'd grown up poor and was more successful than he ever imagined, and that definitely included women. They were all models and actresses, the kind that walked into a room and would take your breath away. It was all about getting the prize that others couldn't have. But when the megabucks came rolling in that changed, because now he was the prize – the gargantuan pot of gold that would give them everything they wanted.

"I just don't feel anything," he muttered. "There's no challenge anymore. Now they're all stalking me and the thrill of the chase is gone..."

Rod leaned closer with his cold blue eyes. "You know this isn't a good look for you, buddy boy. You're a master of the fucking universe, so you're much more appealing when you're cocky and arrogant. Do yourself a favor, don't pull this wimpy shit at the office..."

Trevor waved for another martini, the glumness still in his voice. "When you can have any woman you want, there's nothing special about any of them."

Rod stared at him for a moment, taking a slow sip of his drink. He lowered his voice, leaning closer over the polished wood table.

"Well, buddy boy, it turns out you've spilled your whining tale of woe to just the right person. I've been there myself so I'm going to help you out..."

"What do you mean?"

"I was just where you are and a friend hooked me up with a dating service that's only for the one-percenters. And if you have to ask how much, it's not for you."

"Why so expensive?"

Rod gave him a wink. "Because you get what you pay for, buddy boy."

"But why would I need a dating service if I can have any woman I want?"

"Because it's guaranteed. It's super-secret, the best of the best, and off the grid. It's like you've been driving a Rolls Royce and you're given the keys to a car that's a hundred times better."

"Is this the martini talking?"

"Absolutely not, it's your best fucking friend who's going to show you the promised land. I had my first date two months ago and she's the one. I know it sounds crazy, but I can't stop thinking about her. You gotta trust me, this is just what you need."

And on he went, gushing like a love-struck teenager about the incredible woman he met through the service. He described her appearance and personality, how he was already head-over-heels in love with her. He said she would fill the rest of his life with ecstasy in ways he could only dream about. Trevor listened to every word like it was a life-changing sermon meant only for him. It was a side of his friend he had never seen before, and he desperately wanted to feel that way too.

"You have to be recommended, so I'll give them a call and they'll call you. I know you're a bottom line kind of guy and that's what you'll get. They'll find exactly the woman you want, just like they did for me.

I was going to tell you tonight that you can expect an invite to my wedding in the next few weeks."

Rod gave him another wink and a giddy smile that showed his happiness.

The call came two days later. The voice on the other end was a young woman, direct and businesslike. She gave him the address and told him the evaluation process would take most of the day. He still wasn't sure, but he was desperate, so he decided to give it a shot. The million-dollar fee wasn't a problem, so he cleared his schedule and arrived at the agreed upon time.

He entered the giant glass tower and an elevator whooshed him up to the top floor. The young woman didn't give a company name, just a room number. He walked down a long hallway comprised of doors with ornate gold names until he came to one with no identification beyond the number she'd given. He pressed a buzzer and the door swung open. He stopped a few steps inside because he was surprised by what he saw. The room was completely empty except for a single chair on a black wool carpet.

"Good morning, Mr. Malone. Please have a seat and we'll be with you very soon."

It was the same woman's voice he'd heard on the phone, coming from a speaker he couldn't see. He sat in the chair, and nothing happened for almost ten minutes, until another door automatically opened.

"Please stop at our business office first, the second door on the left," the woman's voice said.

And again, this smaller room was completely empty except for a chair and table. There was an interactive screen on the table and another unseen voice guided him through a series of financial questions, ending with an agreement that the fee would be immediately paid in full. The questions were more probing than he'd expected, but whenever he asked a question, the response was always the same.

"We have our requirements, Mr. Malone."

The voice directed him to another room and this one was different, more like an examination space in a medical office, with an older man in a white coat waiting for him.

"Great, I finally get to meet a real person."

The man nodded. "Yes, I get that a lot." He gestured for Trevor to sit in a chair with cushy white pads. "So," he asked in a monotone voice. "What brings you to us?"

For the next hour Trevor explained the problem as clearly as he could, his whole history of pursuing beautiful women and how great it was, until it suddenly wasn't. And that's the part he described in even more detail, how women chased him now instead of the other way around. He missed the challenge, the romantic hunt, even surprising himself at how strongly he felt. The white-coated old man asked questions along the way, prodding and probing like a therapist.

"I'm surprised you're not taking notes," Trevor said.

He waved his wrinkled old hand out to the room. "You're being filmed and recorded. We don't want to miss anything. If you feel like a lab rat, that's an appropriate response."

Other tests were conducted as Trevor was hooked up to a machine measuring mental and physical reactions through a series of questions. He was shown pictures of women and queried about the traits he desired. It was more rigorous and intense than any job interview he'd ever had.

"We're almost finished" the old man finally said. "There's just the hypnosis session left."

Trevor's face showed his surprise. "Hold on, I think that's going a bit too far. I'm sure I've told you everything you need to know."

"Mr. Malone," the young woman's voice came in from the unseen speaker. "Please understand, there can't be any secrets that prevent us from giving you exactly what you want. As I said when we spoke the first time, we guarantee complete satisfaction."

When he exited the giant glass tower, the sidewalks were crammed with workers heading home. As his limo drove through the heavy traffic, he felt a sense of anticipation at what would come next, a tinge of excitement he hadn't felt in a very long time.

A week later the young woman called and told him where to go, a restaurant with an Italian name. Before he could ask how he'd recognize his million-dollar date the phone went dead. He didn't know it at the time, but this was the first of other challenges to come.

His limo motored him to the address he was given, but the restaurant wasn't there. They slowly circled the block without any luck, and he decided to get out and search on foot. His frustration grew until he glimpsed a shadowy sign in an alley with the name he was given.

He walked in and it was empty except for a young woman sitting at a table. At first glance, there didn't seem to be anything unique or exceptional about her. She was dressed in a plain white sweater, with long black hair. But when he stood in the doorway his heart suddenly leapt at the sight of her, in a mysterious way he couldn't explain. She was beautiful, but it was so much more than that. He walked to the table and she watched him with a startling gaze. It was like she could see into his soul and didn't care about anything else.

For the next hour he was under her mysterious spell. He did most of the talking and she just listened with that soul-piercing gaze. Surely, she knew how rich he was, but it didn't seem to matter. She didn't gush or flatter him like all the others, their selfish yearnings easy to see. Instead, she revealed nothing, and that made the spell stronger, wrapping him tighter in its enigmatic grip.

As the night went on, the strange and ferocious attraction he felt didn't seem entirely normal. It was much too intense and all consuming. The only answer could be the service had discovered everything about him they needed to know, including the secrets hidden in the depths of his psyche. They'd done this to fulfill their promise to find his perfect match. Every part of her seemed to connect to a part of him – a long ago memory, a hidden desire, a subconscious dream.

And then she was gone.

She excused herself for the bathroom and never came back. He waited until he couldn't anymore and ran to the bathroom, banging on the door. When no answer came he threw it open but she wasn't there. He realized he didn't even know her name and that made him even more frantic, quickly searching the rest of the restaurant for the woman he now knew he couldn't live without.

But she was really gone.

He called Rod the next morning to tell him what happened, but his secretary had disturbing news. "I'm sorry Mr. Malone, he hasn't been to the office the last three days. We don't know where he is, so we've alerted the police."

Trevor didn't make a connection between the disappearance last night and his best friend because he was in full panic mode now. The next disturbing surprise came when he called the service and no one answered, letting it ring continuously as more panic rushed through him.

He cursed the traffic as his limo fought its way to the giant glass tower and he finally reached the door of the service. But the number was gone. He banged on the door until his fist was raw, with nothing but total silence coming from the other side.

The days that followed were torture. He called Rod's office every morning without any update on his whereabouts. His best friend was gone, along with the mysterious woman he couldn't get off his mind. She haunted his every waking moment, with her long black hair and pale face becoming even more alluring as he dreamed of her through the night. That strange and ferocious connection he felt left a hole in his heart nothing else could fill.

And then she called, late one night, when her mesmerizing face was glowing in his dreams.

"I hope I'm not disturbing you..." she said in a soft voice.

"Where did you go? Why did you leave?" He had so many questions, but one was more important than everything else. "When can I see you again?"

And that's when she said it, in that very soft voice. "Well, to be honest, I'm not sure you're my type..."

"What do you mean?"

"I don't know. You seem like a nice enough guy, but there are a few things I'm not sure about."

She thought he was a bit overweight, his slicked hair looked greasy, and he only talked about himself. She didn't wait for a response. The phone went dead. A few days passed and she called again with more quibbles and concerns, then more a week later, then more after that. From the very first call he was willing to do anything she wanted and wasted no time making the changes. He went on a radical new diet, shaved his head, and spoke much less, never about himself. But she said there were more changes and he did that too.

Everything else in his life became meaningless. People were talking, of course, wondering what had caused this bizarre transformation, turning superstar Trevor Malone into a ghostly version of himself. What they didn't know was everything he was taking away was getting him closer to the mysterious woman without a name.

When all this was done, and he was virtually unrecognizable, he asked if she had any other concerns, and the answer was no. He fought back tears and pleaded with her in a trembling voice to see him again. But the phone went dead with a brutal silence he'd come to dread. His excruciating heartbreak lasted only a few more minutes when his phone rang again.

"Mr. Malone, we hope you're pleased with our service so far," the young woman with the business-like voice said.

"*I need to see her...*" he croaked.

"Of course, very soon, I promise."

He'd stopped going to the office, never leaving his bed, moaning like a prisoner in a concentration camp. Two days later the woman from the service called again and gave him another address. His limo raced him to a desolate part of the city he'd never been before. It was way downtown next to an abandoned pier, a rusted steel building that looked abandoned.

He'd stopped questioning the baffling machinations that had brought him here. His life didn't seem completely real anymore. He was different, driven only by the all-consuming desire to be with the woman who had cast an unbreakable spell over him.

He staggered from the limo, sweaty and frail in unwashed clothes, his shaven head peering at the black building in front of him. He didn't know how much more disappointment he could bear if she wasn't inside. But he'd come this far and nothing would stop him.

There was no buzzer, so he banged on the rusted steel door, his pounding heart ringing in his ears. No answer came, but he kept banging over and over, to no avail. He began to weep, slumping against the door to stay on his feet. When it suddenly opened, he tumbled inside, falling to the floor. He was still weeping when a hand reached down to help him up.

"Mr. Malone, we're so glad you came."

He recognized the young woman's voice from the service. She had thick black glasses and short red hair.

"*Is she here...*" he moaned, wobbling to his feet.

"Yes, Mr. Malone, she's here."

"Where?"

"Inside, but first you should meet the others."

"Who?"

"Others like you. Please follow me."

She marched down a hallway, Trevor stumbling behind her with barely the strength to walk. The lights inside the building were low.

"What is this place?" he asked.

"It's the final fulfillment of our service," she answered in that familiar businesslike voice. "We pride ourselves on giving our client's exactly what they want, even when they think they have everything money can buy."

At the end of the hallway, she led him into a cavernous room with the same low lighting. Shadowy figures mingled about, some gathered at a dusty bar against a long wall, others sitting on frayed lounges and chairs. The voices were hushed and private, the mood strangely intimate. He looked around, searching for the million-dollar date he'd give a hundred million more to see.

"Hey, buddy boy..." a raspy voice called out. Rod staggered over, a stunning blonde helping him walk.

Trevor immediately saw he wasn't the same either, just like him, but even worse. One of his arms was gone and his head was swollen and bruised. That's when he saw the others in the dimly lit room looked the same way, disfigured men with beautiful women. There were eye patches, gruesome scars, and missing limbs. It was a surreal collection of mutilated men and the women they couldn't live without.

"Mr. Malone, if I may," the woman from the service said. "We have some final business to attend to."

Rod nodded with a grim smile and hobbled away, his cold blue eyes sunken black pits with crusted blood, holding on to the love of his life for support.

"Your selection's name is Rebecca," the woman from the service said. "She's looking forward to seeing you, but she has one last request to prove how much you want to be with her."

She led him down another crumbling hallway where the gloom was heavier. He heard weeping screams and a grinding noise, like a merciless machine in a slaughterhouse. But he knew she was close, so very close. The thumping of his heart was so loud he thought it might burst. As he got closer to the screams and the grinding noise, he wondered how much more he would give to be with the woman he wanted more than he could possibly bear. He remembered her face when they first met and how deeply she kept haunting his dreams.

The answer was... *everything*.

MONSTROCITIES

An offering of the shocking and strange

BEHOLD MY SON

I'm a God-fearing woman, so I have sacred beliefs about how people should behave. It's been with me from my youngest days, when I sat in a candlelit room while my parents read a leather-bound Bible in reverent voices. I didn't know it at the time, but their words created the strict and narrow path I would come to follow without question. We rose before daybreak and toiled over our craggy patch of land, struggling to give birth to crops that were often withered and dead. But the Bible gave us the strength we needed to face those grueling days.

Children are filled with so much hope and mystery, you need to know this right away. They believe they live in a boundless world, and it shapes their mind in hidden ways. The leather-bound book was a hallowed text that promised miracles for which I desperately yearned, but it was also the source of nightly spectacles that raged in my sleep. Fire and brimstone visions burned bright and bold, like crackling dreams hurled straight from God. I saw seas ripped open, the dead rise up, radiant angels, and banshee demons. I witnessed the power of God, capable of both merciful goodness and crushing cruelty. My slumbering hours were a fiery phantasm that lasted till dawn.

Not long after my childhood years, I married a scarecrow like boy from three farms away. Our meager land was given by his parents, and our lives fell into a daily routine of work and prayer. It was all I'd ever known, just now with the added task of being an obedient wife. I was ill-equipped for what that meant. My husband was even more somber than my father, but it was a quality I saw as a blessed trait. He was a servant of God, and his solemnity was evidence of that. Our life was lived close to the land, and our marriage was bonded by that, and of course our shared devotion to God.

But our faith was tested when we set about the mission of starting our family. The doctor delivered his judgment in a mumbling voice I didn't fully understand, but his opinion was clear. My female flesh was an imperfect vessel for giving birth. Not impossible, he said, but not far from it.

The sky was a rumbling shroud during the drive back home. I stumbled upstairs and collapsed into bed with a sobbing wail that lasted for days. My husband brought me water and bread and clenched my hand. Our misery was so wretched we couldn't bear to look at each other. It was like the world had suddenly ended. My hysterical crying finally subsided, but only because I saw in my feverish dreams when hope is gone, nothing is left.

That's when I reached for the leather-bound book my parents had gifted me on our wedding day. When a miracle is needed, I knew where to look. I returned to my daily chores but spent most of the other spare moments clutching the book and praying with an intensity I hoped even an all-powerful God couldn't ignore. My knees were red and raw from kneeling on the splintered wood floor, but the pain was evidence of the faith I wanted to prove beyond any doubt. My husband was broken in the same way, working alone in the barn late into the night.

We were deep in sleep when a torrential storm roared in and began to batter our tiny home with a deluge of water that lasted for days. The thundering sound was apocalyptic, clearly a sign of some kind, but we didn't know what. I continued to pray with a fury that equaled the storm, hoping against hope that the God I'd given my life to would grant me a miracle child, just like his own exalted son.

And so, it came to be.

No one was more surprised than the mumbling doctor who'd told us it was close to impossible. He stared at us with the shock of a non-believer, but now I was blessed with a child so it didn't matter. I already knew it was a boy because my burning dreams showed me his glory tethered inside me.

The joy of creating life was rapturous in a way I can't adequately describe, knowing I was bringing a gift into the world that was clearly anointed by God above. But we were tested again at the bloody eruption of birth, when he choked like a fish snatched out of water, gasping and shaking, struggling to survive. And this is when I learned that miracles in this new age could take a very different turn than the ancient parables in the leather-bound book. What I knew about the modern world was random at best, because my life had been so focused on God.

The mumbling doctor and frantic nurses rushed him away and I feared the worst. But even my fears didn't prepare me for the horror of what we saw through the hospital window. He was ensnared in a tangled web of wires and tubes, trapped in a beeping cradle of medical machines. His naked flesh was pierced and wounded, a crucifixion I couldn't stop. The look on his face was an agony to witness. He was fighting for his life in a prison of madness, and I was close to madness myself, wondering how God could grant us this miracle, then torture our souls.

My solemn husband never spoke, his scarecrow like body hunched and trembling. He was whispering something I couldn't hear, so faint it sounded like a sickly murmur. I knew he was a dreamer too, his troubled moans slipping out in the dead of night. We all communicate our desires in different ways. For me it was prayer, his was more private.

During the days, weeks, then months that followed the torture continued as our child waged a battle against the ravenous demon of death itself. He seemed too frail and weak to emerge the winner, but that's when I realized God's wisdom in this. We're all tested during our time on Earth, and this was going to be his. God had given him the beeping machines and twisted tubes to help his fight, but the outcome was up to him. Without the machines he would surely die, but now he had a chance to rise up and live.

And so, he did.

After his brutal ordeal in the hospital, he finally came home, but not alone. The mumbling doctor said he needed the beeping machines to keep him alive. My heartbreak was only bearable because our mission to have a family was finally achieved. The wires, tubes, and metal machines were now a permanent part of his body, just like his tiny arms and legs.

During his youngest years, the physical changes were mostly inscrutable, creeping and slow. But his beloved life had been saved, so nothing else mattered. The machines kept him a prisoner, so everything was brought to him. He was fed and washed, attended to with loving care.

Perhaps it was because of his sheltered life that the outside world held so much allure. We bought him a small TV, then a computer, both of which he accepted with a blurry blink of his eyes. That's how he learned about the unknown landscape beyond his room, through the eerie connections with other machines. My childhood had been lonely and friendless, but he lived in a different world, roaming an invisible web that stretched out to the ends of the Earth.

Behind his closed door the sounds began to change too. Our isolated farmhouse used to be ghostly quiet, with just the swirl of a passing wind, the splatter of rain, or my nightly prayers. But now the louder beeps and crackling whirrs from inside his room made our weathered old house sound like the grinding guts of a mysterious machine.

The changes became more apparent as he grew from a child to a young boy. His room was now clogged with a thicket of wires snaking across the floor, and there were also bizarre contraptions he'd made himself, taking pieces and parts from other machines to create something new. Now he was out of bed, and that was part of the miracle, standing on bony legs that were wobbly and weak. There was also a flickering glow in his eyes that seemed to quiver and pulse. His voice had always been raspy and hoarse, but now it had a sharper edge.

And this is when my midnight dreams returned with a vengeance. But on this rainy night it wasn't fire and brimstone hurled from above, but something much darker and unknown. It was like a chasm had cracked open and a colossal monstrosity of metal and wires lumbered out. I woke up bathed in a cold sweat and peered around the shadowy room. The rumpled bed was empty beside me, but that wasn't a shock. My husband had become a night owl, spending even more time alone in the barn.

For some reason I needed to see him right away and recount my dream. I staggered down the stairs in bare feet and passed my precious son's door. The whirrs and beeps were even louder, like nothing I'd ever heard. I stood silent for the barest moment, and it chilled my soul. I know that hope and mystery are tangled together in endless ways, but this new sound was a shock I couldn't ignore.

I ran out the back door into the rain and across the muddy yard. I burst into the barn and the flickering sputter of a fire appeared. I saw my husband nearby, the crackling shimmer of flames swirling around him. He was chanting in a language I didn't understand, clutching the headless body of a black bird. I knew about ritual and sacrifice from the leather-bound book, and that was surely what I was now witnessing. Arcane symbols and unknown beings were etched in the dirt around the fire.

My husband looked up and met my gaze with a look I'd never seen before. And this is when I witnessed the horrific sacrifice that had been made for our miracle son. It was branded on his face like a nightmare. He wasn't a servant of God anymore, if he had ever been. He'd given away his sanity to serve something else.

He threw the headless bird into the fire, and the rain thrashed wilder outside. He kicked clumps of dirt into the flames, killing its jagged glow. He staggered towards me in heavy steps, but it was clear from his faraway gaze I wasn't part of his plan. I followed him out of the barn into the pounding rain. A crack of thunder boomed around us, sounding like a beast from another world.

And that's when I saw the pulsing light in our son's room begin to move. I watched through the dirt-smeared windows as it moved down the hall, then out the back door. I then saw the change was complete. I had been given a miracle child like the son of God, but my creation wasn't divine. It was flesh and blood, metal and wires, a new age creature cobbled together from blasphemous parts. His eyes glinted brighter than any fire, as he stumbled through the torrential rain and splattering muck, a tangled trail of tubes and wires dragging behind him like the ripped-out intestines of an infernal machine.

And so, his pilgrimage began.

The news of his arrival quickly spread as a growing horde joined in behind him, apostles and acolytes eager to create a wired new world. They were all believers in the sprawling glory of the tangled web that stretched out to the ends of the Earth. And now years have passed and a part of me knows my son is a monster. But he came from me, and that's a blessing I can't ignore. He was almost dead, and now he's not.

After a long day toiling beneath the cawing black birds, I still say my nightly prayers, kneeling on the splintered wood floor. Our farmhouse is ghostly quiet again, and a fire still burns in the barn at night. My scarecrow like husband has lost his way, but my belief in the leather-bound book has never wavered. It might be another strange and mysterious miracle, but I continue to be his obedient wife.

THE MONSTER MAKER

He was sitting alone at the back of the bar, wondering where the years had suddenly gone. Slumped over in his usual seat, he stared at the glass of bourbon on the table in front of him, desperately hoping it would help him make sense of this strange new world.

The bar was two blocks from the Paramount lot on Melrose, a shabby dive hidden away in an unmarked alley so the tourists wouldn't find it. It was where some of the old timers still working on the lot liked to go before heading home. Paramount was the only major studio left in Hollywood because the machinery of making movies had moved to other places, just like everything else about the movies.

He sipped the cheap bourbon, felt its harsh taste swirl down his throat, then returned to the memories floating in his head. He'd come to view his anger as the only acceptable reaction to the misery of his life, but that didn't make it any easier to get through the day.

Especially this one.

It was always a surprise to his coworkers when he revealed his connection to the glory days of Hollywood, a time when great men made monumental movies by the sheer force of their will and flesh-and-blood talent, instead of the pathetic way it was done today.

His grandfather was Jack Pierce, the make-up genius who'd created the greatest movie monsters of all time. Boris Karloff played Frankenstein and the Mummy, Bela Lugosi was Count Dracula, and Lon Chaney Jr. was the Wolfman, but it was his grandfather's make-up that had truly brought these creatures to life. He was the godlike figure who created monsters the world would never forget.

He remembered his grandfather sitting in a chair, describing how he'd created these movie marvels, and many others, never giving in to the stupid demands of anyone who didn't understand his genius. He'd fought relentlessly with actors, directors and studio executives to protect his vision. He was an artist to the core, a passionate champion for his exalted creations.

With his grandfather as his inspiration, he'd decided early on to follow in his celebrated footsteps, and that had been the driving ambition of his life – to create new monsters that had the same power and grandeur as those from the golden age.

Getting his first job wasn't hard, because of the family connection. He'd worked at different studios over the years, rising very quickly, before being hired by Paramount to run their make-up department. There were a few good years along the way, but none had reached anywhere near the soaring heights of what his grandfather had achieved, because the movies had changed, and the monsters along with it.

He remembered his grandfather explaining his secret in a whispery old voice.

"Never forget that what's scary about a monster is it used to be a man, so you should never cover up the horror of what that feels like. The audience should always be able to see the agony strangling its tormented soul..."

But over the years, everything changed, and not for the better. He'd worked on countless movies and TV shows, but none had given him the chance to use his skill the way he envisioned.

The sad fact was he couldn't when the studio thought a great monster was a brainless hulk stumbling around in a hockey mask. Where was the pain and pathos in that? The magnificent artistry of his grandfather's monsters had been replaced with moronic madmen chasing bratty teenagers.

The only real achievement he'd been proud of was when he'd married his wife, a raven-haired beauty who'd moved from the Midwest with the hopes and dreams to become an actress. But her dreams didn't come true either, and that had only added to his pain. They'd struggled together as lovers and friends, but the combined disappointment of their crushed dreams turned into a lingering cloud haunting their lives.

When she'd died last year, the doctor said it was liver disease, but he knew the real reason, and it wasn't medical at all. He knew it was because the hovering cloud had finally been too much to bear, smothering the precious life out of her with choking despair. And that's when a part of him had died too.

"Ready for another one, Pete..."

He looked up with a bleary gaze and nodded.

He wondered if the waitress could see the new gloom in his eyes, because along with all the other endless disappointments in his life, the latest had occurred just hours ago, and was even more crushing than all the rest.

"We really appreciate what you've done," the studio executive had said, not even looking up from the papers on his desk. "But we need some new blood around here, so let's both agree it's time to move on..."

And that was that, he was thrown away like unwanted garbage, without the respect of seeing the face of the person who did it. The movies had changed alright, because the people who made them now were crass and loathsome without even the hint of a human soul.

When the bourbon came back, he took a bigger gulp. The black cloud that killed his wife was still there, ashen and hazy, swirling around him. His head slumped down, when the front door suddenly swung open and sneakered feet shuffled in.

As usual, he'd had too much bourbon, but he recognized them right away, as they strolled past the bar, then plopped into seats at a table nearby. They didn't acknowledge him, but they never did, even though they worked at the studio too. Whenever he saw them, they were always excited, dressed in jeans and Japanese anime t-shirts, babbling super-fast about stuff he could barely understand.

"Dude, the new program is killer, the pixels rock..."

"It's all about the renderer, my friend..."

"The almighty god of CGI has kicked some butt, that's for sure..."

He listened to them prattle on, as they ordered beers with names he'd never heard. He waved for another bourbon, feeling his anger churn even hotter, because the sneakered group was what he'd come to despise most of all. In the old days, making monsters was a human art, flesh against flesh, all of it done with just two skilled hands and a simple box of tools.

But that had changed too.

Now it was usually caffeinated kids banging away on their computers, creating monsters out of pixels and bytes. They weren't even real monsters anymore, just lifeless mirages made from computer fairy dust.

The magic was gone.

The majestic soul had been ripped away.

He took another gulp, because he saw the hovering cloud was creeping in closer and feared it might smother the life out of him, and he'd be joining his dead wife before the day was done.

Then he heard his grandfather's ghostly whisper reaching out to him. He listened carefully, because at first he could barely make out the words. But soon he began to make sense of the murmuring sound. It seemed his grandfather had a plan so glorious he wished he'd thought of it himself. But his grandfather was a true genius, so of course it came from him.

He stumbled to his feet, swayed back and forth, then staggered past the table with the babbling geeks. They didn't even look up, because he was never important enough to warrant their attention.

But now he had a new mission. He was going to construct a glorious creation that celebrated the good old days. He staggered out the front door, stumbling into the Hollywood night, eager to create his new monster.

He holed up in his small house for the next few days, barely eating, preferring the numbing elixir of cheap bourbon instead. The only light came from the glowing TV screen showing his beloved horror movies playing on a shimmering loop. He had hundreds in his collection, but watched the old classics for the purposes of his plan.

He'd seen his grandfather's greatest achievements, Frankenstein, Dracula, the Mummy, and the Wolfman, countless times, but he watched them again, hunched in the dark, gaining strength and purpose from the grainy old movies.

That's when he came up with his own theory about monsters. He slowly realized in the boozy darkness, with the ashen black cloud still swirling around him, that monsters were what we fear the most about what's inside us. The monster we're fighting is actually the scariest part of who we really are. But he pushed this away as he focused again on his grandfather's brilliant plan.

He took a perverse delight in using his laptop to find out where the geeks from the studio lived. They worshipped blindly at the altar of technology, so it was only fitting that he use that to put his plan in motion.

His grandfather had once confessed that his favorite monster was the Invisible Man, because the worst kind of fear is when you know something scary is lurking close by, but you don't know where. He wasn't actually going to be invisible, but he would be the next best thing, cloaked in a perfect disguise that held no fear at all, until it was too late.

This brought him to his most cherished possession, the dusty old make-up case his grandfather left him. By today's standards, the case was a faded relic, but it was his tangible connection to the glory days. The big wooden box was filled with grease paint, make-up pencils, brushes, clay, and other tools of the trade. Most were decayed and crumbled, but he used what he could. Then he finished his disguise with his own make-up case, a perfect joining of his grandfather's art with his.

He left his house after dark with the handwritten addresses on the front seat next to him. He'd brought along a flask filled with the only friend he had left to keep him in the right frame of mind.

As his grandfather's plan unfolded, he watched it like one of his beloved old-time horror movies, but now he was the star, and that made it better. At each house, or apartment, he rang the bell. When the t-shirted geek answered the door, he was always thrilled to see no fear on their face. Why should there be when the figure in front of them was just a frail old man. If they'd known their movie history, they would have recognized the face as Jack Pierce, the man who'd created the most famous movie monsters of all time.

It was just make-up, of course, but it was perfectly applied, using an old photograph of his grandfather to transform his face. And that was the genius of his grandfather's plan, to reach out from the great beyond and show this misguided new world the proper way to make a monster.

It took until just past midnight to gather what he needed and head back home. Then, after a restless sleep, he woke up before dawn and applied his next make-up disguise. He drove to the studio lot with his flask. When he saw the familiar face of Bennie Wilson, one of the old-time security guards, he waved him in.

And now he was coming to the end, when he was finally going to be able to showcase his talent in a way that truly honored the good old days, when it was flesh against flesh, talented men getting what they wanted.

When the studio executive who'd fired him strode into his office and sat at his desk, he slipped out from his hiding place and quickly did what his grandfather

103

had told him to do. Then he opened his suitcase and began to work. He assembled his Frankenstein creature with meticulous care, using the severed body parts he'd gathered the previous night. The work was bloody, but so be it.

When he attached the studio executive's head, the haunting black cloud suddenly parted, so he could fully witness the glory of his work. He stumbled back, chugged the rest of the burning elixir from his flask, and there it was, exactly as he'd hoped.

A new kind of monster...

And he saw a look in its eyes that would have made his grandfather proud. Two bloody orbs filled with anguish and pain. It was the look of a monster that knows it used to be a man.

THE HOLY GHOST

At what point does pain become so unbearable a single word is incapable of describing the agony? He'd been splayed on the sulfurous soot and ash for so long, he'd lost all sense of time. Had he been there for years, decades, centuries, eons, or something closer to the bleakness of eternity?

He no longer knew.

Everything had been burned out of him long ago, his earthly memory, his lost humanity, and every last shred of his soul. The latter was the greatest contributor to his unending horror, leaving a gaping emptiness inside him. For some unknown expanse of time, he'd been a whimpering heap in the wretched pits of hell, with no sensation except for the pain that was so much more than pain. He was an ash-covered carcass of scorched flesh in this unholy and indescribable place. Other scorched bodies were scattered around him, some still flailing with anguish. Most were as crusted as he, underworld roadkill where everything was damned.

Then, with a startling softness, he felt a strange force creep in without any warning at all. When all you've felt is thundering agony without any chance of reprieve, it was all the more shocking because it was new. Even more surprising was what happened in the moments that followed, as the unseen force lifted him up from soot and ash into the burning air. The sunken black orbs of his lifeless eyes slowly cracked open. And there it was, in all its infernal glory, the underworld insanity of hell. He'd heard the legion of wails echoing around him, felt the unbearable sizzle of the fiendish heat, and been constantly rattled by the bellowing roar of some monstrous god. But now he it saw it below. It was madness indeed, surreal and demented.

His charred form continued to rise through the burning haze. There were colossal volcanoes of craggy bones gushing spews of crackling fire. Gargantuan fissures and craters were crammed to the top with screeching demons. The ground wasn't really ground at all, but the grime and decay of decomposed flesh, an infinite wasteland where misery knew had no end.

And now, in the midst of it all, he saw the towering figure of the Dark Lord looming in the distance. The appalling monstrosity stomped through the burning terrain on cloven hooves bigger than some of the mountains.

Then he was seized by a new notion as he floated up through the cinder. Was it possible he was leaving all this behind, that his body was ascending to another place? It gave him a feeling so strange he couldn't give it a name. It struggled to take hold inside of him, a desperate wish that his relentless misery might be diminished in some small way.

At the same time, he felt his scorched flesh crumble away, tumbling and swirling down through the fire to Hell below. It was his corporal shell being left behind, so something different could take its place. The fiery realm was now murky and red, like fireworks sputtering out.

On he rose, higher and higher, passing through mammoth layers of rock and earth and molten ooze.

His outer form was completely gone, and a flicker of something remained.

He felt as though he was passing through the barriers of time itself, as faint memories began to take shape in his emerging consciousness. He couldn't know how long the strange journey took, but it didn't matter because it was taking him away from Hell. He rose up through a final barrier of earth and rock, to a place his gathering memories recognized - the earthly realm where he'd once lived his human life.

A grey sky hung overhead with a blurry sun only faintly visible. After the roaring red horrors of Hell, this world seemed bland and drab, drained of color. Skeletal birds flapped and cawed overhead. Then his ghostly attention was drawn to a howling mob trudging down a long dirt road. They were fifty strong, soldiers making up the greatest part, dressed in ceremonial attire. They stopped nearby, their breaths hoarse and ragged, suddenly parting to reveal a stumbling figure among them. He was naked and bruised, his trembling body covered with his blood. A crown of thorns had been viciously shoved on his hanging head, causing blood to stream down his long brown hair and over the panting hollows of his face.

There was a brutish man with a thick coarse beard standing nearby, a long leather whip hanging from his waist. The whip had tiny shards of iron and bone tied to the ends, and he knew it was the source of the tortured figure's bruises and welts.

He felt his senses were sharper now, as if the shedding of his flesh strengthened his spiritual essence. He realized the brutish man with the whip was the man he was back in this earthly realm. His name was Tiberius, a Roman Centurion. Then a distant memory took form, and he shuddered at what was to come. His spectral shape hovered in the darkening air like a flickering light, an invisible witness to the sadistic spectacle unfolding below him.

The tortured figure with the flayed flesh was dragged to a craggy hill, along with two sniveling thieves who the howling mob decided would share the beaten man's fate. Three giant crosses nailed out of rotted wood rose up from the barren ground, hanging crookedly in the darkening mist.

The sun was now hidden, banished behind rumbling clouds that had charged in as if summoned from the heavens above. The mob roared like an animal, spitting and hurling taunts at the three prisoners, coating their bloody welts and slashes with slime. The man called Jesus was shoved against the middle cross, the thieves on the other two. His ghostly senses shuddered when he saw his earthly form stride to the middle cross with the burning fire of hatred in his eyes. A crude iron mallet was slapped in his hand. The man called Jesus was hoisted up like a sack of flesh. Two other soldiers stretched his trembling arms out against the rotted slabs of wood, his naked legs left dangling above the ground.

And then it all became clear, as he watched who he once was pound rusted nails into the sacred flesh of the man he now knew to be the son of God. Bones cracked and blood spurted as the unholy crucifixion was inflicted on the hanging figure. This was an act of insanity and brutality, vengeance and depravity, all done as a drenching rain began to wash over the three men, sending their blood swirling away.

Yes, it was all very clear.

In Hell there were always more devious ways to ratchet up the pain, to make it even more unbearable than just a single word could describe. For him, the tortures of Hell had become an endless monotony, and that wouldn't do. So, he'd been sent back to earth to remind him of his despicable sins. He already felt the tug of the underworld summoning him back with the memory of why he was there.

But he felt something new, another spectral presence had suddenly arrived that was as ghostly as he. But it was glorious, not of this world. The force quickly enveloped him with a feeling so radically different from what he felt in Hell, it overpowered even the numbing wretchedness of his missing soul.

It happened in an instant, as his return decent was already underway. He had one last fleeting glance at the hanging body on the cross, and a final look at the part he'd played in the blasphemous slaughter.

His spirit passed through the barren ground, back through the underground slabs of earth and rock and molten ooze, until he once again felt the fiendish fires of Hell crackling below him. His crusty outer shell drifted in like floating black embers and assembled around him. The pain of Hell returned, and now it was even more extreme than before, spiked up by the memory of who he was and why he was here.

He'd killed the son of God.

He passed down through the burning air and churning smoke, as the demons howled and the roar of the Dark Lord bellowed across the underworld. He descended back to the grime and decay of decomposed flesh, and once again misery enveloped his whimpering body without a shred of mercy. But then he felt another sensation that was completely new in the unforgiving pits of hell.

That's why the Dark Lord bellowed louder, sensing its presence. He glared into the gloom with his cavernous eyes, feeling a pain that was more than just pain, because his underworld region had been infiltrated by an unwanted transgressor. The man who killed the son of God felt his torturous pain begin to ebb away, because he'd been given a holy treasure that was hidden in that place where he once again had a soul.

Forgiveness.

MAGIC MACABRE

"Nothing is every truly missing," my father would say. "It's just hidden in a place you haven't looked yet."

In the history of magic, he wasn't one of the greats, but the greats always talked behind closed doors about the confounding tricks only he could do. He'd wandered the country in his beat-up old car peddling magic and miracles as The Great Mysterio. In small town theaters, rickety old carnivals, and backwoods country fairs, crowds would gasp in astonishment as he performed the impossible right in front of their startled eyes. With a deep voice and long hair, he wore a black cape shimmering with symbols that were like a mysterious message from some unknown beyond.

The local police came calling when the newspapers piled up too high on the uncut front lawn. It took a bit of detective work, but they tracked me down, and that's when I'd gotten the call that my father was missing. They'd found no clues about where he might have gone. He had a reputation as a sullen recluse who rarely ventured out, and nobody knew about his unusual past.

"You might want to come and look around," the sheriff had said. "Maybe you'll see something that could help."

"Of course," I muttered.

"When was the last time you visited?"

"A couple of years ago, I think."

"It must have been a strange house to grow up in."

I paused for a moment, imagining a small-town cop roaming around inside my childhood home.

"You're right, it was..."

The next day I was driving through a rainstorm and remembering how strange everything was when you had The Great Mysterio as a father. Magic was all he ever cared about, and it affected our lives in every way possible, like a cloak invisible to the outside world. He'd desperately wanted his only child to care about it too, and it had been a constant struggle between us.

During the scattered few weeks when he'd come home from his barnstorming tours, he'd always try to show me a trick or two, hoping it would ignite in me the same devotion. But I always just shrug and walk away, bringing a heart-broken look to his face. During my teenaged years, I could see it disturbed him even more, like I was ignoring a sacred gift that was more important than I could possibly imagine. When I left home to pursue my own life, the gulf between us widened further, so all we had left were fading memories of a father and son who had never felt that special bond.

Then Mom died and he got stranger still, choosing to spend his remaining years as a recluse in our peculiar old house. I returned less and less, because it was like we were strangers now, a father and son who lived in different worlds. He was still obsessed with his magic, stumbling around in frayed pajamas and his tattered black cape, mumbling incantations to himself.

The rain had finally slowed to a watery haze, and the rest of the drive took me on twilight highways, darker suburban roads, then finally out to the isolated small town where he still lived. Along the way, change

112

had come, like everywhere else, with new malls and endless chain restaurants. But when I finally reached the town of my birth, it still looked the same, rural and bleak, like a forgotten place from another time.

I turned into our driveway and saw the house was wrapped in blackness at the far end. It looked like a creepy present I thought I'd never have to unwrap again. It seemed smaller, but was still a spooky sight, which is why my father bought it in the first place. He said it was the kind of dwelling where a witch or wizard might live. The windows were arched, the faded frame crumbling and black, crooked iron spires poking up from the roof.

When I stopped in front of the house, I thought about another troubling memory I'd always tried to keep trapped in the past. For most of my life, my father had haunted my dreams like an unwanted ghost. I hadn't told the sheriff that I'd already been summoned back home by the spectral glimmer of my father calling out from my dreams.

I found the key in its usual spot, hidden under a crumbling gargoyle pot with a long dead plant withered inside. I pushed open the heavy front door and flicked on the lights. My father's style was what you'd expect from a man who thought of himself as a modern-day sorcerer. During his travels, he'd collected oddities and brought them back home. It was a creepy assortment of all things magical and mystical, so I grew up in a house filled with the impossible. The lights never got very bright, my father preferring shadows and mystery in his home, instead of the brightness of the outside world.

I wandered through the musty house as memories swirled in my head. There was no sign of anything out

113

of the ordinary, except for the strange contents of the house itself. It smelled dusty and stale, like no one had lived there for a long time. Most of all, it felt devoid of human presence, like the dimly lit rooms and hallways were now just a forgotten repository for my father's strange collection.

Then I heard a sound, so faint I could barely make it out. I froze and listened to the silence hovering over me. The sound came again. It was my father's voice. At first, it seemed like it was coming from that eerie night-world where he'd haunted my dreams. I told myself it wasn't real, just a trick my mind was playing. Then it came again and again, creeping from somewhere inside the house.

"I'm here..."

I immediately wanted to run away and drive back to my normal life. Escape is all I'd ever wanted inside this house, and now that feeling was even more desperate. But the insistent voice was a more powerful force that wouldn't let go, luring me like a whispery beacon through the shadowy halls.

And now I had a realization as I stumbled past the dusty oddities my father collected during his life. They were all about magic and mystery, but they were also about something else. I suddenly knew with a stunning awareness that there was so much more about my father I didn't know. He'd assembled this house to be a haunting clue about his true nature.

"I'm here..." his voice whispered again in that urgent hushed tone.

I was pulled in a stumbling trance to the back hallway where the bedrooms were, the whisper becoming louder, keeping pace with the pounding in my heart. Then it went silent as quickly as it had arrived, and I was left in an empty hallway with no further urging on which way to go. But then I knew, because I was standing under the almost invisible hatch leading to the attic. This was my father's private sanctuary – his magician's lair - where he'd created his confounding tricks and miracles. If there were any secrets or clues to be discovered, I knew that's where they'd be.

I pulled the frayed cord dangling above me and a wobbly wood staircase dropped down with a groaning thud. With every part of my body still yearning to run away, I watched my feet slowly ascend the shaky wood stairs as if they belonged to someone else. At the top, I stopped because it was so ferociously dark. I reached out and found a rusty chain cord. I gave it a tug and a single bulb began to glow, but barely enough to reveal the cobwebbed space.

What I then saw almost stopped my heart. The attic was a magician's lair alright, but it looked like it was from another world instead of our own. There were twisted devices and bizarre contraptions scattered beneath the feeble light. They all looked to have been created by beings not shackled by science or any of the other laws of our world. I stumbled around staring wide-eyed at the grotesque creations.

Then I came to an object that was the exact opposite of everything else in the mysterious room. It was a simple wood chest that was barely cracked open. I stared at it for a moment, wondering why it would be here with all the other bizarre contraptions.

Then it came again, my father's voice.

"I'm here..."

My heart almost stopped because the whisper came from inside the faded old chest. It took me a stretch of time that could have been seconds, or much longer, before I could summon the will to reach down and grab the top of the old-fashioned chest. It opened with a moaning creak and a cloud of dust wafted out. I coughed a few times and rubbed my eyes, then stared back down. The chest was empty except for a cardboard box. I bent down and lifted it out.

I didn't recognize what I saw at first because it came from a time I'd long forgotten. It was a magic kit my father had given to me when I was ten years old. The faded cover showed a plastic black wand and other rudimentary tricks, but I'd never bothered to look inside. As I held it in my hands, I remembered my father's disappointment at my constant refusal to ever accept any of his attempts to get me interested in magic.

"I'm here..." his voice said again.

And now the cardboard box began to shake in my hands with some unknown force. It dropped to the floor and popped open, its plastic tricks tumbling out. Then something else appeared, an eruption of black light, yawning out of the box with an otherworldly power.

A cosmic doorway then cracked open, revealing a nightmarish region that looked to have been created from fear itself. There were shuddering monsters and howling monstrosities roaming a heartbeat away from our own world. And my father was there, still cloaked in his tattered black cape, an unknown link from one beyond to another.

"Nothing is ever truly missing," he'd said. "It's just hiding in a place you haven't looked yet."

As this madness consumed me, I crumbled to the floor in an unconscious heap for a period of time I had no way of knowing. When I finally stirred again, the yawning doorway had closed, but not without leaving behind some changes. I staggered downstairs and stopped in front of a grimy mirror. I was wearing my father's black cape and my hair was now a ghostly white.

That's when I realized this was my father's greatest trick. Growing up, he'd let me believe I had a choice about what I was going to do with my life. He'd given me the magic kit when I was ten years old, and he knew that sooner or later I was going to open it, and that's when I'd join the family business.

I spent the next year in the attic preparing for what I knew I had to do. I was going to travel the country in a beat-up old car peddling magic and miracles in small town theaters, rickety old carnivals, and backwoods fairs. I was a herald of sorts, an opening act for what was going to come next, a magical new age. As I drove away from my childhood home, I knew that was going to be the grandest amazement of all when the monsters appeared.

He awoke before dawn, as was his usual custom. Being a spiritual man, he'd always found the darkness and solitude in the last hour of night a time of great comfort. Without the revealing glare of the daylight hours, he was free to imagine a very different world. His life was nearing its end, but he was still clinging to a hope that always surged strongest when the world around him was hidden from view.

He padded down the creaky wood stairs, his old age a nagging ailment he couldn't ignore. But he'd learned his waning years were also a gift, one he treasured with a growing reverence. He'd come to realize one can only truly cherish the miracle of life when there's the chance it can soon be taken away. Like everything else, the glory of living is never fully appreciated until you fear it won't be there anymore.

He quietly prepared his cup of black coffee in the kitchen, careful not to wake the others. His beloved wife and daughter were still sleeping upstairs. Neither shared his affection for this somber part of the day. With the hot coffee cupped in his hand, he slipped out the front door and settled into the rocking chair on the tiny front porch. He took a deep sip and gazed out into the warm murkiness nestled around him.

There was no hint of the moon in the still black sky, and only a few stars were visible overhead, so there wasn't much to see. But he still took comfort in what he knew was there, a surrounding thicket of woods with a long dirt road leading to the house. He'd always preferred the solitude of living a good distance away from any neighbors. A faint rustling shivered in the darkness nearby, then another one deeper in the woods. The gloomy night hours were when the wild animals felt freer to scurry out, roaming unseen without any fear.

He'd lived many places in his life, but this final home had become his most cherished. They'd ended up in a scruffy little town in the tangled sprawl at the southern end of the Appalachian Mountains. It was quiet and private, just like the predawn darkness he loved so much. He took another deep sip of the steaming hot coffee, then finally released the emotions churning inside him. Even thinking about his beloved daughter started his old heart beating faster.

What struck him the most was how their life together had flashed by so fast. He'd watched her sprout up like a precious flower, becoming more beautiful with each passing day. They'd named her Beatrice because it sounded independent and strong, a name that described perfectly the eighteen-year-old girl she'd become.

And just like with his waning life, his love for her was heightened even more because of the momentous occasion that would take place on this very day. He'd always believed in the importance of ceremonies, because they were a marker of faith in a chaotic world. But this one was even more important, because his daughter was leaving the protected sanctuary of their family and beginning her own journey into the world. This single event was going to steal away most of the joy in their lives, because their beloved Beatrice would now be gone.

When she'd gushed at the dinner table six months ago that she'd met a special young man on-line, he'd been deeply perplexed by her willingness to engage in this long-distance connection. He'd struggled to understand this new way of meeting people, because he'd always lived his life in the flesh-and-blood world. But she'd convinced him the young man named Ted

Chauncey was her chosen one, so he'd finally acceded to her ardent wishes.

Of course, he would perform the ceremony himself, in the small church he'd presided over for the last ten years. He could think of no other sacred undertaking that was more important for him to shepherd than this one.

Theirs was a poor community and the crumbling old church was no different. But he was a loving father who wanted the best for his daughter, so he'd reached out to his fellow brethren to help him paint the worn structure a fresh and glowing white. It had taken the better part of three weeks, but the transformation was nothing short of miraculous. The craggy brown wood was covered with a shiny new coat of luminous white. The weathered old church was now pristine and pure, a perfect showcase for his daughter's coming together with this unknown man.

In fact, she'd been so excited when she saw it, she'd decided that the ceremony should be white too. She'd even picked all the flowers herself, racing from one sun-splattered field to the next, filling woven baskets with sweet-smelling daisies, lilies, and violets, then carrying them back to the newly painted church.

This had brought a smile to his face because it reminded him of himself. His beloved daughter wanted the world to be perfect in a glorious way, without all the ugliness. He admired that more than he wanted to admit, but it also came with a lingering feeling of regret.

Every parent wants to leave behind a better world for their children, and he hadn't done that, not by a long shot. While he knew it wasn't a fight he could win alone, it was still a painful fact to confront. As a spiritual man, he'd always had faith his side would win, but it had become overwhelmingly obvious that wasn't the case. On this day most of all, he dreaded that his daughter would be living in a dismal new world more dangerous and threatening than the previous one.

Back in his younger days, he'd been a much fiercer champion fighting for what he believed in, but that inner strength and resilience had waned with his body. He accepted it as the inevitable march of life, each generation getting its chance to wage a great war, then gradually fading away so the next generation could rise up and continue the fight. Now he was left with only the aching hope that his beloved daughter would not be a witness to the end of days. In the paramount struggle between good and evil, she was the next generation, the next desperate hope for a better world.

When the first hint of light spilled over the jagged darkness behind the trees, he heard soft footsteps behind him, then the gentle scrape of the door.

"Papa..." came the soft voice that always sent a flutter through his heart.

And there she was on this momentous day, her blue eyes blinking, her willowy blonde hair tumbling down to her waist. Whenever he looked at her, a part of him still saw the fragile little girl who had brought so much joy into their lives. But now she was on her way to becoming a woman, a hallowed event that would take place later that day in the glowing white church.

As he rose to his feet to give her a hug, he kept thinking about how it was going to be her world now, and all he could do was hope for the best.

"Are you sure he's the one?" he whispered in her ear.

"Yes, Papa, I'm sure," she whispered back.

He hugged her tighter, wanting the warm embrace to last forever, but she gently pulled away.

"Papa, I want you to be happy for me..."

"I am," he said.

But he knew from the glimmer in her eyes that she didn't believe him. The real truth was, a part of him was excited for her, but a greater part was worried and despondent. How could he not be, when he was losing what he loved most in the world?

When the last moments night slipped away, it was another hour or so before the town stirred and woke up too. It was a small and bleak backwoods community with a scramble of ramshackle stores and rundown houses.

He'd met Ted Chauncey the evening before at a small gathering to celebrate the young couple's coming union. It was a modest affair, with wine, baked turkeys, and homegrown vegetables.

The young man had journeyed alone because of tragic personal circumstances. He was an only child and his parents had both been killed in a car accident just a few years before. He wasn't unpleasant to look at, with a flop of brown hair, and deep-set eyes. But there was also a quality about him that caused Beatrice's father a growing unease, a hungering look in his eyes and a raspy edge to his voice. He ate with gnawing bites and grinding teeth, tearing into the food with a lusty zeal.

The preacher knew all too well that appearances could be deceiving, but the true nature of a person could never be totally hidden if you knew what signs to see.

But another quality had also been readily apparent from the first moments he'd seen them together. The young man was deeply in love with his daughter, about that there could be no mistake. He'd gazed at her with open adoration, watching her the entire night with a wanting look. For her part, the gaze was equally direct, seeming to want him just as much.

He was staring too, but with more furtive glances, as the young couple held hands and mingled with the guests. At least now the connection was flesh-and-blood, which he'd always believed is the proper way. A few times during the party, others had pulled the preacher aside to share their feelings in private, no doubt motivated by the glum look he wasn't successful in hiding.

"He's a strong figure of a young man," Zachary murmured. "I think she's chosen well."

"I know what you're feeling," Sara confessed quietly in his ear. "I lost my Herbert too. But we have to let go, as hard as it is..."

To all, he'd just nodded and offered a thankful smile, but it still didn't diminish the pain in his heart, or the suspicious unease about the young man he couldn't shake. It was true that he had to let go but knowing that didn't make it any easier. At least the sacred coming-together would take place under his loving guidance. He silently told himself that he had to ignore the ache in his heart so he could usher his daughter out into the world with as much faith and hope as he could muster.

He also knew the true power of any ceremony was its ability to connect with something far greater than just the occasion itself. Every sacred ritual was a call to a higher power, whatever that power might be. It was a faith-driven plea for blessing and grace, and this is what he tried to hold steadfast in his thoughts.

They'd spent the morning in an anxious dance, all rustling around the small house, getting ready. His wife helped Beatrice, inside her bedroom, both darting out from time to time to fetch something that was suddenly needed. For his part, he answered the phone and chatted with well-wishers. He already knew by heart the words he would proclaim at the church, but he still repeatedly mumbled them to himself. He did this in the same place he'd started the day, sitting alone on the tiny front porch, staring into the woods. Lastly, he ironed his long white robe, wanting it to be as perfect as the daughter he loved more than life itself.

The morning started bright and sunny, but a clump of clouds drifted in around noon, and stayed overhead, casting a darker pallor across the land. He left for the church after a late lunch, giving his beloved daughter another long hug.

The intensity of what he was feeling kept surprising him, but it was a lesson he'd already learned well. You only truly realize how much you love something when you come to understand there's a chance it can be taken away, and that possibility was now a certainty looming just hours away.

On the winding drive to the church, there were waves and nods as he motored past. He'd picked this remote town because he wanted to spend his final years with like-minded neighbors, people of common faith. Everyone in town had watched Beatrice grow up too, so he knew the small church would be completely filled, with another eager group waiting to greet her outside.

He kept reminding himself that the ceremony was a celebration, but the ache in his heart still refused to cooperate. He just hoped he'd be able to summon a more cheerful demeanor when the time came.

He'd spent the last hour in his private room across the hall from the door to the altar. His thoughts raced over his daughter's life, and his too, bringing a flood of emotions. Beatrice's childhood had gone by so quickly, he wished he could live it all over again and savor it in the way it deserved.

But life isn't like that.

Already he heard the murmuring voices and padding footfalls entering the church. He sat awhile longer with his private thoughts, then slowly pushed himself up to his feet. Along with the heaviness in his heart, the rest of his body sagged from the weight of the many years he'd lived. He reminded himself it was going to be her world now, and his time to fight was coming to an end. He took a weary breath, shuffled across the hallway, pushed open the door leading to the altar, and eased down into the large wooden chair next to the pulpit.

He waited until the exact stroke of six, then rose up and took his place in front of the altar. Taking a quick breath, he gazed out at the pews packed with familiar faces. This was important because every sacred ceremony needed to be witnessed by true believers to mark its communal significance.

And then it began, with the opening of the glowing white doors at the front of the church. The young couple walked in, then walked together down the aisle like a newly discovered treasure for all to see.

His beloved Beatrice was a vision of startling beauty, like a fairy-tale maiden conjured from another time. Her white dress was homemade, but it had a shimmer that sparkled even more than the luminous interior of the freshly painted church.

Ted Chauncey strode at her side with a look of hungering love, as if he could barely keep it contained. His flop of brown hair was neatly combed, and he was wearing a white suit, at the request of the beautiful young woman he loved. When they stopped in front of the altar, the conflicting emotions were still battling inside, but he forced himself to play the role his beloved daughter so desperately wanted. He raised his wrinkled old hands overhead and gazed down with a radiant smile. Then he spoke the words he knew by heart from a distant time when it was a far better world than now.

A time when they *ruled the Earth.*

And now his beloved Beatrice was already changing, becoming something else entirely. When the young man suddenly realized something was wrong, it was already too late to avoid his fate. The hungry look in his eyes was replaced by heart-stopping fear.

As a shapeshifter, her choices were many, but he saw she'd chosen the form that was the surest to unleash uncontrollable horror. Her transcendent beauty was shrugged off like a cloak that was no longer needed. Now she had claws and fangs and bloody red eyes. Though she looked like a nightmare to Ted, to her father she was even more beautiful, because now she wore her true face.

The coming-together ritual that followed that was a savage affair. She gnawed and slashed at the burly young man like he was a slab of meat, flinging splashes of blood to the luminous white walls and floor of the church. What had been pristine and pure moments before was now splattered with red.

The preacher watched on, proclaiming the incantation. Every ceremony is a call to a higher power, and this one was no different, a sacrificial offering to dark gods.

In a forgotten age, they'd ruled the world, and the humans were the inferior species. But the balance of power shifted, because the humans had become a loathsome legion that covered the earth, and the shapeshifters' numbers had dwindled. Recorded history became a horrific testament to their harrowing fight to escape extinction. They were seen as monsters, and treated as such, beheaded, burned, lynched, staked, and slaughtered countless ceremonial ways.

He was a holy creature who'd fought the great fight as a fierce and noble shapeshifter in his younger days. But now he was old, and he'd decided his final stand would be in one of the human temples, a symbolic stake in their heart, instead of his own. The others in town were his brethren, living their final days too, sending their young out to fight the great fight. But now it was more of a dying hope than a righteous crusade.

The young man named Ted Chauncey was a bloody mess ripped apart on the church floor, and Beatrice was already shifting back to her previous form. She was covered in blood, crimson streaks dripping down her white dress and smeared on her human mask. He'd finished his cosmic shout-out to the dark gods and dropped his wrinkled old hands from above his head. He stumbled down from the raised platform of the altar and wrapped his daughter in a final hug. He desperately wanted to hold her in his arms forever, but she gently pulled away.

"I want you to be happy for me, Papa..."

"I am," he whispered with a breaking heart.

There were already tears in his eyes as he watched her march away down the bloody white floor. She was going to continue the fight he'd never come close to winning. From now on, the daughter he loved more than life itself would be living a warrior's life in the shadows, because when you're a monster that's one of the few safe places left.

UNDERWORLD

This is a story about love, but it's not a love story. It's a story about the unknown horrors hidden from the everyday world and discovering that monsters exist. Most of all, it's about a very important question you need to ask yourself.

What would you do to save someone you love?

I met Tracy the second year after I'd moved to New York City after college. The details aren't important, because when it's love at first sight that's all that matters. She had wild red hair, an amazing smile, and I knew right away she was the person I wanted to spend the rest of my life with. When I looked in her eyes it was like I could see a dream I never knew I had but wanted to come true.

We'd both grown up in small towns and moved to the city with the same kind of youthful hope and excitement. I worked on Wall Street in one of those fortress-like buildings where the pursuit of money was paramount. I felt like a warrior charging into battle every morning in a subway car that roared underground. My dad owned a hardware store in Alabama, so the city was a whole new world bigger and more thrilling in every way imaginable.

Tracy was from Michigan and worked at a fashion magazine as an assistant editor. She loved her job but wanted to write novels, so she was always scribbling ideas in a notebook. She was incredibly beautiful, with a great sense of humor, and I can't remember a single time she didn't have me laughing. There was a part of her I felt like I knew completely, and another part that was always surprising and mysterious.

We couldn't have been happier, moving in together after just six months. It was the end of August with the heavy haze of a hot city summer still lingering in the air. Our new home was a fourth-floor walk-up on the Upper Westside, two blocks from the giant sprawl of Central Park. It was a quiet street and we already had friends who lived close by.

Tracy did all the decorating. On weekends we'd roam through neighborhood flea markets and nearby stores searching for whatever she thought would look good in our new home. She called her decorating style "young and in love." Her favorite discovery was an old photograph of the city. She said the picture was just like us, because we'd both started out in a dreary place, but now we both amazing. I did all the heavy lifting, lugging boxes and furniture up the four flights of stairs to our apartment.

My favorite times were when we were lying in bed, talking about our future together. Our small-town lives were fading away. Being in love is about building a life together, and that's what we were doing. We talked about the kids we'd have, the trips we'd take, my spectacular rise to the top making tons of money, and all the great books she'd write that would make her famous. We talked in the dark as the city's night sounds loomed outside.

"I love you," she'd say.

"I love you even more," I'd say back.

After work, I usually had more to do at home and that's when she'd go for a run in the park. She'd been on the track team in high school and college, and still loved to run. I remember her coming through the door with sweat glistening on her body, an exhausted smile on her panting face. She always came over and gave me a kiss before going to the shower.

But this night was different.

This was the night she didn't come home.

What I remember most of all is the shock of suddenly wondering if something bad had happened. I kept waiting for her to walk through the door like she always did, sweaty and smiling, but she didn't. I called her cellphone over and over, but there was no answer. I thought of all the reasons she might be late, trying not to think of the worst-case scenarios, until I finally couldn't take it anymore and ran out the door, pounding down the stairs two at a time.

I ran the two blocks to Central Park as fast as I could, in a wild dash through the people in front of me. I lumbered into the bushy darkness and started calling her name, scanning the shadows in every direction. I frantically called the apartment to see if she was back, but there was still no answer.

And now a gnawing ache was growing inside me. The worst kind of fear is realizing the most horrible tragedy can happen and there's absolutely nothing you can do to stop it. I spotted a cop coming my way and ran to him.

"My girlfriend is missing. She was jogging in the park, but she should have been home by now. It's been almost two hours..."

The cop was old and rumpled, with a tired gaze that looked like he'd just woken up. He stood for a moment staring back. He rubbed his eyes and let out a weary breath. "Okay, let's just relax for a second. She probably met a friend and they stopped for a drink."

131

I shook my head because he didn't seem to understand how serious this was. *"No...* she always takes her cell phone and she definitely would have called me by now."

He rubbed his eyes again and a different look slowly came to his saggy face. It was a look of concern and sympathy, but something else too, something darker and unsettling he wanted to keep hidden. He glanced up at the massive skyscrapers near the park, and the look got even darker. He leaned closer like he was sharing a secret.

"Young girls shouldn't run in the park at night," he said in a low voice. "But they won't make a law about it, so we do the best we can..."

"What are you talking about?"

He glanced around at the shadowy stream of runners jogging past. The night sounds were there too, but now they seemed different, like muffled screams and distant howling. He leaned even closer and whispered so softly I could barely hear him.

"You seem like a good kid, so I'll try to help you out. There's a bar called The Black Sheep three blocks from here. There'll be a guy sitting in the back room. Tell him what happened, he might be able to help you..."

I was still scanning the park for Tracy because none of this made any sense. You can't just disappear with so many people around.

"You're a cop, isn't that your job?"

But he was already walking away.

"What's he look like?" I shouted out.

"He looks like someone who's seen the end of the world..."

132

There are moments in most people's lives when you think you know where you're going, but an unexpected detour suddenly appears, and the path ahead is completely different. I'd believed with all my heart that Tracy and I were going to spend the rest of our lives together, but now my heart was pounding with the fear this might not be true.

I ran as fast as I could out of the park to The Black Sheep without thinking about whether it was the best course of action. I burst into the back room and immediately saw I didn't have to pick the mysterious stranger out of a crowd. A slouched figure was sitting alone at a grimy wood table, a glass of dark liquid clutched in his hand. In the dim light he looked more dead than alive, with droopy skin and long white hair. He raised his hand and took a long gulp from the glass, then dropped it back down with a shaky thud.

I didn't stop to ponder the strangeness of seeking help from this slumped old man, because my heart was pounding so hard I could barely think.

"Excuse me, sir..."

That's when I saw the cop was right.

He raised his head with a struggling weariness and gazed at me through the dusty light. His bloodshot eyes were almost impossible to look at because they were filled with so much misery. I had never seen a more tormented face. I didn't move any closer, keeping my distance a few feet away.

"My girlfriend is missing," I stammered. "A cop in the park sent me to you..."

He kept staring at me with a ghostly gaze, then closed his eyes as if he was trying to summon strength from somewhere unknown. If he'd suddenly keeled over and dropped dead on the floor, I wouldn't have been surprised. But his eyes cracked open again. He reached for the glass and drained the rest of the dark liquid.

"We don't have much time," he wheezed, pushing himself up.

He was taller than I would have guessed, and bone thin. He was wearing a dirty black suit that looked two sizes too big, and I saw two leather holsters hanging inside his wrinkled black coat. He led me out of the back room with a shambling gait, his head drooped low, his white hair hanging to his shoulders.

When we got outside, he stopped on the sidewalk and pointed a bony finger at the skyscrapers. "That's where they live, because they think they're gods..."

He led me down the block to a place where limos were parked, then into an alley. A door at the far end was marked with a sign that read, "The Hellfire Club."

We descended a flight of stairs that led to an underground room filled with old men in dark suits, and beautiful young women sipping drinks. An antique bar glowed at one end. The women were all scantily dressed, with fiery red lips and stiletto high heels.

"The door to hell is always tempting," the old man muttered, heading for a hallway hidden in the shadows.

We walked down a long corridor lined with doors, some closed tight, others wide open. Through the open doors, I could see old men and beautiful young women engaged in bizarre and sordid acts. This is when the mysterious old man told me a dark secret in his raspy voice.

"The rich have always done what they want, but there's one horror above all the others. It began many years ago. There was so little left for the poor they

134

could barely survive. So, some went underground, and now they've become something else. The rich don't care as long as it's kept a secret. They give them what they want to keep them away..."

I didn't ask what that was because all I wanted was Tracy and nothing else. We continued down the corridor until we came to another door. He pushed it open and we descended more stairs to a musty cellar. He led me to a ragged hole in the wall.

"There are entrances to hell everywhere," he said. "You just have to know where to look..."

I watched his old body climb through the hole. None of this made any sense, but there was a single question pushing me forward.

What was I willing to do for the girl I loved?

I took a breath and crawled into the hole. There was a bright beam of light shining from a flashlight he'd pulled out from inside his baggy suit.

"Where are we going?" I whispered.

"To the underworld," he croaked back.

The beam of light glowed down on a metal ladder that plunged into absolute darkness. The strength the old man had summoned back in the bar seemed to have finally arrived, because he quickened his pace. We clanged down the metal ladder until we came to the bottom where the black gloom was suffocating. He swept the beam out and illuminated an abandoned subway tunnel.

"This is where they live," he said, pulling out an old-style pistol from one of the holsters.

We followed the tracks to a decayed crack in the wall.

"There's a whole other world down here that's been kept a secret. It's a maze of tunnels and caves.

135

There's the city up there, and this unknown hell below..."

As I took this in, there was movement in the darkness nearby. The old man jerked his flashlight and shined it on a pack of giant rats scurrying past. They looked more rabid and vicious, like an unknown species the above ground world had never seen.

"Who are you? Why are you doing this?"

He didn't answer right away, stumbling through another crack into another tunnel. When he finally spoke, his voice was as haunted as the look in his bloodshot eyes, each word like a weight he could barely lift.

"My name isn't important. What's important is that we've both lost someone we love. My daughter didn't come home one night. I searched and searched, but it wasn't any use. Then I discovered the horrible secret hidden below the city. It was too late for me, but I know how it feels to lose someone you love..."

We navigated the underground maze for a short time, and that's when they began to appear, poking up from the mud and dirt. I saw bones, gleaming and white, crunching and brittle beneath our feet. I didn't have the will to ask what they were and the old man didn't say.

The trek became eerier, as the underground terrain suddenly turned more primitive. Everything was craggier and muddier, like a primordial landscape. Along with the muddy bones, there were other objects lying on the ground, clothes, bicycles, and toys. And that's when I realized this underground world solved lots of mysteries about what went missing from the world above. And then it came, with a suddenness that was more terrifying than anything I'd ever encountered.

I heard some kind of grunt, or growl.

It was low and harsh, inhuman, like a vicious animal or unknown beast. The old man stopped in his tracks and swept the white beam into the darkness. Nothing was visible, but he yanked the other gun from his holster and handed it to me.

"They know we're here..."

I had just enough time to remind myself why I was in this horrible place when they appeared in a lightning fast swarm, scampering across the muddy ground and down the black walls. Another sweep of the flashlight showed almost a dozen, and their mutated forms. They were human once, but not anymore, with bulging luminous eyes, shriveled bodies, clawed hands, and dirt-smeared fangs that looked prehistoric.

Most of all... *they looked hungry.*

The old man fired first, and a creature fell. I fired too, but without a hit. A collective screech blared out as they continued their scuttling assault from all sides. This was beyond fear, beyond what even a nightmare could show. The old man's aim was true, slamming others squealing to the ground. But my hand shook so much I wasted bullets.

The old man trudged on at a quicker pace.

"We have to hurry... it's not much farther..."

I stumbled behind him, and now with a feeling of unbearable dread. Tracy's plight might be far worse than I could ever imagine. She'd gone out for her nightly run just hours ago, and now she might be down here with these creatures. I wiped sweat from my eyes, but that's all it took, as my foot hit a jutting bone and I fell.

137

One of the creatures was on me in a flash.

They say insanity comes when the mind is pushed beyond the limits of endurance. The dirt-crusted creature scurried on top of me, gnawing at my flesh with muddy fangs. The stench of its breath was a spew of mud and decay.

Then its head suddenly snapped away with a sickening crunch, and I saw the old man above me, a part of the creature's head splattered on his shoe. He yanked me back up, and we were off again, the creatures now hiding in the darkness.

And I suddenly had a new respect for this gaunt old man who'd lost his daughter. Real courage is the ability to face unfathomable fear and still go on. He trudged through the mud and slipped into another opening. I tottered behind him, both of us staying low until we reached the end of the cramped burrow. I coughed at a strange smell nearby, fighting to keep some sense of clarity. And that's when I saw it, a tiny piece of Hell hidden below ground.

We were in a cave that had the same primordial feel, but the black mud was even more unnatural, almost like it was a living thing that could rise up and devour everything else. There were many more of the abominable creatures, but now they were hunched and silent, as if this cavernous hole was a sacred place.

The old man nudged me, pointed his gun at the soaring walls of the cave. A slow sweep of the flashlight showed glimmers of whiteness stuck in the mud around us, like some kind of colossal, primitive art. And then I realized what it was meant to be, skyscrapers made of gleaming white bones. They were crude and crumbling, but the intent was clear.

I felt a horrible clenching in my stomach, as I stared at the wretched creatures and the ghastly underground realm they'd created. It was hellish and bleak, but maybe not much worse than the one their ancestors endured in the above ground world.

The old man beckoned for me to follow him.

I heard the whimpering sounds first as we stumbled across the mud, then I saw the yawning black hole. The hunched creatures didn't move. They seemed to be frozen in some kind of primal prayer. And then, out of all the sights I'd seen so far, none were more sickening than what I saw next. I stood beside the old man and stared down into the giant pit. It was deep and dank, with barely visible bodies writhing at the bottom. My heart was pounding so hard I wanted to scream, but I kept staring down at the bottom of the pit, because I had to be sure.

And yes, there she was... my beloved Tracy.

But when I saw her shattered gaze, I knew she'd been pushed beyond what her mind could endure, and she wasn't the Tracy I remembered anymore. Her hair was still wild, but she'd never make me laugh again. That's when I felt a bony hand hit my back.

I tumbled over the edge of the hole and plummeted down to the pile of bodies. I instantly scrambled to Tracy and wrapped her in my arms, our hearts thumping against each other. I never wanted to let her go, but I finally pulled away, and stared back up at the ghostly old man still standing at the edge of the pit. He was staring down at me with his bloodshot eyes that looked like they'd seen the end of the world.

"*Why*..." was the only word I could croak.

"My daughter isn't dead," he called down. "I lied about that. But I sold my soul to save her. The

139

creatures must be fed, that's what I do. But I'm not a monster like them, I'm just a man who knows how it feels to lose someone you love. I've taken your life, but I've also given you something greater in return..."

I pulled Tracy tight again because I realized what he was saying. The pain of what was going to happen next couldn't be as cruel as the pain of never having seen her again. At least now we're together, and that was better than anything else. When I glanced back up, the ghostly old man was gone, as if he'd been part of a morbid dream. Then I heard the creatures stirring again, and their ravenous faces circled around the top of the pit. This was an unholy sanctuary, and the sacrificial ceremony was about to begin.

I hugged Tracy as tight as I could because I loved her more than life itself. But I hope you didn't make the mistake of thinking this was a love story, because the creatures were already crawling over the edge of the pit, scuttling our way.

THE LAST HALLOWEEN

The bushy black trees covered their house in daytime shadows. They'd always shunned visitors of any kind, shuffling through the gloom with creaky footsteps. They were weak and tired, clinging to each other because that's all they had left. Old age had crept up with the barest of warnings and now it wouldn't let go. A gusty wind moaned outside. They'd retreated from so many things the world had become a neglected haze rarely glimpsed through the cracks in the blinds. But this night was different, the October eve called Halloween. An early chill had brought a sudden shiver to the autumn air.

They'd dreamt about it all year, a nocturnal reverie that was finally here. But their dreams were nightmares that howled and screamed until dawn. The outside world had become even more unbearable through the waning years, so this was the slumbering sanctuary they embraced with a primal need. It was where they sated what was still left of their cravings, a nightly wasteland where they could roam unbounded and free.

A hazy sun had just died outside and the sky dimmed to a morbid hue. The blustery wind moaned again. A cloudy moon was rising and the stars glowed like beacons from beyond. Day had ended and Halloween night was here.

Tonight, their house was a beacon too, to lure the scurrying prowlers who would be coming soon. Pumpkins crackled with fiery eyes and clattering skeletons hung from trees. Gravestones were strewn about, crooked and crumbling like the dead they were meant to mark.

For far longer than it was safe to admit, on this October eve they'd made their home a Halloween house.

They always traveled during the darkest hours, staying away from prying eyes. Rumbling down forgotten back roads, they wandered from one small town to the next, finding a house at the end of a lane with a thicket of woods out back.

They never stayed longer than a few years, and most of the people in town didn't know them. But there was always one constant wherever they lived. Every year, on Halloween night, burning pumpkins and hanging skeletons lured trick-or-treaters to the creepy old house that was always dark. They hobbled down the stairs to the basement. Old age had sapped their strength and every morning was a nagging reminder of how little time they had left. The smoldering beat of their hearts was getting weaker, their shuffling bodies hunched and frail. This was part of the reason they clung to each other, along with the ancient love they shared.

But they'd come to accept a brutal truth. This would be their last Halloween. After so many years had passed, the sadness of this was darker than anything else.

Their fading memories were another loss. They'd come together and never parted, sharing a secret life as the world around them had changed. Beauty is always in the eye of the beholder and the daylight world had become an abomination they could no longer abide. That's why they rarely ventured out, or even peeked out from behind the closed blinds. It would just be a reminder that this was the end of their days and the world they despised would carry on without them.

There had always been monsters, but they'd lived in the shadows until it was time to strike. In that long-ago time, they'd roamed the world like wicked warriors, staying just behind the line where darkness meets light. Their shadow realm was a place of chaos and mayhem.

But when you spend so much time hiding, you eventually lose your place in reality. That's when the myths and legends came into being. Make-believe stories replaced the terrifying truth. And now their number had dwindled to the point of extinction, and that would be the end of all the haunting mystery lurking in the world.

So, this was all they had left, a single October night when children mimicked them for sugary treats. Their glorious existence had become a frivolous night of cheap costumes and candy. But they wanted it to be much more than that. They wanted the future to be a shocking return to real horror. They wanted to bring back the good old days, so they relentlessly clung to a single belief.

Real monsters are hard to kill...

They reached the bottom of the stairs with a surging sense of excitement. The rest of the house was dull and dreary, but down here there was no need to hide their true nature. Their lair was filled with the blackest kind of shadows and other macabre belongings only a monster could love. They'd covered the walls with a tapestry of carved grotesqueries, so it felt like home.

Halloween began as a ritual to resurrect the dead. Animals were slaughtered and bonfires lit, offering up a fiery invitation for the dead to return. But like everything else, its reason for existence had changed, becoming just another holiday and not a mystical call to the dead. Bringing back the monsters had been their feverish desire.

Failure, though, was scattered around them like the crumbling gravestones outside. The bones of sacrificed animals were heaped in a corner and the ash of burnt wood piled in another. The same remains were left behind in the other houses, a gruesome wake of anguish and loss. Yet they still had hope, so they went about the preparations like they always did. It was a solemn undertaking, one they revered for what it could bring.

The night before, they'd climbed up through the cellar door and hobbled into the tangle of woods behind the house. Night was the only time they could hunt anymore, so it was a sacred pursuit. Back in those long-ago times, hunting was their sole purpose, making it a cherished endeavor. But now their frailty made it almost too difficult.

After many failed attempts, they finally grabbed a baby deer and dragged it back to the basement, placing it in a cage against the far wall. They knew it was a paltry offering, but it was all they had. At least the pile of fallen branches they'd gathered was not as modest.

How times had changed. In those long-ago days, they could savage a village while the terrified screams still rattled the air or shock a lost traveler alone at night. They could cross the line between darkness and light faster than the eye could see. The lost and alone were the easiest prey, but the strong were always more satisfying.

The ritual was arcane, and the passage of time had clouded their minds, making it harder to perform. The sacrifice was essential, and the elemental fire critical as well. More important though were the incantations, which had to be exactly right. But they'd forgotten so much, memory of the ritual had faded. They'd tried and tried, but nothing worked, and now their desperate hope was close to dying too.

They torched the pile of wood and watched it cast eerie shadows in the underground room. The flames spewed a billowing haze as they dragged the trembling deer from the cage. It snorted and struggled but its death was swift, its body cleaved open with their hooked claws. They blared out the guttural chants in a chorus of screeches and howls. They tried to remember the exact summoning, but they'd failed countless times before.

And then the impossible happened.

Just like in one of their nightmarish dreams, ghostly vapors swirled up in bizarre configurations. Monsters were now escaping from the underworld. Their thumped faster, waiting for the spooky miracle to fully take form. It was a sight they'd never witnessed, the closest they'd ever come. But the macabre shapes faded just as quickly and now they were gone. The couple shuddered at being so close, but now knew what they had to do.

Clearly, a different kind of sacrifice had to be made, and a bigger bonfire too. They climbed the stairs, the fire still crackling below, then huffed up another flight as fast as they could. They put on their costumes as quickly as possible, the bland and boring

145

human disguises they only wore when necessary. The undertaking was revolting and painful. Covering up their true forms was a shameful process.

The world had forgotten what an exquisite creation a real monster was, a crusty apparition with misbegotten parts and pitted black eyes. A real monster could fill your heart with heart stopping fear, a shambling carcass with withered wings. Any extreme is always shocking, and their spectacular horridness was beyond even that.

The human disguise was a makeshift ruse they always used on Halloween so they could witness the revelry. When they pulled open the front door, they'd pretend the make-believe monsters were real and they didn't have to hide anymore. They'd imagine a wild new world that only existed in their nightmarish dreams.

Outside, giggling voices and padding feet could be heard. They hobbled downstairs and unbolted the door, its dusty barrier scraping open. The pumpkins burned with fiery eyes and the clattering skeletons hung from the trees.

They looked like a tired old couple that should have stayed in bed on this cold night. Their hair was tangled and stringy, their clothes dirty and frayed. The adults stared at them with open suspicion, because they hadn't been as careful as years past. But the miniature monsters didn't care because they were too eager to fill their bags with sugary treats. Smoke suddenly erupted up from the fire below, and now there was no need for the hated disguises. They ripped them off to reveal their ghastly forms. The smiles and giggles became horrified screams.

The couple began howling too, the ancient chants to raise the dead. But they needed more than just puny blood from the daylight world. If a macabre miracle was needed, the blood of a macabre creature was needed too. And now their Halloween house wasn't a house anymore, it was a bonfire roaring in the night. They both rammed blades into their hearts.

The kids and parents had scrambled away, but their shrieks and screams could still be heard. Strange shapes swirled up from the underworld, joining the fiery pumpkins and hanging skeletons. The dead monsters were back, a dark legion to haunt a wicked new world.

A BEAUTIFUL HORROR

How best to begin her story?
How about this.
What's a beautiful girl like you doing in Hell?

They say that beauty is in the eye of the beholder, which is why she stared down at the body of her husband with an approving gaze. To others, the hacked flesh would have been a sickening sight, but not her, because it was all about being a good mother.

She'd been sexually abused as a young girl, so when she discovered her husband had done the same to their daughter, her rage was ferocious and swift. A butcher knife from the kitchen had done the trick, turning his foul flesh into a blood-soaked mishmash of human organs.

She'd been blessed with beauty, long brown hair, bright green eyes, and a tempting figure. But she'd found it was more of a burden than a gift, because it brought the wrong kind of attention from groping boys and mean-spirited girls. Her father's midnight transgressions had been only one part of the misery she endured growing up, until she was finally old enough to get married and escape to a hopefully better place.

She'd never truly loved her husband, but the marriage had served its purpose reasonably well, until the discovery of his despicable secret on a snowy winter night. So, she did what any mother would do to protect her daughter. She attacked the evil with all the rage in her body and sent it to a place where it couldn't hurt the precious and innocent child she loved.

So how did she end up in Hell?

Her own death was a messy affair too, as she was clumsily dragged through the justice system by a lawyer who didn't come close to making her situation better. She was sent to prison like the worst kind of criminal, ripping her away from the daughter she loved. And then the unthinkable happened two years later when her daughter was killed in a car accident. That's when she realized her life had no meaning or purpose anymore, so they found her the next morning hanging by her bed sheets. Even with her face a ghostly pale, she was still beautiful. But with that kind of record, a brutal murder and a blasphemous suicide, it should be no surprise where she ended up next.

But first, a few words about the true nature of Hell.

While it has a monstrous landscape crackling with fires of unbounded fury, its real source of agony is its desire to inflict unbearable pain. The volcanic peaks, boiling oceans, and the scorched terrain are merely a wretched stage to showcase the real horror. For each banished soul the suffering is unique and different, a fiery penance to fit the crime. That's why her greeting in Hell was the screams of young girls.

If beauty is in the eye of the beholder, then the adverse is also true, so for her the sight looming in front of her couldn't have been any more horrific. It was the yawning underworld of Hell swirling around her like an infinite nightmare, a seething maelstrom of debauchery and abuse. She saw demonic shapes and frail young girls engaged in wicked entanglements. Even the ashen smoke and sizzling fire seemed to echo these couplings wherever she looked. A glance overhead revealed even more in the scorched black sky. She caught glimpses of her husband and father eagerly engaged in the same foul deeds with sobbing young souls. The thunderous whimpers and wails from the legion of girls were an unbearable anguish.

Then it got even worse.

If beauty and horror are in the eye of the beholder, then what she saw next was an even more depraved rendering of Hell's true nature. Through the volcanic fire and smoke, she saw burnt shapes staggering towards her with the same shocked stare, advancing like an underworld army on an unholy mission. An urging deep in her body lifted her up to her feet. The surging force was like nothing she'd ever felt, equal parts pain and pleasure, but on an inhuman scale infernal in its dark allure.

The figures shuffling towards her through the blistering fire and haze were all naked women. Then something darker began to take shape, coming together like the pieces of a puzzle. The massive feet were first, then the ankles and legs, all built from the horde of dead women climbing on top of each other, all the way up to the wobbly head. Then it was done, a towering monstrosity glowing grotesquely in the fire and gloom. It was ghastly and profane, a soaring abomination of damned souls, splattered with soot and ash. But beauty is in the eye of the beholder, so all of Hell shook with a satanic roar.

She became part of the abomination, hanging on tight, when she saw the prodigious form striding out of the black mist and crackling fires. It towered with twisted black horns and cloven hooves, cavernous eyes burning hotter than the sputtering fires. Whatever part of her was still connected to her past life had to be severed, because the sight of the Dark Lord left no room for that world.

The Dark Lord had spent an eternity in Hell, so he'd learned a few things about suffering. His carnal cravings assaulted his mammoth creation, inflicting his own dark desires in the most demonic way possible, invading every part of the shivering mass. Tiny bodies fell off like flakes of flesh and splattered on the ground, but on he went, ravaging the mass of tortured souls.

When the depraved deed was done, he strode away and the degraded tower of flesh crumbled apart into the soot and ash. Laying splayed out on the scorched ground, she felt a flicker deep inside, a searing realization that Hell had taken her forever. The flicker was gone as quickly as it came, and she was suddenly seized by a profound new longing growing in that place devastated by loss. It was glorious and strange, wonderfully forbidden, and she realized she couldn't take her eyes off the mountainous Dark Lord striding away through the fire and smoke.

Because beauty is always in the eye of the beholder.

WE HAVE OUR WAYS

In my younger years, I began to wonder if I would have become a different person if I'd grown up somewhere else. All I knew of the world was our lonely village deep in the woods. What lay beyond could only be seen in my dreams, lifting me over the giant trees that loomed around us like a primeval wall.

I wasn't a rebellious girl, knowing that would never be tolerated. My curiosity, though, always lurked beneath my compliant manner. It was a secret I kept to myself and felt no misgivings about that, knowing there were other secrets in the village far greater than mine. But on the rare times when I asked my parents a question, their response was always the same.

"We have our ways..."

They were a stern pair, like all the Elders, not given to frivolity or needless amusements. Their somber nature was reflected in their dress. Even during the heat of the summer, they were cloaked in the stitched black clothes they made themselves. Floppy hats were worn by the men, casting their faces in a constant shadow. The women covered their heads with a dark cloth or the same low hanging hat. Every day was like a day of mourning, without the knowledge of who had died.

There was a night though when my curious nature lured me in a dangerous direction. I had just turned ten and the day began like any other, rising at dawn for a humble breakfast and household chores, then down the scorched path for another day of instruction.

We'd always been told the woods were a sacred place for reasons that were never explained. But we were also warned never to enter their vast and gloomy sprawl. We were a community of ancient laws and passing the border into the woods was a strict command above all others.

The titanic trees should have provided caution enough. They looked like mighty creatures fashioned out of gnarly wood and fluttering leaves. As if this wasn't enough, a passing wind would bring unsettling sounds drifting out from their hidden darkness. The Elders never explained this, treating the matter with a collective silence that flamed my curiosity even more.

There was nothing unusual about the night, except for the summer moon that shone through the clouds brighter than usual. I instantly knew what had tugged me awake, the strange and mysterious sounds coming from the nearby woods. I must have still been half asleep because my actions were something I shouldn't have done. In a slumbering daze, I crawled out of bed and slipped through the window in my room. In the stillness of the night, the sounds were clearer, but still as strange, like nothing I could possibly fathom. I believe it could also have been a midnight dream conjured in my childish mind to answer questions the Elders would not.

I had intended to go just a few steps into the woods to solve the source of this mystery. But right away, as my tiny feet crunched over leaves, I was immediately swallowed by the blackness. My trespassing instantly brought the bewildering sounds scrambling towards me in a sudden rush. I barely had time to regret my folly when murky shapes appeared, peering out from behind the trees. What manner of creature they were was impossible to say, but my heart-pounding fear was already unleashed. The ominous sounds grew faint, like prowling animals stalking prey, and glimmering eyes closed in around me.

Whether I was fully awake or trapped in a child's nightmare, I had no way of knowing. I ran wildly without any sense of direction, stumbling in a panic through the maze of trees.

The frightful episode ended when I awoke the next morning, just before daybreak, on the dew-covered ground at the edge of the woods. I was still groggy and confused without any of the answers I'd desperately wanted. I remembered hitting a tree and tumbling to the ground, then nothing after that. But something had carried me out of the woods.

If my life was a puzzle, the most intriguing piece was our daily instruction. It began as soon as we were old enough to make our way down the long-scorched path to the open area with the craggy wood table. A ragged circle smelling of smoke and ash was burnt into the ground around it. The youngest sat on the crudely built benches in front, the older ones stretched farther back, a gathering of everyone younger than eighteen.

And that was the greatest mystery of all. At eighteen you were gone from the village, off to some unknown place. I wondered if they were sent to the outside world and what they saw frightened them so much they always returned.

Without any announcement or acknowledgement, they simply appeared again and joined the clan of Elders with their somber black clothes, never speaking publicly of their absence. I never bothered to question this because I already knew what the answer would be.

"We have our ways..."

The task of guiding us was entrusted to a strange old man with a shivering voice made raspy by time. At the start of the day, we were already assembled when he shuffled in with a pile of books in a tattered cloth bag. They were leather bound, but so old they looked as if they might crumble away, just like him.

Most of the time his musing barely made sense. He talked about the unknown power of the stars, and recounted myths from long ago about battles between primal forces. He'd stagger about, sometimes slipping into an arcane language that confused us even more. Over the years, it was a twisted tapestry mumbled out in that shivering voice. Despite all this, the Elders treated him with a steadfast reverence as he filled our heads with fantastic tales.

The sameness of the days continued into my teenaged years. Though older and stronger, I was feeling even more like a prisoner. My parents had never offered much comfort beyond the shelter of our home and food on the table. I was grateful for that, but I also felt a yearning that was impossible to ignore.

Then fate brought me an unlikely companion, a sharp-featured boy a year older and a head taller than me, with long tangled hair a shade darker than mine. Our companionship began without words, as if some unknown spirit had brought us together. We sat next to each other at instruction once, then twice, then always after that. Any kind of pairing was strictly forbidden until you were an Elder, so we became another secret hidden to others.

The closeness of sitting together was enough at first, then it became too little. On the way to instruction, the sun was behind the trees and brought an early twilight. Our whispers began during this time. We'd lag behind the others on the scorched path and share our grievances. We became conspirators murmuring about the village and its curious ways.

"I was ten when it happened," I said in a hush. "I snuck into the woods and saw something terrible. There are fearsome creatures making those sounds..."

"I saw something too," he said in the same low hush. "I saw the teacher go into the woods. Whatever's there, he knows what it is..."

From this sharp-featured boy, I'd finally gotten an offering of the comfort I wanted. We found other ways to be together, even if only for a moment, but it was enough to give us an unshakable bond. Which is why the words he whispered one morning ripped open my heart.

"I'm leaving soon..."

And so it was, his time had come, the eighteenth year when he'd be sent away. Our daily routine was unchanged, but this changed everything else. On the scorched path, we vowed to discover the whereabouts of his destination, so our fear of being apart would not be so stark. We determined there was only one place to find that information.

Every fortnight at dusk, the Elders gathered, and we waited two days for the meeting to take place. The teacher's decrepit dwelling was at the south end of the village away from everything else. We met at the edge of the woods just as a fall night was slipping out. This cloak of darkness gave us the cover we needed.

The closer we got, the creepier the small house looked, also surrounded by scorched ground. It was built out of chopped wood like the rest of the village, yet was more withered and remote, like a hideaway from another time. As quiet as we could, we padded across the burnt ground to the front door. We were still talking in our bonded way; the whispers we didn't want anyone to hear.

"Are you scared?" he asked.

"I don't get scared," I answered.

"What about the time you went into the woods?"

"I was younger then. I'm older now..."

He squeaked open the door and we stepped inside. The only light came from the moon and stars, but it was enough to seize us with a sudden fear. The crumbling leather bound books were stacked like crooked totems on the rotted wood floor. The dusty walls were covered with carved designs and drawings that could only have come from an unraveled mind. There were misshapen creatures, vast vistas, and scratched ramblings in that arcane language. There could be no argument to what we saw. The teacher trusted to guide us was clearly a madman.

Though frozen for a moment, we were both drawn to a picture bigger than the others, covering a wall. It was a map of the village, and the scorched areas clearly formed a symbol of some kind. Then we heard it – a creepy chorus coming from outside.

The Elders were chanting.

"We have our ways..."

I never again saw the sharp-featured boy I'd grown to love. Little was said by my parents because their stone-faced glare said it all. I was banished to my room with the barest amount of food and water. I was

157

truly a prisoner, completely alone. My door finally swung open three days later and I was told to get dressed for instruction.

When I joined the others on the scorched path, my greatest fear had been realized. The sharp-featured boy was gone, and a part of me was gone too. From that day on, I never uttered another word. I stopped caring about the village and its bewildering ways. I passed the days and nights in a self-imposed silence that couldn't be broken.

Then a time came when it no longer mattered. I was turning eighteen.

A drizzling rain was falling when we left our dwelling and joined the small group on the scorched path. There were three of us, two girls and a boy, along with our parents in their dripping black hats. The rest of the village was asleep, the ceremony always done at a late time between dusk and dawn. I'd been told nothing, and my silence had asked the same.

Torches sputtered ahead, fighting the rain. The teacher was waiting for us, his hunched body faintly visible behind the wooden table. When we got closer, I felt a shiver both from the rain and what lay on the table. There was an open book I'd never seen before, much larger than the others, and even more ancient. Circled around it was a collection of eerie objects splashed by the rain. They were made of burnt bones and bound sticks.

We stood in front of the table, as our parents disappeared in the drizzling mist, leaving us alone with this strange old man, He began reading from the book in that arcane language, and the power of the stars came blasting down. With a startling clarity, I felt like I'd been released from a lifelong trance and could finally see. There was a crackling glimmer in my eyes, and the rest of my body was changing. too I was becoming something else, and I knew where I had to go.

When I entered the woods, I was greeted by the roaming pack of others who were like me. This was our special time, before we returned to the village and cloaked our changes in somber black clothes. The sharp-featured boy was there, waiting for me to come. I wasn't silent anymore, making that mysterious sound that was a clarion call to the stars. Because now I knew the fantastic tales the teacher told weren't from some mythic past, but from a glorious future that was coming soon.

EXTINCTION

The parched desert appeared otherworldly as Justin Craven stared at the bones spread across the sun-battered ground. He muttered his favorite saying to himself.

"Nothing is ever truly gone."

It had been his mantra ever since he took an archaeology course at Princeton fifty years ago and decided that was how he would spend his life. While the rest of the world was busy creating a new future, he'd always felt more comfortable investigating the enduring mysteries of the past. He'd always believed you have to understand what came before to be prepared for whatever the future might bring. The past was covered up, but it was still there, hidden by the march of time.

He was old now too, not quite a relic, but getting there, with wispy grey hair and most of his life behind him. His bones ached, and that was the impact of time, the inescapable decay of all living things. He'd had a distinguished career, and now his work was all he had left, after his wife Sara passed away two years ago. She had been his beautiful partner, the love of his life, in a way that had never weakened like everything else.

"But nothing is ever truly gone..." he kept telling himself as he held on to her memory as fiercely as he could.

But with age comes experience, so he wasn't surprised when the call came, and he was summoned to the Badlands in North Dakota. An earthquake had occurred in a remote area without any warning. No one was hurt, but the devastation to the land was big.

He'd followed the story with growing interest, especially the pictures that showed the giant crack in the desert floor. When dinosaur fossils were found, he was immediately excited at the possibilities. As the country's leading prehistoric paleontologist, he knew the Badlands were one of the best places in the world to find dinosaur remains. His hope was that the earthquake would reveal important new discoveries.

"It's really something isn't it?" the government suit yawned with a bored expression.

His name was Marvin Cotter and he had the smug look of someone who thought they were a lot more important than they were. He said he worked for the EPA, but he was probably sent by another more secretive government agency to be his babysitter and watchdog. In this day and age, he knew the government monitored anything that was out of the ordinary, even an earthquake in the middle of the desert.

"So, what are you gonna do?" he asked.

Justin ignored the question and stared out at the hazy landscape in front of him. The government suit probably thought this was a waste of his time, standing in the blazing desert heat next to a giant hole with an old guy and a bunch of bones. He'd learned over the years the government didn't care much about science, unless it was a new way to blow something up. It viewed science as just another way to get what it wanted in the short-term, not as the key to prepare for the future.

The earthquake had been an anomaly, coughing up earth and rock like an underground volcano, along with black smoke still staining the air. The spewed earth is where the dinosaur fossils had been discovered. They'd been carefully brushed off and spread out on the ground like a skeletal puzzle.

He tried not to get too excited, because he was already astounded at the sheer number collected. He recognized most of them, but some he did not, and that puzzled him. They were pitted and decayed like all ancient fossils. But he was already hoping there would be important new discoveries to be made.

He walked slowly, staring at the ground. Discovering new dinosaurs would be the crowning achievement of his career. He'd always viewed life on Earth as a complex tapestry, where every creature from the earliest of times was connected in some way.

"*Be careful...*" he snapped at the government suit still trailing behind him. He was stumbling through the bones with no clue to how profoundly important they were.

"So, you're pretty excited about this, I take it."

"I am..."

The suit chuckled. "I used to like dinosaurs when I was a kid, but then I discovered girls."

Justin stopped and shot him a glare. "You know, it would really be better if you left me alone right now, the less distractions the better."

His glare was met with a smirk. "Sorry, but no can do dinosaur guy. Just pretend I'm not here..."

Justin glared again, but it wasn't any use, so he continued his stroll through the bones, staring down with an expert eye that could take a single decayed fossil and immediately conjure what the remaining

162

prehistoric skeleton looked like. Archeology was a never-ending puzzle, and the study of dinosaurs was the most enduring of all. He'd always believed they were the most majestic and powerful creatures ever to stride the Earth.

Still walking slowly, he saw something ahead that immediately caught his eye, a bone much larger than all the rest. When he reached it, he eased down to his knees, softly touching its chalky black surface. It was something completely new to him. He studied it with growing excitement. He knew the skeletal structure of a Tyrannosaurus Rex as well as a surgeon knew the insides of the human body, and this bone seemed to dwarf that creature considerably. Then he saw more ahead, different from the first, but with the same unexpected size. He stopped to study them too.

"What's going on?" the government suit asked impatiently.

"These are new," Justin muttered, mostly to himself. "Not like anything I've seen before..."

"Okay, that's really great. But it's still just a bunch of bones, so I'm sticking with girls. They're warmer and not so dead." The government suit chuckled and waved the smoky haze away from his face.

And then, exactly six seconds later, the first rumble came from somewhere below. The desert ground trembled with a movement strong enough to make everything shake, causing the bones to bounce and roll chaotically on the ground.

"*What the hell was that...*" the government suit yelled.

Justin looked around, trying to keep his balance because he guessed what was happening. The first earthquake had been severe, but it was only a

163

preliminary foreshock, and the main shock was now taking place. It would be bigger and more destructive in every way.

The rumble got louder and the shaking more ferocious, as if a giant underground engine was beginning to grind and roar beneath them. The government suit was already scrambling away, and all the others were fleeing too, screeching off in cars and trucks in exploding blasts of dust and dirt.

But Justin stayed where he was, the bones bouncing wildly around him. He'd already come to a scary hypothesis about the new bones, and he stayed to see what he instinctively feared was coming. Every historic event deserves at least one witness to marvel at its shocking uniqueness. He didn't have long to wait for the larger earthquake to split the ground next to the previous crack, creating a gargantuan chasm that released more black smoke, earth and rock.

A thunderous, ashen roar bellowed up, and this is when he knew his instinctive fear was not some crazy-old-man delusion, but as real as the modern world. The horrific roar blared from another world, a world deep inside the craggy black womb of Mother Earth. He'd spent his life scraping the surface to discover her mysteries, but he hadn't come close to unearthing her most well-kept secret.

He stood his ground after everyone else was gone, his tired old body preparing for what was coming next. The black smoke churned as his radical new theory became clearer in his head.

The greatest prehistoric mystery had always been what had killed the dinosaurs. Most believed it was a giant asteroid that struck the Earth with a cosmic force, but that was only partially true. His theory went beyond that to the real cause. The asteroid's impact had awakened unknown creatures in the deepest depths of the Earth and given them a path to the surface. The sudden and brutal annihilation of the dinosaurs had been from monsters below, not a rock from space.

And now he could hear it - something gargantuan clawing its way up. When the monster clambered out of the open chasm, Justin beheld a behemoth that would even dwarf the Tyrannosaurus Rex. It was demonic, as if it was the secret link to all our darkest myths and nightmares. In the tapestry of life on the planet Earth, it was the unknown species that was the deadliest of all.

But he still held his ground because every unique event in history deserves a witness, especially if it was going to be the end of history itself.

Justin knew in some future time his tiny bones would probably be discovered alongside the dinosaur bones he'd spent his life studying. Most of all, he hoped he'd now see his beloved Sara again, because when the mountainous creature finally crawled out of the hellish hole and stood on the desert ground in all its underground glory, it proved what he'd always believed.

Nothing is ever truly gone.

ETERNAL

All expeditions to the New World were a search for bounty, but this one was different, this was a quest for the greatest treasure of all. The legend found its way back to our settlement in Puerto Rico, and that's where my singular destiny was born.

Ponce de Leon looked like a gaunt scarecrow with a grizzled face, but he was a skilled fighter and fearless leader. I joined him like most of the others, an aging conquistador lured by his messianic zeal for what we'd find. The challenge of exploration had marked all our lives and he'd stoked it again, spinning tales of adventure and reward beyond our wildest dreams.

We were three ships strong, venturing out with battle-scarred soldiers, cavalry horses, and armored war dogs. The roiling voyage took the weakest among us before we even reached land, their sun-beaten bodies hurled overboard and swallowed up in watery bites. We'd all made a far more dangerous voyage a few years before, crossing a seemingly endless ocean. Ponce de Leon had been on Christopher Columbus's second vessel, a harrowing tale he told with drink at night.

166

When landfall finally came, the trek through the jungle was hellish and slow, relieved only by a summer rain that never fell often enough. It wasn't long before some began to grumble we were on a fool's pursuit, and I'd become skeptical too, but kept my mounting doubts to myself. Despair was an unseen enemy that could hobble a mission as surely as a physical attack.

Then calamity struck in the middle of the day, when my skin began to burn in the heat, and I was shackled by some kind of sickness. After two days of staggering struggle, I had to face the fear that my warrior's life was coming to an end. I was left with only one last hope, that the miracle fountain was somewhere ahead.

For weeks we'd slogged through the overgrown thicket and merciless sun, and now our leader seemed to be afflicted, stumbling faster through the trees and wild brush. I watched from the back, barely able to stay upright, so they hoisted me on a horse, which carried me along. Attacked by a jungle malady, blood dripped from my eyes and ears. I knew death was close and only the miracle fountain could save me.

The braying horses were the first to take notice, snorting and stomping, quickly followed by the war dogs' growls, both straining toward something only they could sense. The delirious fever grew worse, and that burning haze blurred what came next.

We emerged from the jungle in a ragged formation, assembling on a high rock ridge above a valley below. Even in the depths of our exhaustion, we were a formidable sight – a sunlit fighting force glinting with swords, clubs, maces, lances, crossbows, and harquebus guns.

Our invasion into the New World had not been as arduous as some had feared. When the primitive Indians saw our forged armor and magical weaponry, they cowered as if we were brutal gods from a frightening realm. And so we were, at least in our minds, becoming what they feared the most.

Ponce de Leon stood beneath the fireball sun and thrust his crescent sword in the air. "Glory be to God and our exalted King!"

Because there it was, a spectacle that offered hope the fantastical legend might be true. Nestled below the ridge was a jungle oasis that glowed like a jewel. A torrential gush of water erupted up from a swirling lake with a golden hue.

It wasn't like anything I'd ever seen before, a wonder beyond wonders hidden away in this uncharted land. A massive mud plateau bounded the other side, with a wood barrier protecting the lake. Shapes were moving in the water and milling about on the muddy ground. I squinted through my feverish haze and saw they were brown-skinned Indians barely clothed in ragged cloth. They looked peaceful and tranquil, drawn to the golden water by the heat of the sun.

Ponce de Leon raised his battered sword again. "We claim this land by the godly right of our King!"

Soldiers mounted their horses and the growling war dogs were unleashed. I stayed on the ridge, too weak and feverish to join the attack. I tumbled off the horse and fell back below a tree, but still within view of the conquest.

At first, I thought it was the burning fever making me see things that weren't there, like a strange dream in the twilight of day. I wiped the sweat and blood from my eyes, crawled closer to the edge of the ridge.

The Indians in the lake rose up and stared at what was coming down the hill, a fearsome and awesome sight. The Indians on land turned and stared up too. It was a bewildering scene, the Indian tribe standing perfectly still, waiting like statues carved from rock. It was surely dread and fear, I thought, seeing they were unable to move. We were clearly beyond the scope of anything they'd ever encountered in their hidden sanctuary. We were marauding gods from a distant land, so resistance was not within their meager means.

The snarling dogs were the first to attack, some racing with blurring claws, others leaping up from a few feet away, both savagely seizing the Indians mostly naked bodies. There were men and women, small children too, all dragged to the ground, their bronze flesh mauled and mangled by chomping teeth. The marching soldiers were next, rifles flashing like lightning bolts. The cavalry horses spread out in flanks, more flashing sparks and bursting smoke.

The tranquil scene turned bloody, Indian bodies crumbling to the ground and floating face down in the golden lake, a sudden and brutal graveyard of death. Still the remaining Indians didn't move, as if their life force had already been snatched away and their bodies discarded. I remained on the ridge, still slumped on the ground without the will or strength to stand.

The fiery sun sank below the trees. It began to rain from a darkening sky, pelting the jungle and bloody oasis. What came next wasn't a complete surprise, because it was something   warriors only discussed when no one else was listening.

The attack was won, but it didn't diminish the bloodlust. And this atrocity was worse than the attack, because it wasn't a battle anymore. That's when I

169

realized an eerie strangeness about the killing field below. The slaughtered Indians didn't make a sound. Even the women and children toppled over without the barest of moans.

Then, right before my eyes, the massacre turned into a nightmare new to our world. The slaughtered Indians began to move. They rose up in the golden lake and on the muddy ground, their eyes aglow with a darkish glare.

Every battle is frightening in its own way, but this was beyond mere fright. The Indians had lost none of their strength in death but were now even stronger, attacking the soldiers, horses, and war dogs. The statue-like Indians who still lived joined in with the same might and mania, the living and recently dead fighting together. To them, we might have been gods, but they were clearly more than human too. Even in their rage they remained silent, as if the ability to speak was no longer needed.

To call it a slaughter doesn't fully encompass what was happening, because it was stranger than that. The Indian men fought with bare-footed speed and monstrous strength, and they weren't alone. Muddy children wrestled stomping horses to the ground and wrinkled old women battered soldiers with crushing blows. The indescribable fear of fighting a savage force shifted to our side. The soldiers swung their maces, axes, and swords, but the Indians were too swift, the hurtling steel striking nothing but rain and air. Some rifles and crossbows found their mark, but their blows were not lethal, not even slowing them down.

The rain thrashed even harder, and a thunderbolt crackled overhead, as if nature itself was joining the battle. I crept closer to the edge of the ridge and peered down. The last fire of the sun was gone, leaving just a little light left.

That's when it appeared, rising up and up in the golden lake. The Indians stopped and turned to the improbable mass emerging from the watery depths. They were immobile again, their black eyes shining with wonder and worship. The remaining soldiers were frozen too, overcome by the hideous sight now towering above them The mass seemed to bask in the rain, its hideous form awash with the golden water. It looked like nothing else on earth, and not just because of its gargantuan size. Colossal appendages splashed out and dug deep in the mushy ground. No eyes were visible, but ragged slits pulsed with a slimy creepiness. It didn't seem to have a single shape, its immense bulk oozing in different directions.

Even in the first blackness of night, I knew its predatory mission. We were a New World, and it was an invader we'd never encountered before. It had come to conquer our primitive land like a god from an unknown realm.

The soldiers knew it too. They attacked with everything they had, bullets, maces, axes, and arrows, all hurtling at the towering beast. The war dogs took to the lake with thrashing paddles and snapping bites. The Indians still surrounded the monster like dark-eyed puppets awaiting command.

But we were too weak and puny on a scale we'd never experienced. Nothing penetrated its slimy hide, all the axes, maces, and arrows splashing and sinking in the water. It raised its prodigious appendages from the muddy ground and a new kind of weapon entered the fray, its whip-like tentacles catapulting soldiers, horses and war dogs into the night.

I heard a hoarse yell and recognized Ponce de Leon in the murk below. He waved his sword again and turned from the creature, stumbling away in retreat. The bloody soldiers limped behind him, a sign the battle was lost. Then I saw Ponce de Leon wasn't leading his men back up the hill in retreat, but in the other direction. They were staggering shadows, barely visible from my distant perch. Fiery shots rang out and I heard the steady crunching of axes on wood.

I had to fight to keep my eyes open because the specter of death was suddenly near. I'd lived a warrior's life, so it could have come at any time, but it was surely here now, wrapping its claws around my heart. My eyes closed, and for a breathless moment I was more dead than alive.

Then I heard a rumbling sound and I knew what was happening. The blasting gunfire and hacking axes had weakened the primitive barrier protecting the lake, unleashing an avalanche of slush and mud rumbling down. The creature's howl was another intrusion into our world, rattling the lake, the ground, the trees in the jungle, and maybe even the stars above.

I heard the slow crunching of boots trudging back up the hill, along with the panting of horses and dogs. I knew victory was theirs, but that didn't mean the war was won. It was easy to crawl behind a tree and stay hidden from Ponce de Leon and the other survivors as they began the long journey back home.

I mumbled a whispery prayer that this was the final battle, but I couldn't be sure. The claws of death squeezed tighter around my heart and a darkness erupted inside me. With my last bit of strength, I crawled to the edge of the ridge and tumbled down the steep hill.

The rain had stopped and a gloomy full moon claimed the sky. The otherworldly being and the miracle fountain were smothered by the avalanche of mud and an eerie silence had fallen. My warrior's death was a heartbeat away, but I was already slurping the golden water from a muddy puddle. My heart stopped, then a light appeared, the gloomy full moon glowing above, and my dying heart was beating again, steady and strong.

And now we come to my destiny.

The miracle fountain has given me the greatest gift of all, which I use for a single purpose. They found passage to our world once before, so it could happen again. For the past six hundred years I've been in countless armies and fought in numerous battles, always slipping away when they wonder why I never get older. I don't worry about the claws of death anymore, so I can be an eternal warrior fighting beneath the burning stars, ready and vigilant if they ever return.

DEPRAVITIES

A collection of the wicked and wild

MIDNIGHT TOWN

A pack of cards is the devil's prayer book…

There are moments in life when you can glimpse your future if you know where to look. That moment came when I was nine years old driving to Las Vegas with my dad. We were on a sun-beaten highway when a distant glimmer appeared ahead, glowing like giant diamonds and jewels. I turned to my dad and I'll never forget the look on his face. He was staring through the windshield at the shining oasis that would be our new home.

At first, I thought it was a look of hope and excitement, that our lives would finally be different. Mom had left with another man, but that was mostly because of Dad's gambling. He was a drunk and a dreamer who always believed his next bet would make him rich, and Mom couldn't take it anymore.

Slumped next to him in the car, I wanted to believe what he believed, that moving to Las Vegas was what we needed to do. "Kiddo, they're not going to know what hit them," he told me.

As we drove through the desert, I caught a glimpse of the strange and haunting future I would never escape. My dad was staring at the radiant sprawl shining ahead, and that's when I saw the look in his eyes wasn't hope or excitement, but the first hint of his madness.

He'd worked as a bartender back home and finally found a job at one of the dives far away from the bright lights downtown. He poured cheap drinks during the day, then gambled and drank in grungy backrooms at night. I knew he loved me, but the madness grew, gnawing away at everything inside him. He was still my dad, but he became a staggering puppet, dragged around by forces beyond his control. I also remember the glaring divide between the brightness of day, and the night world where lost souls chased impossible dreams.

He had never been a healthy man, and he grew much worse, as if his aging body had been infected with all his past misdeeds. He began to mumble to himself when he thought no one was looking, muted guttural sounds that didn't make sense. I waited at home every night for him to stumble through the door after work. His trembling body was hunched, his voice raspy and weak, but he still lurched back into the night, crumpled up money stuffed in his pocket, then staggered back home when the money was gone.

One hot summer night he didn't come home. I was twenty years old and working as a security guard at one of the casinos downtown. My dad's misspent life had pushed me in a different direction, following the rules as best as I could.

Growing up in Las Vegas, I'd heard all the harrowing late-night tales, but thought they were just rumors and local legends. Disappearances were common but kept from the public so the tourists would feel safe. I searched all his usual dives, but the scraggy denizens just shook their heads and mumbled a few drunken words. They probably couldn't have told me where he was even if he was sitting right next to them.

The next day I filled out a report with the police, and it was stuffed in a coffee-stained folder that was two inches thick. I could tell by the look on the cop's face that my dad's disappearance wasn't going to be a high priority, but just another luckless loser who'd vanished without a trace. I lingered in front of the cop, not knowing what to do. He leaned closer and lowered his voice. "Listen, we'll do what we can, but so should you." He took a quick glance around. "Have you ever heard of Midnight Town?"

I thought for a moment, then shook my head.

"Ask around," he said in the same low voice. "Maybe you'll get lucky."

During the days and weeks that followed, I searched for a place I wasn't sure even existed, taking me to places were gloom and shadows were the décor of choice. As the search continued, I began to hear a voice that urged me on. Whenever I hit a dead end, it croaked out and lured me in another direction, guiding me through hidden haunts and secret spaces. What I eventually discovered wasn't on a map because tourists weren't allowed.

I found my dad, but it was too late for him. He was living in Midnight Town and there was nothing I could do. When I stumbled back home, I gulped half a bottle of his rotgut bourbon and fell into a thrashing sleep. I didn't know it at the time, but something had changed in me too, crawling out that horrible night.

The next morning, I called Mom and told her he'd died, surprised to hear her sobbing on the other end. He wasn't a bad man, just a hopeless dreamer whose life had turned into a nightmare.

I still wonder if I've done the right thing sticking around, or if I should have left Las Vegas and all its monstrous secrets behind. I began to drink and gamble, and I'm not sure why. Maybe it was to keep a connection with my dad, or maybe it had always been a part of who I am.

I still believe in right and wrong, but what I saw in Midnight Town was a horror beyond comprehension. I was a cop for a while, but the drinking and gambling ended that. Now I'm a private investigator specializing in missing-persons cases. Word got around that I can find people who can't be found. I've learned the best advertising isn't one of those giant neon signs on the main strip, but a stranger telling you what to do, just like the cop had done when Dad disappeared. That's how I get my clients, from heartbreak and grief, last-chance desperation.

I have a one room office above a tattoo parlor called Final Destination. I don't have to pay rent because I'd found the owner's speed-freak girlfriend. She wasn't in Midnight Town, so it was an easy case, except for when I got beaten to a pulp in a biker bar.

I go to Gamblers Anonymous meetings whenever I can. I sit on one of the metal chairs in back and listen to the raspy voices of the puppet people, trying to guess who will disappear next. They've gambled with their lives, and that never ends well.

I can usually guess by the knock on the door who the person on the other side is. This knock was soft and weak, just a couple of taps.

A middle-aged woman with a drab coat and old brown shoes shuffled in like she was going to a funeral. She talked in a cracked Midwestern voice, fighting off tears. I listened quietly, nodding my head, because I'd heard it before, just a different spin on the same story. Her daughter had come to Las Vegas from a small farming town in Kansas. She'd worked as a showgirl and seemed happy at first but began to change in ways the mother couldn't understand. She didn't call as often, and when she did her voice was gravelly and weak.

"I knew something was wrong," the mother whimpered. "Then she stopped calling at all. I came as fast as I could, but nobody knows where she is. I went to the police, but they haven't found anything. That's why I came to you."

She pushed a picture across my desk. Her daughter was blonde and beautiful, with blue eyes, the small-town prom queen or cheerleader type. I stared at the picture and was already wondering if her eyes had looked different before she disappeared. They wouldn't be filled with her hopes and dreams anymore, but with the creeping horror of madness.

I reached across the desk, took the mother's hand and told her I'd do everything I could to find her daughter. I wrote down her address and the place she worked. The mother started crying, shaking in front of me with the same misery I'd felt when my dad disappeared. She pushed herself up and walked out the door, praying she'd see her daughter again.

I'd decided awhile back if I was going to let my demons win, then I'd do it with a lot better bourbon than my dad drank. I splashed it in a cup and gulped it down, not caring about the taste. The mother was scared something had happened to the daughter she loved, and I just hoped she wasn't in Midnight Town. I might be able to bring her back, but she wouldn't be the blonde beauty her mother remembered.

She'd worked at the Golden Nugget and shared an apartment with two other girls.

"She finished the show, then never came home," the redhead said.

"She'd been acting weird," the platinum blonde said.

I talked to her bosses and old boyfriends, everybody I could find who knew her. She was a girl everybody liked, but for the last few weeks she'd seemed troubled, not the same. When there was nobody left to talk to, I went back to her apartment and searched again, going through her closet and drawers, looking more carefully to see if I'd missed anything. That's when I found her diary hidden in a box with her white high heels.

Inside was a picture in her costume, a red silk dress crusted with beads and glitter. I flipped through the pages because I already knew what I needed to find. There was the usual stuff written in a girlish scrawl, and then the flowery scribbles began to change, turning into meaningless scratches. The last page was ripped and shredded, completely black. I closed her diary, knowing what that meant.

I had to go to Midnight Town.

After the sun went down, I locked the door and sipped bourbon in my office. The liquid burn made everything blurry, which was exactly what I wanted. My senses had to be dulled to face the misshapen horrors again. My demons wanted me to stay put and keep drinking all night, turning me into a puppet. It was never easy, but I forced myself to put the bottle away and padded down the stairs to the darkness outside.

Hope is a strange thing, I thought, driving through the streets to the outer reaches of the city. It can be glorious and bright, filled with the excitement of dreams coming true, but it can also turn dark and haunting, a nightmare made real.

So it was with my first trip to Midnight Town, the place I'd found that wasn't like anything in the known world. It had taken me weeks of searching, going where there was no city left, just the barren desert and the empty night sky. The croaking voice had led me there, but now there was nowhere else to go. I'd reached a final dead end. I was about to turn back, when I saw a flicker in the desert, a colossal shadow that came and went. There were sounds, raspy and wailing, like nothing I'd ever heard.

That's when I found Midnight Town.

Once again, I strode into the desert, and was being pulled toward something I still couldn't see. My shoes crunched on rocks and dirt, and then it was like passing through an invisible barrier that shuddered out of sight. Spread out around me was a jumble of crumbling edifices rotted and black. I'd been here before, but the brutal eeriness stunned me again. My dulled senses did little to help, and I had to close my eyes to brace for the horrors ahead.

I walked into the first crumbling edifice, low and squat like a crypt, knowing this is usually where the new arrivals were, so their humanness was still mostly intact. But the wicked allure of Midnight Town was already evident as they openly fed their desires. They were gamblers and strippers, hustlers and swindlers, murderers and drunks, but now more fevered and frantic.

As strange as it seemed, I'd come to realize that Midnight Town was a sacred place. The victims were lured to this glowing oasis in the desert, believing their wildest dreams would come true. At first, they'd prayed to the heavens above, asking for fame and fortune, but the God they prayed to didn't answer, so they were forced to plead their case to a different entity.

Midnight Town was a sanctuary that didn't play by the rules. That's what the chorus of wails was doing, pledging allegiance to a monstrous power that finally fulfilled their dreams. They gambled and drank, seduced and debased, in ways they'd only dared to imagine in the city of sins.

I stayed on the outer edges, scanning the murk for the missing showgirl, knowing her youthful beauty wouldn't be there anymore. In Midnight Town, flesh was one of the offerings made, creating a change that would terrify the outside world. I roamed through the cave-like crevices and crumbling corridors, thinking again about hope and where its blindness can lead.

I soon found her, not in a red silk dress with glitter and beads but covered in ash, surrounded by pawing men. She was still a showgirl, but now she was dancing like a raunchy puppet, a bump-and-grind freak show. A look of weeping ecstasy was on her face, because her wretched new god had made her a star.

This was the horror for me too. The primal allure of Midnight Town was a force I had to fight, because I could feel my demons getting stronger. I'd always wanted to do the right thing, but now that felt like a burden, an unwanted barrier to what I really wanted. My senses weren't hazy and dull anymore, but burning and bright. I wanted to leave the outside world, and fully unleash my true nature.

But the Midwestern mother's heartbreaking voice was still inside me, and that was another kind of wail I couldn't ignore. I charged through the pack of growling men and grabbed the ash-covered girl by the arm, dragging her away from their clawing hands.

A guttural roar rose from the miasma around us, shaking the ground and crumbling walls. It waw the screams of the other worshippers, knowing their sacred place was being violated. There were more clawing hands from every direction, some that were barely human.

Maybe it was hope that saved the day, pushing me through the howling horde to the darkness outside. I carried her through the shuddering barrier, then across the empty patch of desert to the edge of the city. On the drive back, I called her mom and told her to meet us at my office. She kept trying to thank me, but all she could do was cry.

I waited outside the tattoo parlor and watched the mother's car pull up. When she saw her ash-covered daughter slumped on a nearby bench, she sobbed uncontrollably. I grabbed her by the arms and told her what to do.

"You have to get back in the car and leave this place. Don't stop until you drive all the way home. You have to leave now."

I carried her daughter to the backseat. When the car screeched away, I was sure she was going to take my advice.

Only two hours of darkness remained when I finished the bottle of bourbon and made peace with my demons, promising them in a hoarse voice everything would be okay. I stumbled back downstairs to my car. There were still mumbling bodies staggering down the sidewalks, a drunken puppet parade. I was glad I'd found the showgirl and hoped she'd be alright. I was betting on the mother, but it was probably a long shot.

As I headed back to Midnight Town, I thought about how life is a gamble whether you do it with cards and dice, or your sanity and soul. I passed through the shadowy barrier and staggered back to the crumbling black edifices. I felt weak and confused, but another power pulled me along, or maybe it was my demons pushing me.

The blasphemous horrors of Midnight Town got more extreme the deeper I journeyed inside. The wicked pursuits were more demented, the offerings of flesh more sordid, the betting and gambling more depraved, until I reached a dead end. I was standing in front of a giant burnt wall. A voice croaked out, and the charred wall cracked open like a cosmic mouth.

I entered another realm that seemed infinite in the way only a nightmare can, with no boundaries or borders, just the startling shock of terror and fear. Murmuring shapes were splayed on the ground, praying to whatever lured them here. I searched through the bleakness until I found what I was wanted. My father was no longer human but wasn't a puppet either, he was something much worse. I fell to the ground and joined him in the chanting prayer.

UNCOMMON PLEASURES

France, 1793

At midnight, the Chateau La Coste in Provence had the decaying look of a beautiful woman who was now giving in to the ravages of a decadent life. Moonlight splashed on pitted rock walls and sagging watchtowers, revealing every crumbling crack. To the old man sitting at the window, it had become another reminder that the future always destroys the past, no matter how grand and majestic it was. In his homeland beyond the window, this was even more evident as it struggled through a savage revolution and the Reign of Terror.

He was dressed in a black silk nightgown that glimmered from the light of a nearby candle. He'd been having trouble sleeping for years and found gazing out at the night would often have a soothing effect. It also gave him the quiet and solitude he needed to reminisce and reflect. After seventy years, it was the one welcome gift given by old age. He could gaze out the window and look back at the exquisite wonder of his life. There are no true saints or sinners, he'd always believed, just humble human beings trying to seek out their personal truth in a complicated world.

His grandest achievement, of course, had been his devotion to pleasure. He'd treated it with a reverence above everything else. While others of his noble station were obsessed with status and wealth, he'd never felt so inclined. Maybe he'd just been born differently, and that's why his senses were sharper, his appetites more unbounded and pure. He hated the mundane with a disgust that bordered on revulsion. Luckily, he'd also been born with the unshakable courage and resolve to follow his own path, staying steadfast to its twisted route no matter how radical or extreme.

As he stared out the window, dark memories played out in his head like they did every night, bringing a satisfied smile to his parched old lips. The gloominess of what he saw was not because of his fading memory. On the contrary, it was replaying events from the past exactly as they had happened, in all their shadowy, secret glory.

But on this night his reverie was suddenly cut short when a flash caught his eye beyond the window. At first, it looked like a shooting star, but that wasn't the case because he followed it down through the night sky until it crashed in the gardens behind the castle.

He pushed himself up, reached for the candle with his trembling hand. The castle was all he had left, his final resting place. He was worried about a fire spreading and taking away his home.

"Francoise! Isabelle! Wake up! Quick! Quick!"

Two bodies stirred beneath the plump red covers of his massive oak bed. There was grumbling, but just a little, as the covers were pushed away by the waking forms. The young faces that appeared would have preferred to stay sleeping, but that didn't matter. Anyone who shared the warmth of his bed knew not to question his commands.

Francoise was already on his feet, his brown hair curly and wild. The young man had been his servant

186

for the past five years but was just now out of his teens. Isabelle was slower, a year younger. He'd found her two years ago begging on the streets for scraps to eat, and he'd brought her home. She was dull-minded and stocky, but pleasingly compliant.

His long-suffering wife had abandoned him years ago, her patience and love seeming to dissipate at the same time.

"Marquis, we're coming, we're coming," Isabelle's sleepy voice called out behind him, as he stumbled down the stairs at the end of the hallway.

Seconds later, they were out the back door of the kitchen, moving swiftly across the terrace in back of the castle. A fog had rolled in with the black thickness of smoke, the untended gardens not far ahead. The path was almost invisible in the sudden fog. His foot came down on a rock, sending him tottering off-balance, then down to the ground.

His anger flared because it was another harsh rankle he had with old age. At this sad time in his waning life, his desires usually exceeded his physical abilities.

The servants gently tugged him back up to his unsteady feet.

"Marquis, you're hurt," Francoise murmured.

A cut on his hand dripped blood.

"We have to hurry," he snapped again, ignoring the pain. He had bigger concerns than a small wound, a sight he was more than familiar with.

They reached the end of the terrace, Francoise and Isabelle still helping him along. François had snatched up the candle that was still aglow. Its light illuminated the dark hedgerows in front of them, separating the terrace from the gardens beyond. They reached the gardens, then stumbled to a stop. The sight that greeted them was made stranger by the thick smoke billowing in front of them.

"Marquis... *what is it?*" Isabelle whispered.

He didn't have an answer, or even a guess.

For a long moment they stood in silence, their eyes taking in the bewildering sight. On the ground ahead was a weirdly shaped object smothered in churning, black smoke. Its sliding crash had cut a deep trough into the earth, its smashing path finally stopped by a gnarly old tree.

The object was large, but the thick smoke obscured its shape. And something was crawling through the smoke.

They shuffled closer, very slowly, staring at what emerged from the haze. There were arms and legs, and a head, of sorts, but it wasn't human, and it wasn't an animal. It was tall and thin, starkly white, crawling across the ground like a giant spider. Then it collapsed, fluttering with weakness to the ground. They moved closer, hovering a short distance away. It was shivering, wheezing out a wispy, weak sound.

"Fetch the wheelbarrow," he said to Francoise, pointing nearby.

With the smoke and fog the going was slow. It took all three of them to lift the strange creature and settle it down on the rickety cart. As they did so, the creature's mouth dropped open and a snaky tongue shot out, lapping at the blood, still red and wet on his hand. He instinctively yanked it away, but not without a tingle of surprise, an emotion he hadn't felt in far too long.

They tugged the wheelbarrow across the garden to the dark castle ahead. He wondered with a growing curiosity what manner of life they were carrying inside.

"We'll take it to the basement," he announced when they reached the back door to the kitchen. He saw Francoise and Isabelle share a quick glance but ignored it. Their silly opinions meant nothing to him, and never had.

They clumsily lifted the creature up from the wheelbarrow, hoisted it on top of Francoise's broad shoulders, and he carried it inside. The door to the basement was in the short hallway beyond the kitchen. He retrieved the iron key from its hiding place and unlocked the thick wooden door. Isabelle had the candle now and led them down the twisting stairway to the underground rooms. He picked one of the smaller spaces that were mostly empty of his cherished devices.

We all have two lives he'd discovered early, the side that we show the world, and the private side without any constraints. The underground basement with its catacomb of rooms was where he'd kept his private side.

They lay the creature on a long slab table. As they'd done before, they stood for a moment in silence, staring at its startling strangeness. It was creepy and eerie, not of this world. He wasn't a man of faith, or a man of science, but he had a fondness for spooky mysteries.

They stayed awhile longer marveling at the quivering creature, then he ordered Francoise to sit vigil the rest of the night. Going back to bed, he still had no guess as to what it was, but he knew it was a unique and unknown possession that belonged solely to him.

The next day, he decided the first priority was to provide sustenance, because it looked even weaker than it had the night before. They tried water, cow's milk, bread, cheese, and meat, but nothing elicited any interest. The creature lay limp on the table, looking close to death. He would have sent for the doctor, but the prissy little man had long ago declared his disinterest in coming to the chateau anymore. Then another idea appeared in his head.

"Isabelle, bring in the turkey we've been saving for Sunday supper. Slaughter it, then bring me a bowl of its blood."

She was back faster than expected, cradling a white bowl filled with turkey blood. He took the bowl and brought it close to the creature's head. Like before, a snaky tongue shot out and lapped up the blood in just a few seconds, leaving the bowl empty and white.

"How strange," he murmured.

So now we kept a bowl of blood taken from the livestock on a table next to the creature's head. It consumed it insatiably with an astounding effect. Its body grew firmer and stronger by the week, changing so quickly he decided precautions had to be taken. He bound the now restless creature to the table with leather straps that had been hanging on both sides. As the creature lay bound on the table, he also found a feeling stirring in his body as well. His dark desires were catching fire again.

He was staring out the window two nights later when the urge ignited inside him again. This was the way it had been when he was a younger man. A ferocious desire would suddenly flare up, and he couldn't have peace until he found a release.

He reached for the candle then padded across the floor, leaving Francoise and Isabelle undisturbed in the bed. The tiny glow lit the way as he descended the three flights of stairs down to the underground catacombs. He wondered if the urge had first appeared in his dreams, because he already knew which of his cherished devices he wanted to use. He quickly gathered them from the other rooms, then carried the bundle to where the bound creature lay. He dropped them to the floor, spikes, whips, clamps, prongs, shackles, and knives.

The creature's body was freakish, its skin so white it almost glowed, and he realized this was the cause for the reawakening of his desires. Over the course of his life, his pursuit of pleasure had pushed him far beyond what was considered acceptable. At the outset, he'd discovered a personal truth that guided his way. For him, pleasure and pain were inextricably linked, pain in others was pleasurable to him.

After a lifetime of pursuing every extreme fantasy he could conjure, the human body had ceased offering anything new to explore. He called them his uncommon pleasures, but after so many years they'd become boringly common. That's why the strange creature was so alluring and seductive. Its unknown body was a uncharted playground where he could use his devices in painful new ways.

In the following days, a macabre routine settled in at the crumbling castle. During the daylight hours, the strange creature was provided with bowls of blood that kept it nourished. Its impossibly white body would lap up the blood like a downing person gulping for air. The creature's eyes were milky orbs that pulsed red during feeding. But his care for the creature was not without a selfish side, because it gave it the strength it would need for the punishing nights that followed.

It was always after midnight when he'd slip out of bed and spend the time as he always had. He'd sit in his velvet chair and gaze out the window at the night sky. Only now it wasn't as preparation for falling asleep. He used it to devise new ways for what he would do to the creature that belonged only to him.

The first night he began slowly, probing and poking the creature's freakish body with patient care. Progression was always an essential component when pursuing his uncommon pleasures. He didn't want to introduce pain too soon, because it wouldn't result in the greatest satisfaction. He did it gradually, using his morbid assortment of leather and metal.

Each night he inflicted a higher level, a more excruciating degree of torture. As he increased the severity of his nightly assaults, what he enjoyed most was the new look in the creature's milky eyes. It was a look of absolute, uncontrollable terror.

He padded down the three flights of stairs, eager as always, but on this night, he was greeted by a shocking sight. The creature was still latched to the table by the leather straps, his torturous devices scattered around it on the rock floor. But it was clearly dead, the front of its body gaping open with a ragged hole.

Then he saw the reason for the creature's demise. A smaller creature was on the table next to it, its tiny tongue lapping at the blood. The smaller creature had clawed its way out of the bigger creature, a brutal and murderous birth.

He moved closer, knowing the origin of this unexpected arrival. His erotic progression had included the ultimate assault, using his own body as the bludgeoning tool. This small creature was clearly the offspring of that unnatural union. He saw it was more human in form, but its damp skin was still shockingly white. It peered back at him, blood smeared on its newborn face, and he saw that its eyes were the most striking. They were as dark as the darkest, pitch-black night, and they seemed to be filled with nothing but a desire for cruelty and pain.

The family resemblance was undeniable.

The miracle of the first creature's arrival was followed by another. On the same steady diet of blood, its growth was even faster. Over the course of a year, it grew until its newborn form was taller than his own height.

Francoise and Isabelle seemed to have an instinctive fear of it, but it was a naïve fear he didn't share. After all, a part of it was his own flesh and blood, so he felt a primal connection he couldn't ignore. The creature was strange, but now a part of that strangeness had come from him. Except for the cold blackness of its eyes, and the spectral whiteness of its skin, it now appeared to be human in all regards.

But then he was shown the brutal truth about the creature's nature. When he came downstairs to the kitchen late in the morning, he immediately saw the spilled blood on the floor, then the bodies of Francoise and Isabelle. The creature had been locked in the underground catacombs, but left free to roam. Now it had clearly found a way to escape. The heavy door

193

was wide open, and the creature was on the floor lapping blood from the slaughtered bodies. As he stood there in shock, the blood smeared creature looked up and caught his gaze. He saw a look in its eyes he recognized because he'd felt it himself. Its dark desire had been fulfilled.

While he still felt an allegiance to the flesh of his flesh, he also realized his fate would be the same as Francoise and Isabelle's if it remained in his home. Its brutal desires would no doubt be unleashed again, and he'd be dead on the floor like them.

After nightfall, he cleaned the smeared blood from the creature's face, then dressed it in his finest silk clothes. He took its ghostly white hand and led it outside. The hand was ice cold and skeletal, like a corpse that had crawled out of a wintery grave.

It took some coaxing to get it into the carriage, but then they were off, galloping out the front gate, then down the long dirt road that led to town. He knew what he had to do, but that didn't make this any easier. He wasn't sure if it was love he felt, but whatever it was, it throbbed inside him.

He raced to the most sordid part of the city, then helped the creature stagger down from the carriage. It followed him without hesitation into the rat filled alley and kept its pace when he slowed. Then he did what he had to do, yanking out the metal club hidden beneath his long coat, and striking the creature on the back of the head. As it lay on the dirty cobblestone, it was a vision of ghostly white flesh and seductive black silk. He made sure it wasn't dead, but he also wanted to be sure it couldn't follow him.

There are no true saints and sinners, he'd decided long ago, just human beings trying to find their truth in a complicated world. As the carriage raced back down the long dirt road, he suddenly realized a truth he couldn't deny. He did love the strange creature he'd had to abandon because nothing else could explain the terrible and excruciating pain in his heart.

A few months later, he knew he was dying, and it was just as well. Life had nothing more to give, and there was nothing more he wanted to take. On this night, it was midnight when he slipped out of bed and sat in the velvet chair in front of the window. He hadn't done so in a while, lacking both the interest and strength. For the past few weeks, he'd been confined to his bed, waiting to die. Francoise had brought him news from the outside world, that a different reign of terror was sweeping through the land.

They called it *le Vampyre.*

A thin smile came to his face.

While others had always thought he'd brought shame and disgrace to the once respected de Sade name, he had no remorse. He'd lived an exquisitely singular life, staying steadfast to its twisted route. He'd also learned a valuable lesson about the past, and this was his final thought as his head suddenly slumped to his chest, and his broken heart stopped beating.

It's always the past that creates the future.

THE VIP CLUB

Morgan Malone gazed glumly out at the cavernous room filled with men who had millions to burn. It was the most prestigious club in New York City, a Fifth Avenue sanctum of polished dark wood and creamy brown leather. On any given night, it was the go-to place for the biggest titans of industry and kings of capitalism. If the martinis and whisky were poisoned the stock market would plunge five hundred points.

"What's wrong?" Harold asked. "You look so bored."

Harold was his oldest friend. They'd been roommates at Harvard Business School together, then climbed the corporate ladder to its uppermost heights.

"Everything okay at home?"

Morgan shrugged. Like most long marriages, his had fallen into a humdrum routine, the fireworks long gone.

"How about work? You're still kicking butt and taking names?"

Morgan took the last sip of his martini and nodded for another. A waiter appeared and whisked away the empty glass.

"I've decided to slash and burn our workforce by ten percent, but I'm betting the Board will give me an even bigger bonus this year."

Harold gave him a wink. "It's good to be us."

From the very beginning, they'd both understood how the corporate game was played. It was all about fighting your way to the top, winning at any cost, because that's how you got all the millionaire toys. They shared their dirty little secrets together, confessing their business sins.

"Then I'd say you need a hobby, or something to cheer you up."

His new martini appeared, the crystal glass gleaming softly in the light. "I guess this is the only hobby I have left."

Morgan stared outside through the massive windows. The streetlights had flashed on and the masses were heading home. It was a world he'd lost contact with a long time ago. Other people had become like shadows to him, little more than numbers on a spreadsheet.

Harold pulled out his Gucci wallet, fished out a card, and dropped it on the table.

"What's that?" Morgan asked.

"It's another club I belong to, but you can only get in by referral. It's even more exclusive, very hush-hush."

Morgan looked at the card, holding it up in the dim light. THE VIP CLUB was scrawled in ink on one side, along with a phone number. It wasn't anything like the fancy business cards he was used to.

Harold leaned forward and lowered his voice. "Call the number. It's just what you need to lift your spirits."

"What kind of club is it? I belong to too damn many already."

Harold pushed himself up from his leather chair. They were both past sixty with hair just starting to gray.

"Sorry, old sport, but I have to run."

197

Morgan watched him walk away, weaving through the smoke and the dewy martini glasses, finally disappearing through the giant wood doors. He slipped the card in his wallet, then turned to the windows again, staring at the staggering masses outside.

A week passed before he'd thought about the card still stashed in his wallet. He'd just returned from presenting his proposal to the Board about the drastic employee cuts. He'd long ago stopped worrying how his cutthroat decisions affected others. He wasn't paid the big bucks to be a charity.

He rose up from his desk and walked to the windows. His sprawling office was on the top floor of a steel-and-glass tower, looking closer to the clouds than the world below. He remembered Harold had said the new club would lift his spirits. That much, at least, intrigued him. He'd been fighting a dark mood for almost a year. He walked back to his desk and dialed the number.

The phone rang for a short time without an answer.

"The VIP Club," a voice finally croaked.

The voice wasn't what he'd expected at all, very different from the deferential tone he was used to.

"I was given this number by a friend. Could you tell me what kind of club this is?"

There was a snorting laugh on the other end, like a pig. This was a surprise too, almost a shock, because a man of his position was never laughed at.

"No can do, buckaroo. But if you meet me at the McMurphy Saloon on Bowery and Broome at ten tonight, I'll fill you in. I'll be the handsome bloke with the black cane."

His surprise at the surly voice and the odd request where to meet stayed with him for the rest of the day, as he toiled through the usual drudgery of meetings. Harold had never steered him wrong before, and his desire to rid himself of the dark mood sealed his decision.

His wife was at one of her stupid benefits, so it was just a matter of calling his driver for a pick-up.

When he strolled out of his Park Avenue building, his limousine was waiting at the curb. He nodded to his driver, slipped inside, and wondered how the traffic would be going downtown.

The trip took less than thirty minutes, but the transition was stark, taking him from the expensive apartment buildings on Park Avenue all the way to the grimy bowels of the Bowery.

When his limo pulled up in front of the bar, he had second thoughts about going inside. This wasn't like him at all. He was a man of careful calculation, not one to do anything sudden or rash. He wondered if this was a practical joke, or if Harold was throwing him a surprise party. He saw other limousines parked nearby, waiting in the shadows away from the streetlights.

"Wait for me here," he muttered, pushing open the door.

He wouldn't have thought it possible, but inside the bar was even grimier, a booze-soaked dump. When he walked in, he drew only a few curious stares from the local bikers and other drunks at the bar. Then he heard something tapping on the floor. A short pudgy man with long stringy hair was hunched at a table against the wall. He was dressed in a cheap black suit and a shiny red tie, tapping a black cane on the filthy wood floor.

Morgan walked over.

"This is all rather strange, but my name is..."

The short man quickly cut him off.

"Let's just stop it right there. No names, okay. You got my number, that's all I need to know. Grab a seat, we'll get right to business."

Morgan sat in the other chair at the table, but he was starting to feel that he should just get up and leave. This was clearly a joke and he didn't have the patience.

"Here's the terms for membership," the short man croaked. "You send me fifty grand the first day of the month."

"Excuse me?" Morgan muttered.

"But if you're a dollar short, or a day late, you're out of the club."

Morgan stood, because now he knew he never should have come.

"C'mon, buckaroo. You haven't even asked what the club is yet."

"Okay, what is it?" he huffed.

"It's a service we provide for people like you."

And then it happened, quick as a flash.

An argument at the bar suddenly turned into a fight, clenched fists flying, bodies hurtling into each other, but that was just the beginning. Knives were yanked out, glasses and bottles smashed into weapons, and now it was nothing short of a bloody brawl, dead bodies falling to the floor. Morgan slammed his chair back against the wall and stared in wide-eyed shock. He'd never been this close to such horrific violence. His coal grey slacks and starched white shirt were spotted with blood. Then it was over as suddenly as it began.

For a few seconds, the bloody room was utterly silent and still, followed by the soft scraping of shoes on the floor. Other people began to appear, striding out of the hazy shadows at the back of the room.

Then another shock came as Morgan recognized the faces. They were business titans like him, super rich old men who'd clawed their way to the top of the corporate mountain. Harold was with them, giving him a nod and a wink. They stepped over the dead bodies without saying a word, walked quietly across the bloody wood floor, then strolled outside to their waiting limos.

Morgan was too stunned to move, until he realized his dark mood was gone, and something brand new was taking its place.

The strange little man tapped him on the shoulder with his black cane.

"Let's face it buckaroo, you've done well by yourself, so you deserve some perks not available to the average Joe. That's what The VIP Club is all about."

Over the next several months, Morgan saw in brutal, gushing red exactly what those perks were. A phone call could come at any time, telling him where to go and what time to be there. He'd have his limo drop him off and park a short distance away with the other waiting cars. At the designated place, which could be anywhere in the city, he'd wait quietly with the other club members. They never acknowledged each other or exchanged any kind of communication. They simply stood together staring straight ahead. It was like being in church, where you waited quietly for the ritual to begin.

His first meeting as an official club member was on the Upper West Side, where a head-on collision between a bus and a gas truck created a volcanic bonfire of roasted metal and burning flesh. His next meeting was at a sandlot field where a crazed madman opened fire on middle-aged men playing baseball, gunning them down in a firestorm of bullets.

Each meeting was different, but they were all sudden eruptions of violence and death. As a member of the VIP club, you were always guaranteed early notification and a front row seat.

After a few months, his dark mood had been pushed away so forcefully, he was amazed at the result. Before he'd trudged through every day with a dull mysterious ache, but now all that was gone, replaced by the excitement of belonging to the club.

His wife had been in the hospital for the past two weeks when he met Harold again at their midtown club. Their drinks had just arrived and been placed on the dark table in front of them. Outside, the twilight horde was stumbling home, surviving another day.

"Any improvement with Betty?" Harold asked.

Morgan shook his head.

"It's those damn cigarettes. Without the oxygen she can't even breathe."

They sat for a moment, sipping their martinis.

"I never thanked you for your referral to the VIP Club."

"No thanks needed."

"I just sometimes wonder if it's going too far."

Harold smiled.

"C'mon old sport, look around the room. Tell me what you see."

Morgan gazed out at the cavernous room. He often thought it looked like a place where millionaires went to die.

"I see a bunch of rich old men."

Harold chuckled, took another sip of his drink.

"That's where you're wrong, old sport. They wouldn't be here if they weren't fighters, killers, and hunters. In the old days, they all would have been great warriors and conquerors, but what's missing today is the pleasure of seeing what you've killed dying in front of you."

Morgan thought about this for only a few seconds, because he realized his friend was right, and that's what had been missing from his life. He'd always been a fighter and a killer, because that's how he'd clawed his way to the top. But now the battlefield was a spreadsheet, and the vanquished were little more than annoying numbers easily deleted. All his fights had been cerebral and bloodless, but he'd always secretly wanted much more. That's the service the

VIP Club was providing.

Harold leaned forward. "The Roman emperors got it right. They built giant coliseums so they could watch the weak get eaten by lions."

His wife had gotten worse, so he'd been spending all his free time at the hospital when the call came. At first, he thought about missing a meeting for the very first time, but decided he needed a break, and it wasn't very far. His limo dropped him off at the edge of a small park, then he walked a short distance to the designated spot, a large oak tree with a bushy canopy of leaves.

It was a dark night, no moon or stars, so he felt a touch of disappointment that visibility would be poor.

203

It was always more thrilling when you could see every detail of anguish and pain. He glanced around, surprised that none of the other club members were here yet. Then he heard a sound, something tapping sharply on wood. The strange little man with the black cane stepped out from behind the giant tree.

"Glad you could make it, buckaroo. You and me have some business to settle."

"Where are the others?"

He tossed the cane in the air, caught it with his other hand.

"Don't worry about them. I didn't get your dues this month. That's a problem."

The instant he heard it, Morgan knew it was true. He'd been putting in longer days at work because of the restructuring, then spending his nights at the hospital, so things had been falling through the cracks.

"Yes, of course, you're right. You'll have it first thing in the morning. My mistake."

The short man walked over, shaking his head.

"But that's not the way it works, buckaroo..."

"What do you mean?"

Then it happened, quick as a flash.

The strange little man yanked his cane apart, revealing a hidden sword. He cut through Morgan's expensive clothes, bringing out the blood in streams and spurts. He fell to his knees, then crumbled to the ground, knowing he was about to die a horrible death. He'd never been in pain like this before and was shocked at the searing intensity burning through his body.

That's when he saw them walking back to their waiting limousines. Harold gave him a good-bye nod, then the strange little man raised his sword and gave him a final stab. As he closed his eyes to die, Morgan decided not to fight it, but to give in, because he knew none of this was personal, it was just business.

IN THE DARKEST OF PLACES

This was a lifestyle choice he'd stopped questioning long ago. It was simply a part of who he was, like his taste in food, or the kind of clothes he liked to wear. What people didn't understand was that being tied up during a sexual encounter was a liberating experience. When free will is taken away, submission to your partner becomes absolute. It is about power and control, submission and obedience, and being in control is the part he loved.

He'd taken the scenic route from his apartment in Ipswich, driving down long country roads at the end of the day. It was Halloween Eve and shadows were slipping out. Pumpkins burned with fiery grins and spooky decorations hung from the trees. His excitement for the night ahead was growing the closer he got to his destination. *God bless the internet*, he thought with a smile. With just a few clicks you could find whatever you wanted, even if it was a dangerous taboo. There were no barriers of any kind, all you had to do was know where to look.

They'd connected on a site for people who shared their specialized tastes. He'd instantly agreed to her scenario because it suited his needs. A time and place were quickly arranged. Roleplaying was an integral part of the lifestyle. Adopting another persona was part of the fun.

The ride was under an hour and would have been even less if he'd taken the direct route. But anticipation was also a big part of the process, so there was no need to rush. He spent the time musing about the exquisite delights that were ahead. He thought her scenario was interesting, but it was always about execution. It had to be as real as possible, and that was the part he reveled in. He never held back, always pushing the limits beyond what others might see as too extreme.

He turned into the parking lot of the small church. It looked like it had been there forever, a forgotten relic from the past. The once white steeple was rotted and the stone walls were crumbling. Moonlight was just beginning to fall, covering the abandoned church and surrounding woods.

And now his excitement spiked even higher because this was the perfect setting for the fantasy she described. Their meeting was make-believe, but it couldn't feel that way. Even a tiny flaw could ruin everything. It was all about creating the perfect stage to showcase their deepest and darkest desires.

He was surprised to see the weed-covered parking lot was empty, but guessed she didn't want to rush things either. Every encounter was a kind of shadow play that unfolded at its own dreamy pace. When you're exploring erotic extremes, there weren't any rules, and that was part of the rush. The unbounded unknown is always more thrilling than the straight and narrow.

He spent the time gazing at the woods and creating a series of imaginary encounters. They'd agreed on a basic scenario, but that was just a starting point. The variations they could take were many. But it really didn't matter as long as there were whimpers and moans, screams and wails, a howling anthem of pain and ecstasy. He believed the world we see is a mirage hiding an unseen darkness. He longed for a time when that darkness would take control and he would no longer have to hide his true self.

A light rain began to fall, and that's when he saw headlights crest a hill. The car motored down the empty road and turned into the parking lot. He took a deep breath, because this was a critical part of the fantasy too, the tingling anticipation right before meeting your mystery partner. He stayed in his car as the other car glided to a stop. He watched the front door slid open and a dark figure emerge.

She was completely shrouded in a hooded black cloak and the light from the moon cast her in a murky glow. His heart was racing and he couldn't wait any longer. He grabbed the bag on the seat next to him and opened the door. He hadn't expected the rain, but it didn't matter. It added to the eerie atmosphere they both craved.

Her scenario was simple enough, with the usual gothic trappings that most women into bondage felt an affinity for. She'd be a witch who'd committed blasphemous deeds. He'd be a fire-and-brimstone preacher with no tolerance for the wicked and sinful. She wanted it to be on a night with a full moon and take place in the middle of the woods. The witch had to be punished, of course, and that's what he was carrying in his bag. Then other urges would no doubt take over, and the fire-and-brimstone preacher would have his way with the helpless young girl.

She lived in Salem, so her fantasy had a real-world connection he found intriguing. Growing up in the town where a coven of young witches had once terrorized the churchgoers must have contributed to her secret yearnings. Where his own desires came from had never been a matter of curiosity. His father was a gruff and demanding man, who treated his fragile mother with open contempt. That may have been the origin of his perversity, but he really didn't care. He was who he was, and that was that.

He ambled across the parking lot in the clergy costume he'd ordered online. He felt a bit silly, but it was a small price to pay for what would be coming very soon. That's when he caught a glimpse of the face hidden beneath the drooping black hood. It was stunningly beautiful. He was able to catch only a glimpse because she turned and hurried away. He followed her shadowy form through the drizzling rain, lugging his bag. She quickly crossed the parking lot, waded through a stretch of high grass and disappeared into the dark thicket of trees.

He trailed behind her, led by the padding sound of her feet as she weaved through the gnarly maze. Trudging as fast as he could, the memory of her face intensified. She had the palest skin and darkest black hair. The thought of her tightly bound and powerless to deny his every desire was so overwhelming he tripped and stumbled, then continued even faster. Her startling beauty made his cravings close to uncontrollable, a surging force that had a life of its own.

She suddenly stopped without any warning, the long black cloak fluttering around her. He staggered closer and dropped his bag to the ground. Unlike the gloom they'd just passed through, they were now in a glade with giant trees looming around them. She'd wanted a full moon, and there it was, a misty orb low in the sky. She wanted everything to be perfect, as did he. They were engaged in a make-believe fantasy, but it had to look real.

"My most holy Reverend... I've been a bad girl..."

She was only a dozen feet away, but her voice was so faint he could barely hear it. She tugged off her black hood, letting the rain and moonlight wash over her face. It was a vision of radiant beauty, and he couldn't control his desires any longer. He ripped open his bag, dragged out ropes, a whip, and metal handcuffs. He wanted her tied up and gagged as quickly as possible.

Then he suddenly felt something new, a trembling attraction to this mysterious girl. The force of the feeling sent him lurching towards her, as a quiet rustle appeared in the woods. He stumbled to a stop and peered around, seeing more figures emerge from behind the trees. They were clad in the same long black cloaks, the drooping hoods hiding their faces. They gathered around them in a silent circle.

"What's going on?" he croaked, wondering if this was part of the scenario she hadn't revealed. When no answer came, he became angry, then filled with rage. He hated any surprises that weren't his own creation.

He took another step towards her and heard a brittle crunch beneath his feet. He kicked away the soggy leaves and saw a bone, dirty and decayed. There were others, scattered beneath the leaves. The figures pulled off their hoods, revealing the faces of other young women. They were beautiful and ethereal like her.

The girl he'd chased into the woods let her black cloak fall to the ground. The others did the same. Now there was only their nakedness and nothing else. They stood for a moment before discarding their human bodies. Their ghostly forms were ashen and burnt, the misty rain falling through them to the ground. In this terrifying moment, their monstrous secret was revealed. They'd gathered in these woods as young witches, and were still here, after being burned alive at the stake.

They were on him with a rushing ferocity. Spectral hands ripped away his preacher's collar and it erupted in flames, the beginning of their ancient ritual. The decayed bones shivered like they were coming back to life, and the ghost of the girl he'd so desperately desired gathered what she needed from his bag. Ropes were tied around his arms and legs, binding him tight like one of his fantasies. He screamed with a fury that blared out, but he knew it wouldn't matter. The only witnesses to the coming horror would be the full moon and the giant trees. All his past encounters had been a series of dreamy shadow plays where he got what he wanted, but not this time. He was trapped in a nightmare he couldn't escape.

As their ancient ritual of mischief began, he had one final thought as he screamed for help that no one would hear.

Being tied up wasn't liberating at all.

It was the ultimate horror.

They came for him at the darkest hour of night on the holiest of days, when he was sleeping in his room in the parish house behind the church. He'd always feared it would happen, so when the gnarled hands grabbed him, he was only faintly surprised and didn't resist. He had a saggy face, wispy grey hair, and was dressed in a faded nightgown.

The three hulking figures wore long black coats and low wool caps, even though it was Good Friday and the weather didn't call for such heavy covering. He only saw them by the sparse light streaking through the window, but he already knew who they were.

The Occultus, the Hidden Ones...

Or rather, that's what the whisper croaked in his head.

They dragged him from the bed and dropped him on the floor like a bag of bones. He was half drunk from the night before, the smell of red wine still on his breath. The hulking figures grabbed him again and yanked him up like a wobbly puppet. He caught a whiff of smoke and ash in the air, but that had to be his imagination playing tricks again, like the croaking voice in his head.

"Please," he muttered. "At least grant me the courtesy of wearing my holy attire. I beg you to honor this simple request."

He staggered for a moment, waiting for an answer. One of the hulking figures let out a grunt that smelled of fire and smoke, another sign of his delirious state.

After a lifetime of craven debauchery, his grip on reality was shaky at best, so delusions were a part of his everyday life. When he saw a cleaved hoof poke out from beneath one of the long dark coats, he knew this was just more proof of his mental decay.

He stumbled to his closet, took out his holy vestments and laid them neatly on the bed. He pulled off his nightgown, feeling no shame at being unclothed, because he never did. He put on his priestly attire with meticulous care, a ritual he never got tired of.

He'd always marveled at the power of such a simple act, dressing in garments that made him a figure most people would obey. The holy wardrobe didn't change who he was, but it kept his true nature hidden in plain view.

With the stiff white collar fastened around his wrinkled old neck, and the silver cassock draping to the floor, he reached for his favorite cross and draped it front of his chest. When he turned and faced the three hulking figures, he wasn't a woozy old man anymore, he was something much greater. At least that's how his holy garments made him feel.

But the brutish figures weren't affected by his facade. They grabbed him again, covered his head with a coarse black hood, then dragged him out of the room. His dangling feet scraped down the hallway, until he was outside in the last dark hours of night.

"*It's Judgment Day...*" he heard the voice croak in his head.

He felt the trio of gnarled hands grab his arms tighter, then a sudden flapping sound gusted around him. It was like he was being pulled up into the air, but it had to be another delusion.

213

He was the worst kind of priest, that he accepted without contention. The raid had to be from the church he'd disgraced. So now he was being taken to a secret place where his misdeeds would be addressed in the strictest manner. The mysterious figures were clearly from the Vatican sent to abduct aberrant priests. He was probably in the back of a car driving down the road away from his small country church, and everything else was a guilt-ridden fantasy concocted from his hidden shame.

What was truly unfathomable was how he was able to separate the two warring parts of his life. To do so had to be evidence of some mental disease. What else could explain the deplorable travesty of his life as a priest?

When it suited his mood, he'd fulfilled his holy duties in a manner that was not inadequate. His Sunday sermons addressed the moral ills the Church had always stood firm against, and he attended to his flock in the way they wanted, praying with the sick, consoling the grieving, and giving religious guidance to those who wandered off the holy path.

But there was also his dark side.

In the beginning, his indiscretions were personal and alone. His cravings were satiated in modest ways, with magazines and movies, always obtained with the utmost secrecy. Then they grew more desperate and dangerous, moving to the realm of real flesh. His first molestation was a clumsy affair, but there were others after that, then so many more, and it only got worse.

That's when alcohol and drugs became a part of his predatory ways, then a daily part of everything else. Whatever sleazy force was hiding inside him had finally taken complete control. Even then, he couldn't

214

stop marveling at the power of his holy vestments, which magically shielded him from the judgment of others.

Until now...

The thunderous flapping bellowed in his ears with a windy turbulence. His delusional trip might have lasted for hours until the last moments before dawn, but the heavy black hood and the uncertainty of his mental state left him with no way to know.

Suddenly, his feet thudded hard on the ground, and he collapsed without any strength left. The gnarled hands pulled him up, and the blinding black hood was yanked from his head.

"*What have we here?*" the whispery voice croaked.

It was that time when the blackness of night was finally giving way to the creeping light of dawn. If this was still one of his crazy delusions, it appeared realer than any before.

The three hulking figures were clustered nearby, but the long black coats and low caps were gone, revealing what they really were. The source of the flapping was giant black wings, fluttering and strong. Their eyes were burning orbs glowing in giant carcasses that looked like they'd been roasted in Hell.

Looking around, he saw dozens more, and more priests, all staggering towards a black church. It looked as hellish as the creatures. The walls and windows were the blackest kind of black, and the towering steeple was made of writhing snakes.

"This can't be real..." he muttered to another priest in front of him.

The priest turned and he saw a look he recognized, a loathsome gaze that came from a life filled with perversity. He could smell the cheap whiskey on the priest's breath and see the trembling in his hands. He didn't speak, just stared, then turned back around.

"It's Judgment Day..." the voice croaked in his head again.

The shadowy line of scorned priests staggered across the ground into the black church. When he reached the gaping door, he felt a churning in his soul, like the two warring forces inside him were now engaged in a brutal fight.

When he entered the church, his attention was seized by what loomed ahead in the putrid half-darkness. It took him a few seconds to discern the sight, and when he did, shock nearly stopped his heart from beating.

The floor was covered with snakes and there were no holy adornments left, just the suffocating stench of smoke. When he got closer to the black altar, he saw this was still a place where ritualistic ceremonies were conducted.

But now it was the unholy kind...

What he saw was like death and birth at the same time. When each aberrant priest reached the altar, the darkness inside them became stunningly real. Each shuddered and screamed as a demon leaped out of their body like monstrous smoke. The demons were skulking and scary, with clawed hands, and lusty wet tongues.

Now he was at the altar himself.

"This is good-bye..." the croaking voice said.

The churning grew worse as he felt an eruption deep inside him. It passed through his body and became a demon croaking beside him. Seeing the unholy creature, he knew it had won, and he suddenly realized the overall plan. In the fight between Heaven

216

and Hell, the underworld was going to defeat the Church one disgraced priest at a time, until there was nothing left to believe in anymore. As his faith and goodness sprouted back up inside him, he fell to his knees and began to weep.

LAST CALL

"**C**an I buy you a drink?" he slurred with a predatory smile.

He'd been watching her for most of the night from his wooden perch at the darkest corner of the bar, peering with bloodshot eyes through the smoke, wondering if she'd be the one. He usually went on gut instinct, but the process was methodical, evaluating the women with a shadowy detachment.

There were two others he'd considered, his gaze moving from one to the other, as he sat hunched and silent, quietly sipping his poison of choice, vodka on the rocks. It was like trying to decide which late-night dessert would be the yummiest. He'd fine-tuned his pick-up strategy to the point where it rarely failed, and when it did, it was usually because he was too drunk, reeling up from his chair, then lurching across the floor like it was made of ice.

But tonight wouldn't be one of those nights, because he'd timed everything perfectly, and timing was always paramount. His strategy depended on two essential truths.

The first was obvious because it was a fundamental instinct of human nature. When it came to pursuing women, the male beast was always on the prowl for beauty above everything else, so they only went after good-looking women with a groveling lust. That made the women feel like exotic rarities that needed to be worshipped, not sullied by groping hands. Beauty was the sure-fire aphrodisiac, but it was also the haughty buzzkill luring guys in, then sending them home with a scowl on their face.

Can I buy you a drink?

It wasn't the greatest opening line, but that's all he usually needed because of the second truth he'd learned back in college. He didn't need to be a slave to beauty, because his poison of choice could turn just about any woman into a blurry mirage that would satisfy his needs. He could stroll into any bar, leisurely gulp down five or six drinks, and the ugly duckling he'd winced at before would be something he'd be able to work with.

So here he was, striding through the shadows and smoke, always waiting until last call when the witching hour of desperation kicked in.

Can I buy you a drink?

That was pretty much all it ever took.

The woman he'd chosen turned around and gave him a shy smile. She had a plump face, a smattering of freckles, dull brown hair, and a shapeless body hidden beneath a frumpy dress. But the long night of drinking had turned her into a woozy vision that was better than that. Drinking was the alchemy that turned her into the prize he would take home.

He saw a flicker of hesitation in her eyes, but only for a second or two, because it was also true that most women were suckers for a good-looking guy.

His handsome features had dissipated over the last few years, because his poison of choice had added a ruddy slackness to his face. He still had sky-blue eyes and dark hair that fell in casual curls. He always dressed like he'd just come straight from work, preferring the look of a hotshot lawyer or banker, even though he'd been fired months ago from his low-level insurance job for missing too many days because of his nightly carousing.

"It's late," she murmured, brushing a lump of hair away from her eyes.

He smiled and nodded without trying to convince her. "Yeah, you're right, it's late. No worries. I just thought you looked like someone it would be nice to meet."

And that usually did it, just one little compliment tossed her way as seductive bait she could nibble on. A hopeful look came to her eyes, instead of the glum glaze that was there before. He kept smiling, but not for the reason she would have guessed. He was smiling because it was almost too easy.

The next part was about control, because now he had to casually sit down on the empty stool beside her and pretend to listen to her prattle on and on about her pitiful life, while the urges were twisting tighter inside him.

There'd been times he'd let his drunken guard down and his ferocious loathing for the inane chatter chased them away, like a child suddenly seeing the real face of their new best friend. He wouldn't let that happen tonight. The witching hour was almost ove and the fun part was about to begin.

There was always the hope in every singles bar that tonight would be the night when your romantic dreams would finally come true. For the women in the bar who weren't beautiful, this yearning was more extreme, a gaping hole in their heart, because they were looking for love in a world that had deemed them less than worthy.

"I know it's late. But I don't live very far from here if you feel like a nightcap."

Hesitation flickered in her eyes again, but he wasn't worried. He knew what she was going to do before she knew it herself.

"Why not?" she mumbled, pushing up from her stool with a wheezy breath. "You only live once."

Part of his strategy was to never be a regular at any one bar, to stroll in like a newcomer who had just moved here or was in town on a business trip. He had a dozen or so weekend watering holes spread out from where he lived, an invisible spider web with his home lurking in the middle.

The woman was still prattling on in the cab, a whiny monologue that made his buzzed head throb. He just nodded and tried to tune her out, because this was a necessary part of the game. His apartment was only a few blocks away and he was eager to celebrate another victorious night. The festivities would be held in a more private place hidden away from judging eyes.

As the elevator clunked up, she told him for the twentieth time her name was Edith, as if that were something he needed to know. He was aching for another drink, so when he pushed open the door and switched on the lights, he headed straight to the liquor cabinet, trying not to walk too fast.

"What's your pleasure?" he asked, already splashing vodka into a glass, not caring about ice anymore.

"White wine if you have it."

He smiled, of course he did. He bought it by the case because it was their usual drink of choice. They probably thought it made them seem dainty and sophisticated.

When he brought her the drink, her eyes were darting around his small living room. It wasn't fancy by any means, but he always kept it clean and neat because that's how they liked it. Even now, he couldn't afford to be careless. They were close, but they still had to get to the bedroom.

After three quick gulps from his glass, the blurry haze came back, settling in the room like a woozy fog. She was still blabbering on, but that would end soon, because he'd already seen the expected signs. She'd shimmied closer to him on the couch, resting her hand on his knee with another shy smile. He leaned over and gave her a kiss, because that was the way it always started, very slow and gentle, then not so much.

He stumbled up, pulling her up too. It was a short walk to the closed door of his bedroom. There had been a few who'd stopped at this point, but he knew tonight wouldn't be one of those nights. He shut the door behind them, kept the lights off, and they tumbled together onto the freshly made bed with clean white sheets.

He kissed her again, still soft and gentle, but now he could stop pretending to be something he wasn't. They were all alone, just the two of them. He began to undress her, his trembling hands clutching for the zipper, because already his urges were taking control. He yanked it down with a desperate tug, then shed his clothes with even more urgency. Now they were both naked and panting in the dark.

The sex started out normal, just casual kissing and groping. But it didn't stay that way for long. He wasn't an outright psychopath or a depraved sadist, but his urges weren't far from that. He hunted ugly ducklings for rough sex, the rougher, the better.

In the cloaking blackness, he didn't care what the women looked like because it was all about him. They

222

were just unseen blobs of flesh whimpering beneath him. Their responses always varied, but most were able to tolerate his assaults for much longer than they ever would have imagined. Without the gift of beauty, what they were willing to endure in the search for love was sometimes surprising. Tonight, the woman he'd picked had gone farther than most. He felt like properly thanking her for a job well done, but he couldn't remember her name.

The next morning seemed to come almost immediately. He saw red-splattered sheets which meant the night had been perfect. And of course, she was gone. No awkward goodbyes, no pushing her out the door, just the head throbbing memory of his victory.

He lay in bed, waiting to summon the strength he needed to get up and take something for his pounding head. When he stumbled to the bathroom, he saw the woman, whose name he'd forgotten, had smeared a message on the mirror.

We are who we are, he thought to himself. She'd scribbled the message on his mirror a week ago and now here he was, sitting in the back of a cab taking him to a bar. There was a time when he'd wondered why he was the way he was, but after a while he didn't care anymore...

How can it be bad, if it feels so good?

This development, though, was something brand new.

He'd lured countless women to his bedroom. Some had lasted much longer than others, but none had ever wanted to see him again. The only sound he ever heard was teary panting as they ran away clutching their clothes. He'd also stopped worrying if he'd be reported to the police for his serial assaults. After all, how do you report rough sex, however extreme, without getting painted by the same brush? He'd never felt it himself, but shame appeared to be a wonderful deterrent.

So, this was a first.

When the cab stopped in front of the bar, he wondered if the unexpected had happened, that this woman whose name he couldn't remember found her own kind of pleasure from their one-night stand. He wasn't a commitment kind of guy, or a one-woman man, but the possibility was intriguing.

When he got out of the cab, he saw right away this wasn't the kind of place he was expecting, the usual yuppie watering hole with people streaming in and out. It was tucked away on a grimy side street in a part of town he didn't know. He didn't see the usual after-work crowd, or hear the muffled sound of music. He did see a small metal sign next to a door, so he knew he was in the right place. On that sign was the name she'd scrawled in lipstick on his mirror a week ago, with today's date next to it.

The Red Wine Bar.

He walked to the door and gave it a tug, only to find it was locked. There was a buzzer next to the door and he pushed it. The bar was obviously a dump, so why had she picked it if she was interested in him?

This probably isn't going to work out, he was starting to think when the door finally opened. It took his eyes a few seconds to adjust to the dim interior. He was used to dark bars but this was more like a cave, with huddled bodies talking in small groups. It was quiet, not the usual sounds of blaring music, chattering voices, and clinking glasses.

224

Screw this.

He was about to leave when she appeared, the woman with the name he couldn't remember. He'd gulped down a couple of shots of vodka before coming, but it wasn't enough to even partially obscure her lack of grace and beauty.

"I'm so glad you came," she said.

"What kind of place is this?"

She handed him a large glass filled to the top. "It's a wine bar, but it's more like a private club. I hope you like red."

His anger was still there, but he grabbed the glass and took a big slug, draining almost half. He wasn't a wine drinker, but he felt the familiar warm tingle, so he guzzled the rest.

"It's okay."

Another glass appeared right away, and that went down fast as well. Then another, and the woozy haze started to drift in. The alchemy was almost complete after two more glasses. He was starting to think this place wasn't so bad.

That's when he noticed the woman whose name he couldn't remember hadn't been prattling on like she had a week ago. Instead, she stood quietly in front of him, watching him gulp down the drinks with a hovering patience.

And now the others were coming towards him, shuffling slowly through the murky half-light. They were all women, and while they didn't look half bad now, he guessed the opposite was true in the sober light of day. They circled him, something brutal in their eyes, a dark urge that wasn't much different from his. He knew instinctively where it came from. It was cobbled together from all the endless humiliations and savage mistreatments they'd been forced to endure as women who were not considered beautiful. The anguished resentment had festered inside them and finally surged up into a kind of insanity seizing control of their battered souls.

He knew this because he'd been a part of it.

A flurry of hands dragged him to a chair and held him down, as thick rope was wrapped around his struggling body. Even his wine-soaked stupor couldn't mask the horror of the faces leering around him.

"*What are you doing...*" he screamed.

The mass of flesh didn't answer because they were too busy chatting to each other in their prattling voices, grabbing his body with clawing hands.

"I like his eyes..."

"He has such strong arms..."

"What a cute butt..."

Then he saw the flash of a knife and felt its pain. As his blood splashed to the floor, he knew where the bar got its name. His poison of choice had always been vodka, but even he knew red wine always goes better with meat.

A DREAM COME TRUE

A booming clarion call erupted in Hell and the army took flight like a thundering maelstrom of howling black bats. Massive wings flapped through the ash and haze until they shattered through the soot-covered rock above. Red eyes blazed as they ascended through the endless layers of sulfurous rock. The underworld horde broke through the last barrier with a volcanic roar and their startling appearance threw a harrowing shadow over the world below. It was a sight never witnessed before, but a new age was coming – the end of times, when everything was going to be dead and dark.

The Devil led the throng, a frightening colossus who was even more gruesome in the early morning light. He was the daemon king, the avatar of evil, a blasphemous creature finally free from its prison of fire. The gargantuan shadow from its twisted horns, cloven hooves, and charred wings grew larger the higher it soared. His cackle was triumphant as he glowered down at the non-believers below, who were seeing what they thought was a religious myth suddenly flapping in the clear blue sky.

The Devil unleashed a comet-like fireball and humanity scattered like ants. Millions fried in the blink of an eye, which he took as the first of countless more pleasures to come. The noxious stench of burnt flesh and smoke erupted like a billowing fog, filling the sky with a churning blackness. He unleashed another and the rippling ocean came to a steamy boil, bringing more charred death floating on the surface.

Charging higher, the Devil embraced his freedom as a miracle long overdue. After an eternity trapped in Hell, a realization had appeared deep within his cavernous consciousness. He knew with an absolute certainty that the time had come to escape. He didn't question where this certainty came from because the impossible happened in Hell all the time, but with more agony and despair were as the end result.

Until now.

The struggle between Heaven and Hell had been an ongoing battle since the dawn of time, with victories and losses on both sides. The secret showdown between good and evil had been waged in the shadows by inscrutable forces never revealed to the world of man. The bowels of Hell were now overflowing with damned souls, so maybe this is where the Devil's newfound power had come from, the sheer mass of evil now writhing in the fires.

One of the cruelest perversities was the unrelenting brutality of time. Every second seemed like a never-ending eternity, making eternity itself an infinite horror multiplied even more. The surreal inflictions of pain and punishment were so far beyond the scope of endurance, each second in Hell was an abomination.

That's why his rage at the God who had put him there was so raw. Even now, rising higher in the smoky black sky, his ferocious anger roared like a living beast. The Devil was consumed with a ravenous hunger for revenge that propelled him at a more urgent pace, its monstrous army flapping below like a screeching black cape.

Beyond the endless tortures, Hell had other rewards too, and these would be shared with the God he despised with every charred chunk of its hideousness. After endless eons inflicting unbearable suffering, he was a soulless connoisseur with a devious insight into the intricacies of mistreatment. His underworld power was beyond any threshold even the most wretched human mind could imagine, and this was the power he would share with the God he hated, and his legion of angels too.

A rumbling chuckle rattled deep inside as he imagined the battle to come, the war between his howling horde and the coddled white angels made puny and weak by their whimpering sanctity. While his torturous skills were more myriad and precise, his underworld army was adept at creating misery too. Each damned soul had been forged in Hell to become the daemonic extreme of its unholy sin. They were daemon molesters, daemon slaughterers, and daemon sadists, all reconfigured into a wicked new form.

If the Devil was a different kind of creature, he would almost feel pity for the desecration to come. Heaven was going to be a killing field of mutilated angels wailing over the death of their God.

After the strangling darkness of his entombment below, the new sights and sounds should have held more allure, but he was too eager for the apocalyptic battle to begin. All of creation was a kind of mirage, including the hallowed heights of Heaven and the fiery black depths of Hell, all part of a cosmic riddle. His knowledge of this was part of the puzzle too. It didn't diminish his fury or need for vengeance, it just stopped him from caring about the unknowable line between reality and illusion.

His journey to Heaven was a dreamlike assault that could have lasted an eternity or just a few seconds. The flight passed through an abandoned wasteland of ghostly galaxies, skeletal nebulas, and dying universes. Despite the cosmic necropolis, the vastness of space looked to have been sculpted by God into a phantasmagoria beyond comprehension. None of it mattered, however, because the Devil wasn't interested in puzzles or mysteries, only in the final destruction of God.

Then, without any warning, there it was, the towering gates of Heaven glowing in the blackness ahead. He was not disappointed or surprised, because the vision was precisely what the Devil expected, a majestic white barrier with two radiant angels standing as guards.

The Devil paused for a moment to savor the terror that filled the angels' eyes when they saw the hell-storm flapping above them. He gave the clarion call to attack and the horde of fire-crusted daemons swooped down with an astonishing speed and crashed through the white gates with a monstrous cry.

The ensuing massacre was like a healing salve to all the wrath that had accumulated during his time in Hell. The daemon army attacked without mercy or restraint, savaging Heaven with inferno eyes. Their assaults rained down from every direction as the terrified angels scrambled to hide. But the daemons were too fast, so the swirling squall from their flapping wings was quickly filled with severed angel parts.

The Devil marched through the melee as Heaven became the killing field it had lusted after. He didn't bother to step around the mangled angels but kicked them aside like unwanted trash. Those were the fortunate ones, because others were bound on top of makeshift altars and forced to endure atrocities that could only have originated in Hell. The daemon molesters and sadists were performing their own rituals on the whimpering angels who begged for a mercy that would never come.

The Devil let out another dark chuckle.

Welcome to my world.

Continuing his triumphant march though the death and despair, his mighty black wings fluttered on his back. Where there was once beauty, light and holiness, there was now only destruction. One last fight remained, and then the invasion would be complete.

The Devil saw a shimmering light ahead, so he quickened his pace, stomping over the mutilated angels and past the makeshift altars of abuse. Heaven now looked like Hell, and that was a pleasure he embraced with something as close to joy as he could feel. And now the light ahead was so bright he could barely see.

The sight he finally came upon was shocking and stirring at the same time. The mountainous figure was lying on a bed of clouds, robed and bearded, its face only partially seen. The vision rekindled the burning rage the Devil felt with even more hellish ferocity. He had no qualms about killing God while he slept, so he crossed to his bedside with feathers still matted on his feet.

But then the real horror washed over him. The Devil knew all of creation was a kind of mysterious mirage, and now he knew why. The mirage was a dream, and the dream was a nightmare, and it belonged to God. That meant all the atrocities, the

231

death and destruction in Heaven, and all the horrors in Hell, were just God's nightmare.

Then he knew this with even more certainty as he felt an urge to share his depravity with the sleeping colossus. He reached out with his scorched claws and gently pulled open the glowing white robe. He let out another dark chuckle because this could still be a dream come true.

JOHNNY HELL

When the black van crunched into the gravel lot of the Bonecrusher, he knew his metamorphosis was almost complete. It was a rainy night, the perfect setting for what was to come. Everything was gloomy and wet, like a nightmare. But this wasn't a nightmare to him. It was his fevered dream to become a rock god, and this was the place he'd picked for his glorious ascension.

It didn't look like much, just a cement slab in a dilapidated part of the city. The location was mostly unknown except to the heavy metal worshippers who were already packed inside. For them it was a head-banging temple where they could perform their nightly rituals away from the drudgery of their daytime lives. They needed a place where rage was the only emotion that mattered. He could already hear the mayhem inside, that seemed to come from a much darker world.

The world he wanted to rule.

Though it had only been a few years, it seemed like a lifetime ago when he was a completely different person, unlike the exquisite creation he'd now become. Back then he was just another high school dropout who spent most of his time listening to metal while under the influence of whatever drug he could find. But his destiny was suddenly revealed one night during the raging motherfucker of all acid trips. He was listening to a death metal dirge and the acid ripped a psychic hole in his scrambled brain. The acid was the magic elixir, and the pounding music showed him the way.

Don't just dream it... be it.

That's when he decided to break free from his mortal bonds and become a rock god. He'd always hoped in his frazzled brain there would be something special that would change his life – and this was it. His tiny room in the basement of his parent's house was a cluttered shrine to the hardcore bands he loved: Cannibal Corpse, Fleshgod Apocalypse, Battleaxe, Metal Church, and Grim Reaper. They were the thundering soundtrack that celebrated everything he hated about the world.

And there was more than that.

In the drugged-out womb of his basement room, the most depraved appetites and cravings were set free. Uptight barriers were blasted away by screeching guitars and banshee screams. The nauseating world he felt trapped in was way too boring and rigid, a suffocating prison of stupid morality and middle-class crap. The heavy metal world was chaotic and dark, a freak show of savage rage.

Don't just dream it... be it.

So, he decided to leave the worshipping mob of followers and become one of the metal gods too. But he didn't just want to join the tattooed pantheon of snarling deities, he wanted to push it to an even more mythic extreme.

More drugs were needed, of course, and a band who shared his hardcore beliefs. It all came together in his basement room where he huddled with other misfits he found online. Including him, it was a grimy group of four. He was going to be the singer and lyricist, the mastermind leading the way. None of them were very good, but it didn't matter. They all agreed that deafening rage was more important than art.

And that's when his macabre metamorphosis began.

First, he came up with a new name... *Johnny Hell.*

The other members followed his lead, but that didn't matter either. They were barely part of his vision, useful pawns in his grand design. The path to his deification needed disciples, but their role was secondary. He would be the growling messiah and scream his way to the promised land. He named the band The End of the World.

The van grumbled to a stop in back of the cement slab. He'd been tweaking for almost a week on crystal meth, so his brain was crackling with wild desires. Acid had been the chemical mindblower, but crystal meth was the slashing ax that severed the parts of his life he no longer needed. He didn't look like his old self. His eyes were dark and quivering, like he was seeing startling sights only he could see. His skeletal body looked close to death, a cadaverous figure that could barely stand on shivering legs.

When the money dripped in, he blew it on meth and tattoos. The crank sculpted his flesh into the morbid messenger his vision required. It also dredged up the demented lyrics from inside his head. The tattoos covered his sagging skin like a gruesome stain, all in the deepest red and darkest black. They showed monsters playing bloody guitars and pounding on the fiery mountains of Hell.

They shambled from the van and headed to the back door of the building. The rain soaked his skeletal body and he welcomed it as a holy anointment for the night. He saw the other band members were staring at him with a nervous gaze. His startling metamorphosis was too radical even for them. But there wouldn't be any non-believers after tonight.

They walked in silence down a shadowy hallway, then down creaky stairs to their dressing room. He recognized the band that was playing before them, a thrash metal group from Cleveland. He was tweaking hard and hated their feeble attempts to be hardcore. The more he heard, the more it assaulted his senses. The only way he could get rid of the nausea was to imagine them burning alive.

Don't just dream it... be it.

A dirty bulb hanging from the ceiling barely lit the room, which was just the way he liked it. The wood walls were covered with carved out names of all the bands who played here. He recognized most of them and felt the same wave of revulsion. They were all pale imitations of what hardcore metal needed to be, so now the fire in his brain was thrashing with more burning bodies.

They drifted to different corners of the room and began their pre-show rituals. There was heroin, coke, pot, and pills, all of which he'd shunned as his transformation picked up steam. Only the scorching sizzle of crystal meth gave him the transcending purity he needed. He banged a hit and pulled out his black spiral notebook with the flaming skull on the cover. His trembling hands caressed it as the heart-thumping rush rocketed through his flesh.

The dark road he'd been on the last two years had been strange and brutal, but enlightenment had finally come. His vision was driven by his desire to embody the hardcore rage of metal music and become its almighty god. Only after he'd purified his flesh with

236

the sacramental meth was the way revealed. His faith rewarded him with the power he needed, and it came from the darkest depths of the ragged hole torn in his brain. At first there were just distant cries from far away, but they got louder as his chilling metamorphosis evolved in more tortured ways.

A part of him knew it was insanity, but that only excited him more. This was the extreme he was searching for, a shattering escape from the normal world. The distant cries turned into screams, and the screams turned into a blaring manifesto. This is where his lyrics were born, and that was the power he was given. He scribbled them down in a tweaking rush that could last for days, filling the pages with madness.

He didn't tell anyone about the real meaning behind his lyrics. His message was only for the black-clad horde who followed him like a midnight army. He looked down at the scribbled words and whispered them hoarsely to himself. He could already feel the power of their anger and hate.

A shaggy-haired guy cracked open the door and said it was time to take the stage. The music had stopped overhead, but the hoots and howls still boomed out. He tottered to his feet and felt his hanging head spin. His spectacular metamorphosis could barely hold up his tattooed body, but the hard-charging meth gave him the strength he needed. They walked as a silent group up the creaky stairs. The hoots and howls got louder as the cheering crowd began to chant their name.

"The End of the World..."
"The End of the World..."
"The End of the World..."

When they reached the space next to the stage, he could hear the voice inside him screaming louder than ever. He wondered if it was the voice of a dark god from some unknown beyond, and he was just a slave to its will. For a moment he felt weak and helpless, his faith suddenly shaken, but it quickly passed, and his messianic vision returned.

Don't just dream it... be it.

Nobody else knew tonight's show would be his last, a final ritual to celebrate the mythic extreme he wanted. The magnum opus he'd been singing in fragments was nearing its end. This was his metal masterpiece of exalted anger and righteous rage, so his black clad horde could finally see the promised land.

When they took the stage, he could only see the barest glimmer of the scowling faces gathered in front of him. Matches were lit and the flames gave a haunting glow to the cavernous room. It was their trademark, a fiery salute to... The End of the World.

He staggered to his place at the edge of the stage, wobbling unsteadily in front of the crowd. He pulled off his ripped black shirt and a spotlight hit his monstrous tattoos and skeletal frame. The crowd became a bellowing beast as a metal blare exploded from the stage. Ecstasy consumed him, sending sizzling shivers to every part of his body.

They weren't a very good band, but that didn't matter because their sonic rage washed over the banging heads. He was perched at the edge of the stage like a heavy metal scarecrow that couldn't stop shrieking and shaking. But it was all about the secret message coming from an insane portal ripped in his brain.

That was the power he was given...

When they came to the final song, it was the end of the manic masterpiece he'd scribbled in his notebook with the flaming skull. He'd been a shrieking messiah with only one desire.

Don't just dream it... be it.

When the song ended, he collapsed to the floor, not knowing what would happen next. Then he heard the roar of the growling beast in front of him. He looked up and saw the matches were lit again, and the faces were different now, even more monstrous than his gruesome tattoos.

"The End of the World..."
"The End of the World..."
"The End of the World..."

They set fire to the building with an infernal howl, then rushed the stage with clawing hands and feral eyes. He staggered back to his feet and raised his arms, accepting the crush of worshippers with a tweaking rapture. They ripped him apart, flesh from bone, bone from flesh. At the very last second before his death, all his morbid dreams went out into the world, and this began his ascension.

LOVE NEVER DIES

The Leather & Chains was a desolate roadhouse in a godforsaken patch of the Badlands. No signs were posted because they wanted to keep the tourists away. The building was made out of rotted wood, with no way to view what was happening inside. Buzzards flapped overhead for some unknown reason, cawing predators in the hot desert air.

I was there with the most frightening motorcycle gang of them all, the Hellfire Club. We were big and brawny riding giant bikes that spewed fire and smoke. We'd rode all day beneath a blazing hot sun that died a slow death an hour ago. Twilight was gone and the blackness of night was here, so it was time to have fun. We strode in like dusty devils and headed straight to the bar. The music was heavy and loud, the lights low, and shadows where everywhere. The mysterious travelers who gathered here liked it that way. It was off the beaten track, a secret hideaway for desert nomads who didn't want their recreational pursuits to be seen by anyone who wouldn't understand.

I was on my third tequila shot when she strolled up, holding a shot glass too. Even in the murkiness she was something to see, like a vision I didn't know I'd been waiting for. Nothing was said because we both knew what we wanted, and here there were no boundaries to what that could be. We wanted to be naked and bloody, moaning on the floor, or slammed against a wall. It was like we could read each other's minds, eliminating any need for small talk. Like I said, this wasn't the kind of place tourists would like, unless they had a secret life too shocking to reveal.

I was into the good-girl-gone-bad look, so her pouty lips and wild hair were just what I wanted. Midnight black and tortured red were clearly her colors of choice, a perfect match for the whips and chains hanging on the walls. She looked like a mythic enchantress from the bad side of town, and I was from that place too, hulking and tall, with steel-studded boots.

I nibbled at the tattooed flesh of her neck and pulled her tight. A crushing knee to the groin and a stinging slap across my face came next, giving me exactly what I wanted. Right then and there, we were already in love, a violent match made as far away from heaven as you could possibly get.

We gulped two more shots and headed to one of the private rooms in back. We assaulted each other with a fury most people wouldn't understand. In this little-known desert hideaway, everything bad was why you came. It lasted more than an hour, a writhing entanglement that was both a lusty struggle for domination and a quest to embrace delirious pain. It was a private spectacle no one could witness or judge, as it was meant to be.

When we were finished, we stayed on the floor and shared whispered secrets, feeling a bond that surprised even us. I told her I was the leader of the notorious biker gang that roamed the Badlands like legendary

241

marauders from long ago. I recounted a few of our greatest hits, a mishmash of thievery, violence, and roadside terror.

She listened with an amused smile and a cryptic glint in her eyes. She'd covered her body with a tapestry of occult symbols and designs so there was very little left of her pale flesh. Her hair was a fiery red and she told me she was the leader of a gang too but didn't elaborate. I accepted this because mystery was part of the game, the masking cloak we all wore.

And that's when she died.

I can't remember exactly what happened, but round two was even more violent, both of us grabbing each other with a ferocity that soared out of control. Screams became wails, wails became groans, and suddenly this glorious enchantress collapsed to the floor with a death-rattle moan. I'll never forget the look in her eyes when she gasped her last breath.

What have you done?

I know what you're thinking: What the hell kind of love story is this? She was a really hot chick you said you loved and then you killed her. So try to imagine how I felt from that moment on, because I'd met the girl of my dreams and turned it into the worst kind of nightmare. There was nothing to do except stumble out of the room and tell the raspy old bartender what had happened. His weary nod made it clear this wasn't an unusual occurrence.

By the time I was dragged from the bar, I was too drunk to ride, but that had never stopped me before. I told the others what happened, but their boozy sympathy did nothing to quell the ache in my heart. We lived an outlaw life, so there were plenty of dead bodies left in our wake. But this was different, I'd killed the girl I loved and my life would never be the same.

The emptiness of the desert made the emptiness inside me hurt even more. We left the Leather & Chains with the grinding roar of our pumped-up bikes. They were giant macabre machines that caused fear even in the light of day, with leering skulls, hellish creatures, and red-hot flames. Parents and kids in their boring cars would scream and point at the shock of what was stampeding past.

We found the highway again and rode for a while before veering off into the desert, bumping and swerving over the rough terrain. It was an eerie landscape of peaks and plateaus. We circled our bikes and turned off the grumbling engines. The calls of wolves and coyotes wafted in, a baying night chorus that never went away. This is where we always slept, out in the desert with just the wind and wild animals. Tonight, the sky glowed with a monster's moon, when there was nothing else to be seen, no clouds, no stars, just a gargantuan orb shining like a glimmering eye.

Like all gangs, we had our ways and customs. We loved the heat of the day, but the darkness of night was a sacred time. First, we tended to our bikes, wiping away the dirt and grime. They were as much a part of the gang as us, snarling and mean, big and bulky, not to be messed with. If there were problems that needed attention, Dirty Dave was our mystic mechanic. He never talked except for a few grunts, and that was usually to the ailing bike he was bringing back to life.

It was time for our nightly ritual, sitting on blankets inside the circle of bikes. Slug was our medicine man. He looked like a leather-clad lizard, his face scarred and scaly from the desert sun. His eyes were strange too, like black clouds before a storm. He took out his peyote mix and we passed it around, waiting for the night journey to begin.

From the very beginning, we were renegades who wanted a hell of a lot more than the civilized world could offer. There were way too many rules and restrictions, too much judgment and scorn. We were all about smashing through that and going where others were too scared to go, and nothing did that better than Slug's psychedelic battering ram. It smashed open locked doors and burned down barriers built by the normal world. The wolves and coyotes yelped louder as we rose up and left the circle of bikes.

The transformation began but it was just one part of what was happening. It was like the underworld crawled up into the desert and we howled as it melted away. Now there were other creatures, misshapen and crusty, prowling through the flames. The blaze reached a crescendo, a phantasmagoria of horror and fear, then faded away, as if the mind-blowing spectacle crawled back from where it came. The others staggered back to their blankets to end what was left of the night. It was always a deep and rumbling sleep filled with wild creatures.

That's when I heard it, Love *never dies...*

I didn't know where the haunting voice came from, but I knew who it was. It was my hardcore enchantress, the woman I loved and killed. I called out again and again but there was no reply. I began to doubt if the voice was real, or just a symptom of my longing and pain. I waited beneath the monster's moon, but the only sounds in the night were coyotes and wolves.

I continued to roam the Badlands with the Hellfire Club, but it wasn't the same anymore. Even the roar of our bikes wasn't enough to drown out my inner turmoil. She was wicked and wild, spooky and beautiful, a good girl gone way beyond bad. Seeing her in my dreams made it even more painful. She was gone forever, banished to the earth where she'd become nothing but dust in the dirt.

Weeks later, I heard her again as I stood once again beneath a monster's moon. It was the same haunting voice reaching out to me from some unseen place. That's when I knew I had to find that place.

So I went back to where it all began, the Leather and Chains. I had to find out what happened after we left, where she was taken and buried. We were miles away when a storm rolled in with heavy rain. We kept going and finally reached the desolate roadhouse in a good forsaken patch of the Badlands. We slogged inside and nothing had changed. The music was heavy and hard, with a motley group of mysterious travelers.

I went straight to the raspy old bartender and told him why I was here. I needed to know where she was, the wild and wicked girl I loved and killed. He stared back at me and nodded, as if he knew I'd come back. Without saying a word, he shuffled from behind the bar to the door leading to the back rooms. I followed him down the hall past the private rooms. I could hear the moans and groans, bringing back a memory that changed my life.

We reached the end of the hall and he pushed open a door that took us outside. The rain was still falling, giving the desert a misty look. His gait was shaky as he trudged through the puddles and mud. I began to suspect he wasn't all there as he mumbled to himself in gurgled words I couldn't understand. Then suddenly, a plateau rose out of the rain in front of us. Crude steps had been carved out of the dirt and rock. The bartender staggered up, his hunched body huffing and puffing to the top. That's when I saw markers spread out in the soggy dirt.

"She's here," he croaked.

We were in a graveyard hidden at the top of this desert plateau. But the markers weren't regular tombstones with names and dates. They were macabre statues and totems being drenched by the rain. Some were creatures not of this world and others were bizarre configurations made out of rock.

Then I heard it again, louder this time.

Love never dies...

At a marker a dozen feet away, the dirt shivered and shook, then broke apart, skeletal hands clawing up from below. The rain drizzled to a stop, revealing another monster's moon. The skeleton was now above ground, a trembling horror stumbling towards me.

I recognized her immediately – my one true love.

She then revealed her secret in that haunting voice. She was part of a gang too, a coven of witches that roamed the Badlands like us, enchanted desperadoes using magic and sex as the source of their allure. The bartender shuffled away, leaving us alone in this hidden graveyard. As his hunched body reached the edge of the plateau, there was a fleeting glimpse of what he really was, a flash of tentacles trailing behind him. I shrugged away my disguise too, revealing my true form. I was ash and smoke, fire and brimstone, the leader of a motorcycle gang from Hell.

She staggered towards me, a skeletal temptress with barely any flesh. I could see in the hollow holes where her eyes used to be she was still mad at what I had done, but I also knew that didn't matter anymore. I took her in my arms and we tumbled down to the graveyard dirt. Beneath the monster's moon, we both began to pant, because make-up sex is always the best.

"**M**y God, Gretchen," he moaned. "*Not him...*"

"Oh, get over it for God's sake."

He clinched his hands into fists. He wasn't a violent man, or overly emotional, but he hated that tone in her voice, bored and annoyed.

"Look, I'm sorry, okay? It happened. Life is like that, Carl... *things happen.*"

He felt his anger nudging up again. He'd just learned she was screwing their next-door neighbor, an arrogant low life named Tommy Callico. Tommy's wife had just called, in tears. "Do you love him?"

She laughed and leaned back in her chair. "Not likely, honeybun. I mean there's not much there. He's a blue-collar kind of guy and I need a man with... well, you know... a bit more polish."

For her, words were rarely used for their actual meaning. She communicated with a whole range of other techniques. The taunting tone of her voice was one. The raised eyebrow was another. That mocking laugh.

"I have to think about this, Gretchen. I have to think how I feel."

"Of course, you do, dear, because that's what you do best."

She crossed her legs, rested her arms along the sides of her chair. After all these years, she was still beautiful. The long dark hair was shorter now, but she still had that smile, her incredible blue eyes. There had always been something about her that was unpredictable, and that's why he fell in *love* with her. Opposites attract, and she was his opposite. They'd met at a party in college. Right then and there, he'd decided he wanted to be with her the rest of his life.

"I suppose we'll have to move. You know, I really can't believe this..." His head began to throb, but he tried to ignore it. He needed to stay focused, because that's how you solve problems. After all, that's what he was good at: taking in disparate information, sorting it out, analyzing, discarding, synthesizing if necessary, then reaching a logical conclusion.

"No, Carl, we're not moving. I like it here. I like this house and I like this town."

"But we see each other all the time. I mean, Jesus, he still has my lawnmower..."

She lifted her right hand and began to inspect her nails. She always kept them in excellent condition and loved to experiment with new shades and colors.

"Look, we're adults, okay. We'll just pretend this never happened and go on with our not-very-exciting lives. We'll just say hello to the Callico's when we see them, and nobody will be the wiser. It'll just be dust under the carpet, as they say."

Satisfied with that hand, she held up the other, staring at it like it was a work of art.

"Just like that?"

"Of course, honeybun. Just like that."

"But why, Gretchen? There must be a reason."

"I told you. It just happened."

"But why him? The man is an absolute thug. I mean, listen to the way he talks."

"I know, and he even has a tattoo on his butt. Can you believe it?" She'd said this in a lower tone, then immediately realized the obvious implication. She dropped her hand. "Carl, I'm sorry. I shouldn't have said that. That was a really stupid thing to say right now."

He'd heard the word "tattoo" and a picture instantly appeared in his head. He saw his beautiful wife and his thuggish neighbor lying in bed together, his stupid tattoo next to her naked body. He stared at her, completely ignoring the words now coming from her mouth, because she didn't communicate with words. He was staring at her smile. It was small and private, trying to hide something. Seeing that smile, he knew with absolute certainty she wasn't sorry about anything. In fact, she was enjoying herself, playing a game he was finally seeing.

She held up both hands and stared at her nails again.

"Gretchen, I need to ask you a very important question right now."

"What's that, honeybun?"

"Do I have your word this won't happen again?"

"My word?"

"Yes."

"Like you want me to cross my heart or something? I know, I'll sign a piece of paper and drip blood on it. How does that sound? Would that make you feel better?" She rose from her chair, gazed out the window for a moment, then turned back around. A look of barely concealed disgust darkened her face. "You know what, honeybun? You really are the most predictable man in the whole entire world."

As he watched her walk away, he thought about the cruel simplicity that defined their marriage. They were opposites in every way.

There are stages to solving any problem, that he knew all too well from the many years he'd worked as

250

a research scientist. First, accurately define the problem, specify what needs to be solved, changed, deleted, or improved upon. He knew what the problem was with a heart-breaking clarity.

His wife didn't love him anymore.

His plan of attack now had clear and definable guidelines. He had to somehow change the circumstances that had prompted this evident erosion in her feelings for him. The second stage was always more random and formless. Don't actively search for an instant solution. Instead, send the problem down to your subconscious for a while. Then, more often than not, the result would be a flash of insight, a leap in logic to a new way of thinking. He focused on both these stages in the weeks that followed, giving much more thought to the reasons behind the obvious fracture in their marriage.

The conclusion he finally reached was painful to confront. What his wife had originally found appealing and worthy in his personality, she now found predictable and dull. He was a brilliant man who'd dedicated his life to his career. He'd done very well, but there was nothing in his make-up that matched his wife's unpredictability and exuberance towards life. After much soul searching, he'd reached a conclusion his wife probably reached many years before.

He was utterly boring. That was the brutal truth. It showed in his eyes. They were brown and drab, always a little scared, because that's who he was. He was a somber looking man who had never strayed even an inch from the straight and narrow. And his wife had come to despise him for it. After three weeks, he knew the second stage was over when he awoke one morning with a man's name swimming in his head.

251

The name was Dr. Gulliver Fryde.

A meeting was easy to arrange, requiring only a general explanation of his credentials and area of interest. He'd come across Fryde's name in a journal a few months earlier. Back then, he'd merely tucked it away in his memory, not giving it much thought. But now the name had resurfaced again for a reason. By training, Fryde was a criminal psychologist, with a specialty in sociopathic behavior and criminal dementia.

"The Man Who Knows Monsters," was the title of the article. It detailed his accomplishments in studying the brain patterns of his subjects. He'd been able to compile a database of extreme psychotic behavior. The hope, of course, was to discover some measure of preventative care, and even a cure.

But his hope in meeting Fryde was entirely different, because this was his leap of logic to a new way of thinking. The secret was always to take disparate areas of learning and combine them to create a new avenue of action, a creative springboard to a radical new solution.

Fryde adjusted his glasses and looked out the window of his cluttered office. They'd just finished the banter that prefaced these types of meetings, sharing background, professional interests, and a few common complaints. The reason for his faraway gaze was the previous question he'd just asked about the specifics of his database.

"Well, I'm still a long way from where I want to be."

"Aren't we all?"

"But I'm very pleased with the progress I've made so far. You're familiar with the new developments in memory coding and analysis?"

"Somewhat…"

Fryde took a sip from his coffee mug. He was a short man with a droopy mustache and balding head. "It's a simple matter really. We scan the brain and duplicate the encoded memories on a computer. What I've been able to do is strip away the memories that deal with the aberrant episodes. That way, I can use the computer to do an analysis of the relationship between the deviant behavior and the core psychological need it fulfills."

He listened attentively, knowing much more about the technology than he let on. After Fryde rambled on for a few more minutes, he interrupted with another question. "What exactly do you classify as deviant behavior?"

"Yes, of course, excellent question. That was the critical consideration. For the optimal results, I decided to only focus on the top quarter percentile, the absolute worst of the worst."

"How so?"

"Well, without getting into too many details, it includes mass murderers, acute sexual perversion, extreme body mutilation, catastrophic cruelty, torture deviants, and degenerate sadism."

"I see."

Fryde smiled.

"So, you think this data may be helpful to your own work?"

"Truthfully, I'm not sure, but it may."

He smiled too because he wanted Fryde to feel important. His company did work for the government, so he had the necessary clearances. These he used to entice Fryde further. It also allowed him to be purposely vague about why the data would be useful.

Fryde merely nodded, saying he understood. "It will take a couple of days to get the process going, but I should be able to send you a coded compilation by the beginning of next week."

He stood up to go, then paused. "One last question, if I may."

"Of course."

"Do you think they know what they're doing is sick, or do they rationalize it in some way? You're the expert, so I'm curious what you think."

Fryde looked off into space again. This time his voice was distant too. "Oh, they know it all right, and they couldn't care less."

Problem defined, solution identified.

Stage three was almost the exact opposite of stage two, being more rigorously systematic and goal oriented. Determine what needs to be done, then do it.

He wasn't without doubts, however. In the next few days, he reviewed his analysis and the radical solution his subconscious suggested. But he couldn't ignore the obvious feeling of excitement This was the intellectual thrill that accompanied all journeys into the unknown. Non-scientists couldn't understand this feeling. It was the thrill of creation, because being a creator was the elegance of his solution. He was going to take what was missing in their marriage and create something new.

He was a high-level research scientist who worked for a technology company specializing in biological applications. Regarding the details of what Fryde had discussed, he knew all the technology involved quite well. In fact, he was simply going to reverse the process. He was going to take the memories on the database and deposit them back into a human brain.

His own.

As a scientific solution, it was simple and direct. His wife clearly hungered for a more daring and adventurous partner, but he was psychologically incapable of fulfilling that need. Hence, he had to change.

Of course, he didn't expect to wipe away a lifetime of rigid conformity and tedium, but he did hope to burn away that bland, dull look in his eyes. With Fryde's technology, he'd be able to experience a part of life he'd never dreamed possible. He wouldn't just tip toe off the straight and narrow, he'd catapult himself into a primal new landscape with infinite possibilities. There'd be no laws, no rules, no limits of any kind, just desire and freedom, uninhibited release. And all this without risk or pain. No laws would be broken, no realities altered. The only thing changed would be him.

Even if it was just a new twinkle in his eyes, that would be enough, though he hoped the borrowed memories would rattle his inner psyche and change him even more. A bit more daring, perhaps, and a lot more spontaneous, without that invisible straitjacket he'd been trapped in his entire life. How could they not?

His inner mind was neatly ordered and exceptionally dreary, dull as dirt. He was brilliant, but that didn't matter. He wanted to be daring and adventurous. He wanted the ability to be truly, truly angry. Unfortunately, these were emotions and qualities he simply didn't possess. With any luck, the

255

borrowed memories would change all that, if only just a little. If he wanted to stretch his capabilities even an inch, he had to drag his psyche as hard as he could in the opposite direction. If this was a desperate act, so be it.

He loved his wife. Problem, solution.

The data file arrived at the beginning of the week as promised. By now, he was thinking of little else. His wife had done as she'd said, not mentioning the incident again. She also carried around a new air of indifference. A few words here and there, but little else.

Last night he'd discovered the lawnmower was back in the garage. A note was taped to the handle, "Thanks, Tommy." He ripped up the note and threw it in the trash.

Thanks, Tommy.

The obvious question was the gratitude for the lawnmower or his wife?

The moment of practical implementation had finally arrived. As he lay in bed reading, he could hear his wife humming in the bathroom. At least two or three times a week, she indulged herself with a long, hot bath. Like all married couples, they'd fallen into countless routines over the years, and this was one. He loved to read science journals in bed, and she loved the warm comfort of a bath at night. She always hummed to herself, splashing quietly in the water like a little girl.

Thanks, Tommy.

He began to feel a nudge of anger again, but it wasn't just anger at his wife's betrayal. It was anger that he couldn't feel more hate and rage. He knew what another man would do in his place. There would be yelling and screaming, then violence. Another man wouldn't just rip up the note, he would storm next door roaring for a fight.

Even now though, he thought about all this without the rage that should go along with it. He simply wasn't that kind of man. He'd wondered about the exact nature of the sights that awaited him but was never able to conceive anything vivid in his mind. That would have to wait.

"Still awake, honeybun?"

"Yes, I'm reading."

"Tomorrow's Saturday, any plans?"

"I've got some work to do in the morning, but that's about it. You?"

He waited for an answer, but none came, just humming and the quiet sound of splashing water.

After eating breakfast alone, he carried his briefcase downstairs to his office in the basement. This was part of his routine too. Most weekends he would work for a couple of hours at home. The office wasn't much, just a desk, a laptop, and a file cabinet. The rest of the space was cluttered with dusty old furniture and boxed-up clothes.

He eased into the leather chair and opened his briefcase. The data file had been sent to his office and he'd immediately forwarded it to his home computer. But that wasn't all he needed.

There was another part of his plan, and that's what he took out of his briefcase.

A small plastic bottle.

The boost.

Inside the bottle were a couple of light blue pills called Harginon. He twisted off the top and popped them into his mouth. This part of the plan had come to him only a few days before. Harginon was a psycho-hallucinogen that would intensify the experience. So rather than just viewing the borrowed memories inside his head, he would ram them into his brain with a psycho-active chaser. The drug was new, its range of capabilities still being tested, so he wasn't absolutely sure about the combined effects. His hope was that it would greatly increase the impact of the images.

He turned on his laptop, quickly logged in, and accessed the file. The method of inputting the memories was new. The link was done with a specially designed modem and two neural patches that were attached to the skull directly behind the cerebral cortex.

He heard the padding footsteps of his wife in the kitchen upstairs. The basement door was locked, but he was confident she would have little interest in disturbing him. He also expected her to find a reason to be away from the house the rest of the day. Finding ways to avoid being with him had become one of her regular routines.

A glance at his watch showed it was 9:40. He attached the patches, then activated the file and closed his eyes. In the first few seconds, he saw nothing, as the footsteps shuffled softly overhead. He tried to relax but was too nervous. His fingers began to twitch, and he wondered if this was a reaction to the drug. There was still nothing but darkness, so his mind began to wander. He thought about his wife and how much he loved her, because all this was for her.

The first memory suddenly blazed into view...

Charging into his brain with a shocking brightness... a naked man burning alive... his charred body crumbling into chunks of black ash... then more

258

after that... skin slashed... eyes gouged... mutilated faces with rictus screams... they came and came... sick and disgusting... bloody and perverse... the acid like chemicals ramming them deeper and deeper into his cranial core... he watched in inescapable horror... then helpless despair... but on and on it went... until the searing shock finally faded away... and the numbing despair too... because he was beginning to see something else... a ferocious new beauty that made his eyes gush with blissful tears...

The glow from the overhead light seemed brighter as he yanked off the patches and stumbled to his feet. He stepped away from the desk and peered slowly around the room. The stairs were a dozen feet away, rising up to the closed door at the top. He turned away because something else caught his eye, a ray of sunlight hitting the basement floor.

He staggered to the light, his body stiff and sore. He blinked hard several times, with a strange feeling that was new. When he reached the sunlight, he found a shorter set of stairs and two horizontal doors. He stumbled up the stairs and pushed open the doors.

He blinked again.

Because there it was.

A whole new world...

The colors were so startling and bright they stung his eyes. It was the sun-drenched grass of his backyard, but now it was so much more. It was a new landscape of infinite possibilities. He looked at his hands; they were different too. His fingers were thicker, longer, and stronger. He fell to the ground, snorting in the intoxicating smell of the glowing grass. He felt absolutely free and wildly alive, no longer human. His old body was a fading memory. He clawed his new hands into the grass and pulled himself forward. His nose flared at the new odors. A sound drifted by, and he strained to hear. It was coming from a window on the side of the house.

Looking up, he saw a woman he'd known in another life, but now he did not. He knew other things though, and he giggled to himself. He was the first of his kind, madness from machine. But others would come too, he'd make sure of that. He'd unleash them into this dull and dreary world he now hated in a way that was impossible to describe. He moved faster through the glowing green grass to the window and the woman. His pants were off, and his groin was on fire. A few seconds more and the fun would begin.

He giggled again, crawling up from the grass to the open window.

Free at last...

MISSING

Trying to describe how it feels to lose a child is futile because everything changes, especially you. The hole where your heart used to be is a bottomless pit of loss and despair. Most of all, you're trapped between the living and the dead where even the brightest day is cloudy and dark.

His name was Oliver and he was seven years old. Small and funny, with curly blonde hair, he was fearless in the way kids can be when they think they're going to live forever. No one ever does, of course, but seven is barely the beginning of what life should be.

I toiled as a government lawyer in a fortress like building the locals called the Tomb, a fitting name given its monolithic shape and the mysterious work hidden inside. Some days the drudgery was so numbing I'd bolt the door to my office and turn off the lights, slumped like a corpse in the dark. There was little interaction with the other workers beyond a slight nod in the dimly lit halls. No friendships were formed or alliances forged. It was a dismal place in every regard.

My return home was usually when Oliver was already in bed. "Daddy," he'd murmur in a sleepy voice. "I've been waiting for you." I'd sit on his bed and wait until he went to that slumbering realm full of dreams. I'd stay for a while and try to imagine what those dreams would be, desperately hoping his life would have a brightness mine did not. I should have spent more time with him and not trapped in that dismal office.

"Something's wrong," Sara blurted on the phone late one day. "Oliver's sick. I'm taking him to the hospital."

"What happened?"

"I don't know... *I have to go...*"

I jumped up from my chair and ran through the long corridors of the Tomb, my pounding feet echoing off the heavy stone walls. And this when my world began to change in ways I barely noticed at first. The taxi chugged through the streets at a torturous pace and the vast grey city seemed muffled and strange. A weird haze drifted in, along with curious shapes and shadows.

When I reached the hospital, it wasn't much better. I wandered through a serpentine maze seeking my son. Others were searching too, a shuffling parade of faraway gazes. I was panting when I finally reached my destination. An old doctor was mumbling to himself as he did the examination, his brown spotted hands looking ancient and frail. My heart was pounding so loud I barely heard what he said, when Oliver was suddenly wheeled away, his feverish face stricken with fear. As I watched him go, I saw he knew he wasn't going to live forever, or even much longer than the rest of the day.

We sat in a waiting room with other hollowed-eyed figures clenching their hands. I picked up a magazine that was five years old, a wrinkled relic from the past. The tears in Sara's eyes made it look like she was drowning and my gasping breaths made it seem like I was too.

Sometime during the night, a much younger doctor took us to an office with a rickety skeleton hanging in the corner. He announced Oliver's condition like he was speaking another language, so we wouldn't know how hopeless it was. Sara let out an ear-splitting scream like she was giving birth, but it was the opposite of that, she was losing her child. We were taken to another room where he was lying in bed. The feverish fear was gone but only because he didn't have the strength to show it anymore.

"Momma..." he whispered with the weakest of voices. "Daddy..." he moaned even weaker than that.

The feeling of utter helplessness was the beginning of a punishment that would steadily get worse. We sat all night and most of the next day watching nurses come and go. Every second was an eternity, a slow-motion vigil no parent should ever endure. Oliver was draped in a faded white sheet with only his sickly face uncovered, a gruesome sight made even worse by the flickering light pulsing overhead.

He died at the end of the day without any warning. I could tell the nurse had seen a lot of death when she pulled the white sheet over his head as simply as if she were making the bed. That was the moment my heart began its tortured descent into a dark void without any escape.

The funeral was a wretched affair. I was paralyzed with misery and loss when a sound crept in, struggling to be heard. But I didn't care about that or anything else.

Some say madness is not a mental aberration, but rather an ability to see and hear what the ordinary world cannot. They claim it's an enhanced capacity beyond the known senses to witness matters the rational mind can't conceive. With Oliver buried and gone, I began to consider this as a possible explanation for my emerging condition. My world had changed in some bizarre fashion, and now it began to unravel in ways impossible to ignore.

In at least one surprising turn of events, I now welcomed the staggering numbness of my job because it perfectly suited my emptiness. I continued to labor on arcane legal matters that changed people's lives without their awareness or knowledge. That's when I began to muse about how naïve and powerless we really are. If I could do this from my unknown subterranean office, I wondered what other hidden forces were pulling the invisible strings of our lives.

There was no reason to hurry home anymore, so I decided to seek solace in drink, stopping at a pub called The Black Swan every night after work. I'd never noticed it before – or rather never needed what it had to offer – a tucked away haven for the lost and discarded.

I'd sit at a table in the corner, drinking pint after pint. I'd lost weight from not eating, but I didn't care. My life had been assaulted in the worst way possible and my physical decay was a symptom. With my cadaverous body wasting away, it wouldn't be long before I looked like the rickety skeleton hanging in the young doctor's office.

My melancholic mood was so strangling I thought about ending it all one night and drinking myself to death in the pub. That's when a shambling figure walked in and stood for a moment looking around. He was wearing a frayed black coat which made the white collar around his neck more visible. He moved with an unsteady gait to an empty table and began to drink with a pace equal to mine.

I was not a religious person but something dragged me to my feet and I staggered to his table. I was so bereft of hope I lurched in front of him like a dying man lost in the desert. My desperation was all I had left. His face was haggard and sullen, peering up at me through the dusty light. He took a long gulp from his pint and nodded weakly to the empty chair across from him.

Without the slightest hesitation I spewed out my story, babbling in a hoarse voice about how my grief had become like a monster inside me. If I sounded like a madman, I hoped the reason would at least be clear. I'd lost the flesh of my flesh, my treasure in life, my beautiful boy. When I finished in a trembling state, he said nothing at first, his gaze so distant and dark I wondered if he'd heard a word I said. He drained his pint and waved a shaky hand for another.

When he finally spoke, his quivering voice had none of the comfort I sought. He acknowledged my loss, then recounted a tragic tale of his own. He was the pastor of a nearby church, bringing light to darkness, and faith to the forlorn, but something had changed. The once packed pews had steadily dwindled to just a few followers. He ventured out to seek the cause, rapping on the doors of his missing parishioners, but they didn't open. And now the pews were completely barren and his last sermon was delivered to scurrying rats. He'd spent the past week sobbing in his abandoned church like an orphaned child. We sat in silence until the pints were empty, then I stumbled up and out the door.

Outside, the night sprawl displayed a new configuration, like a puzzle with pieces missing. On my way home, familiar sights were gone. This is when I heard the sound again. It was stronger this time, but still unknown in the strange quiet of the night.

The unease continued when I reached my house, almost passing it by because all the lights were off. After the funeral, Sara had been avoiding me, as if my presence would drag up more anguish than she could possibly bear. If I padded through the house in search of her, she was already slipping away. At bedtime, I'd find her under the covers, breathing as quietly as she possibly could, hoping I would think she was already asleep.

Except now I was determined to find her because she was all I had left. My plunging despair had cast me adrift and I needed an anchor before it was too late. I flicked on the light next to the door but the house remained dark. I called her name, moving to a lamp just a few feet away, but it wasn't there, or the sofa beyond that. I crept deeper into the house, needing Sara to help me with the aberrant condition now eating me alive. But the very next second, I was seized by a terrifying panic and it swallowed me up in a crushing blackness.

When I woke the next morning, everything was back to normal. The terrifying panic was gone, replaced by a throbbing sensation of further emptiness. I was late for work, so I hurried out in the same wrinkled clothes. I hadn't seen Sara, or any evidence she still lived here, until I looked back from the street and saw her peek out from behind a curtain.

I'd never been close to my co-workers, or anyone else for that matter. They were drones like me,

266

controlled cogs with a purpose none of us fully understood. I had no idea what they did and I'd come to suspect this was by design. On this morning, my delayed arrival and disheveled appearance brought no acknowledgement. There were no nods or even a passing glance as I stumbled by, as if I'd suddenly ceased to exist, or was the unwitting target of a cruel prank.

I worked as best as I could, keeping the door locked and staying alert for any suspicious activity in the hallway. I viewed my paranoia as more evidence of my madness, and even more proof came soon after that. A page I needed in a legal tome was missing. Other folders and notes were gone too. My manic search became uncontrollable. I hurled papers and smashed books, falling to the floor in a shuddering heap.

I tried to open the door, but it wouldn't budge. When it finally did I tumbled out into the hallway. It was empty, not another worker in sight, or the faintest sound to be heard. More than ever, the byzantine building felt like a tomb and I was the only one left. I dashed through the empty halls and burst out the massive front door. There no one outside either, and what little light was left in the day vanished as well. No more proof of my madness was needed.

I saw the distant light of The Black Swan and ran. I stopped at the door, hoping to hear clinking glasses and muffled talk, but there was nothing there either. I twisted the knob and walked inside. The likelihood of my mental and physical collapse was almost certain. Like everywhere else, the pub was empty.

Then I saw I wasn't alone after all; a dark figure was slumped at the farthest table. It was the sullen priest, sitting so still he looked dead. I staggered towards him, and that's when I heard him weeping. He raised his head and I saw right away there was madness inside him too.

I'm not sure if he said it aloud or I surmised it just from the sight of him. I'd lost my son and he'd lost faith in his Heavenly Father. I began to weep too, and that's when I heard it again, the mystifying sound calling out to me from some faraway place. I tried to dismiss it as another tangled thread in my mental decline, until the priest croaked he could hear it too.

There's a belief that some mysteries are better left unsolved, that the toll it would take might be too great. But we were beyond that, the despondent priest and I. We spent no time discussing the strangeness of our shared connection, deciding instead on what we needed to do.

We hurried through the empty streets to his abandoned church. In the reconfigured city, it looked like it didn't belong anymore, a part of the past that was no longer needed. The priest offered his car for our plan, and I waited behind the church for his return. When he came out the back door, he'd changed as well, leaving behind his holy attire, now dressed in clothes as rumpled as mine.

We left the city in his rattling car, two lost souls on a quest without a known destination. We talked for far longer than it seemed possible, the night slowly giving way to the light of the next day. We tried to remember better times, but the devastation we'd both suffered thwarted any attempt to find solace in the past, and we finally fell into a brooding silence.

The city became a fading mirage and we wondered if it had ever been completely real. The faraway sound was our only beacon carrying us through the barren terrain. Any sense of time or place was gone, as if it had been a mirage too. We began to feel an unspoken dread that our quest was a meaningless trek that would end in oblivion. We seemed to be in a place beyond desolation, beyond anything that would appear on a map.

It was night again and a radiance shone down from the stars. We were morose and silent when a startling sight came into view. There were others like us, traveling by any means possible, a rumbling horde on the same mad pilgrimage, the same nightmarish dream crusade. We charged across the empty expanse to a baffling sight in the distance. It appeared to be heaps of junk, a haphazard mountainous mess. And then we saw it was anything but, it was a colossal gathering of lost things.

It didn't matter if it had sprung full blown from our madness, the epic onslaught of seekers closed the gulf as fast as they could. They'd all heard the call in a puzzling summons they didn't understand, but now they did. The misshapen mass was a chaotic collection from the smallest treasures to the grandest of mysteries, but size and shape had nothing to do with their value. That was measured in the yearning of those who'd found this impossible place. To them it was closer to the reality they wanted than what they'd left behind.

It's often said we don't know what we have until it's gone. I stood with the priest in front of the mountain of lost things as he raised his gaze to what he could see beyond the stars. He began weeping again, but this time with a joy that brought him to his knees. That's when I heard a whispery voice.

"Daddy... I've been waiting for you..."

AFTERWORD

*T*he shriveled old shapeshifter wheezed a sputtering breath as it decided what to become this one last time. A menagerie of the impossible filled its crumbling mind. Its weariness was a burden it struggled to resist, but it accepted that death was an inevitable part of the cosmic design. It knew with an unshakable certainty its existence was nearing its end, so this last metamorphosis had a significance that made the choice even more profound.

It had come to this world and unleashed a parade of mysteries that couldn't be explained by the rigid boundaries of science and logic. It was the opposing foe to all that was dull and dreary in a land shackled with stifling bonds. But now its fabled strength and transformative powers were fading glimmers inside the dying husk the world had never seen. It shuddered because it had changed too. Its presence had transformed this world, so the prospect of death was even more sad.

It was a monster, of course, but only because monsters are defined by those without any knowledge of true strangeness. It had been born in a place of darkness and dread called Horrifica, and it had splattered its marvels with a reckless wonder. It had never been seen, but it was the maker of myths, the creator of fear and astonishment, the mystical source of all that was scary and unknown.

And now there was time for one last revelation.

271

Its shriveled form began the changing process that was always wracked with the pain of a brutal birth. Its cherished life was coming to an end, but billowing black wings suddenly burst out, along with the stench of fire and death. It rapidly grew, stomping up through the shadows and rock, to the world it had blessed with its mysteries.

It charged into the air with a thundering flap, soaring through the wispy white clouds and blue summer sky, still growing and growing, until it looked like a mythic black angel above the spinning world below. The heavens shimmered with a startling intensity as its gargantuan wings dropped down and caressed the sun-splattered orb with a surprising tenderness, cradling it like a newborn child. Then it was gone, gone forever, ending the legendary reign of Horrifica.

Sheldon Woodbury worked for some of the top advertising agencies in New York City then returned to school to get an M.F.A. in Dramatic Writing from New York University where he also taught screenwriting. He's an award-winning writer (screenplays, plays, books, short stories, and poems). His book COOL MILLION is considered the essential guide to writing high concept movies. His short stories and poems have appeared in many horror anthologies and magazines.

Thank you for reading! If you like the book, please leave a review on Amazon and Goodreads. Reviews help authors and publishers spread the word.

To keep up with more Nightmare Press news, visit us at:

Nightmarepress.net
Facebook
X
Instagram
Nightmare Press Network on YouTube

To interact with authors and other readers, join the Nightmare Press Fans & Authors group on Facebook